VINNIE: a love letter

BY RONALD PRESTON CLARK

TO AUGUST ISAIAH JOHNSON

I love you, nephew. Always and forever.

"When you have a love for anything, you'll go to the extreme to maintain that love. That's what love does. Love drives you to do whatever you need to maintain that connection." - Michael Jordan

I

Where is he?

Clusters of adults sprinkle irrelevant conversations into one another's ears. I hear the lackadaisical tone in their high-pitched voices, all surrounding the elegant grace of my mother, Annette, her glazed brown skin shines even within the cloud of breath that engulfs her. The sheer volume of words trickling into her ears, I know it is nothing she wants to hear.

Where is he?

He was supposed to be here by now.

My principal, Ms. Georgia Washington, taps her foot against the hardwood floor, snacks on bite-size edibles as the time she wastes becomes more and more of a concern. My art teacher, Ms. Brenda Scott, scurries back and forth from outside to in, caters to the many parents and students who patiently wait on the person I seem to wait for every day. They do not know patience quite like I do.

Everyone waits for him. Ms. Washington. Ms. Scott. My classmates wait for him like they did when I was in kindergarten. Or was that third grade? Or fifth grade? Or seventh grade? Or all grades? They all run together like dysfunctional sentences, I cannot even differentiate anymore.

My mother waits for him.

I wait for him.

I am always waiting for him.

My mother runs interference. Puts words in the ears of those who matter as to why I cannot seem to move at this moment. My lip quivers but it is simply involuntary. My hands shake but that is natural, is it not? Natural despite the abilities I possess with the same hands I cannot seem to control at this moment, in these moments.

My mother really tries. Not tries as in effort. But tries to calculate how many times we have been in this position. How many times she has nursed multiple conversations with people as they continue to wait for something she nor I seem to ever be able to produce.

My father, Thomas Smith.

I, his 14-year-old son, Vinnie, kiss my scarred knuckles. Reflex screams to punch a wall but I refuse to let anything more than a little sweat, a quiver and a shake be seen by judgmental eyes. I cannot be the only one in this room who has dealt with the inability of a parent to show up.

I hear words spoken – from the mouth of Principal Washington.

"He is simply brilliant."

My Art teacher, Ms. Scott.

"I have never seen a skillset like his at that age. I am astonished every time he presents something new. I almost want to have a class with just me and him. I might learn something myself."

A classmate whose name I do not remember despite us knowing each other since kindergarten.

"Dope."

All of their eyes seem to be open. They see it. But why can't he? Why can't he ever just, see it? It, literally being my newest painting. It, figuratively being the emptiness of what outsiders would see as a father and a son. I only see a man and a boy.

And so, I stand here, in a familiar position. Alone, with only him to blame for my melancholy exterior and my mother here to wash away the residual effects of his absence.

I hear my mother's voice.

"It isn't always like this. He just works a lot. He's an ambitious man, what can I say?"

I can say a few things, but words are why we are here in the first place. Need more actions. More detailed responses. My vocabulary – influenced and affected by two hours of reading every day – is still not sufficient enough to properly describe my feelings towards my father. Words just do not do my feelings enough justice. It must be shown. It must be witnessed. It must be everything my father is not – present.

I take a deep breath, turn and lock eyes with my mother. She nods a nod I have seen an innumerable number of times. She knows I must continue without him. I know I do, too. Does not take away from this aching urge to add more red to the color scheme of my knuckles.

In front of the class with a half-smile on my face, I present my painting.

"It isn't much really. A collection of colors and thoughts intertwined with this growing perception that today's child is not raised with the same values as past generations. And I believe that to be true, mainly because two parents who actually know they are parents is always better than one real and one fake parent, not coming to an agreement on how they should raise the only thing they have created together that is any good – their child."

Principal Washington dares to respond.

"I don't know whether to clap or give you a hug."

"Neither would suffice. But I can't prevent you from having a human reaction to such an unhealthy situation."

The room is still. I can hear my mother's heartbeat. Ours are synchronized. I spend so much time with my head to her bosom that I memorized her palpitations then trained my own to follow. This could be fact or conjecture but either way it speaks to you, does it not? My heartbeat recognizes itself in another. It recognizes itself in her. And without her, my heart does not know its function. It loses its way. And because of this, synchronization is everything.

But back to this room. This room that vacillates between silence and intrigue. My classmates shake their heads – not of disbelief for that would insinuate that they

5

have beliefs – but in a sheer act of not knowing what to do with me and my non-traditional self. They cannot turn away from me, but they cannot understand me either. I would not want them to.

I just want him to.

Clap. Clap. Bravo. A congratulations of sort. For those that are here and that can see.

I just want him to.

My mother's voice.

"I guess that's it, huh?"

"Yeah, I guess."

Another voice. This one deeper, with a familiar twinge of remorse.

My father's voice.

"Did I miss anything?"

His son's response.

"Wash, rinse and repeat… the answer to that question from the last time you asked."

You see, Pops is always on time.

II

"You're late."

A layered regurgitation of past events continually infiltrating the present. James Baldwin's sentence structure still resonates in my mind at this time, so do not mind that last sentence. I felt an urge to scream within an intellectual cage. Baldwin always seems to fit in those times.

I did not actually say, 'You're late.' My mother may have. Either way it would have been a waste of breath. Ever known someone whose presence never necessarily meant they were there? My father has perfected this craft. He has molded his fatherhood into trying to convince my mother and I that what he is able to do is enough.

The painting does not even look the same at this point. All its vibrancy evaporated upon realization that the most important eyes to be laid upon it were not going to be laid upon it at all. It gave up on attempting to be at its best. It gave up on attempting to be loved and adored, showcased for the rest of the world to see. It has given up. It has looked up to me, taken its cue from me, so none of this comes as a shock, now does it?

My mother is the one who put the paintbrush in my hand. A black woman whose essence is everything our ancestors would have wanted her to be. Something like a goddess on earth, mocking us with her constant ability to be more than human within the restraints of that humanity. I, her son, simply want to provide her with the warmth and love necessary for a being such as her to continue to function.

So, I paint. She smiles. I paint some more. Her joy is evident. She takes my hand in hers, guides my paintbrush in regal strokes, the paint listens to her every direction at a level I have not reached yet. This is our time together. The time in which my life is the most colorful, most full.

Yet, the darkness his shadow provides can swallow even her sunshine, even within a flashback to a beautifully designed memory such as this one. But we must leave this place now, and return to my father's shadow. It is not done covering the present with its unwavering swirl of parental ineptitude.

He looks at his watch. Checks the time, as if he has been here forever. He wants this to be over. I want *this* to be over, too.

My mother looks in my direction. She wonders the same thing I wonder. Yes, I do have something to say.

"It was over before you arrived. It's been over for some time now. But I guess a thank you is required in this situation since you wasted gas to get here."

"Yes."

I imagined another conversation taking place in this moment. I really did. But my imagination is responsible for the vast majority of fond memories that include my father. I must create a position for him within my memories for him to have any substantial impact. His gravestone will read, 'In Loving Memory?'

I am sure he held me in his arms at times when I was a baby. I am sure he tossed a ball around with me when I could barely run. I am sure he did – something. But the more I independently operate, the more he feels the need to not be a parent anymore. I will never understand the trigger in fathers to back off.

Do not ever stop loving me!

Excuse me. My throat hurts. That scream clawed at my vocal chords. Whenever I see him, I scream this. I scream this over and over again. He does not hear me. He does not listen to words. But I have not found the proper actions necessary to get him to recognize his glaring flaws. He cannot see my necessities. He cannot see my needs. But what is most painful is differentiating between cannot and will not. Maybe cannot can be forgiven. Maybe. But will not? Will not? Naw, I ain't having that.

Do not ever stop loving me!

I can get so consumed by this, all of it. To the point that I no longer notice the words being stated around me.

By classmates.

"I have only ever seen his dad on, like, maybe, three occasions. He don't be around like I would want my daddy to be."

By Ms. Washington.

"There is so much potential here for something beautiful. Vinnie is calling for him, but Thomas refuses to listen to his cries."

Reading makes me cry. And music makes me cry. It makes me cry like a baby. I break down. I have no choice in the matter. When I hear and see these stories of young men begging for the chance to even know their father, let alone be loved by them, it breaks my heart. For mine is standing right here, yet I still have an emotional reaction to their stories, and they don't know their father at all. I know his name. I know his occupation. I know his bank account number. I know what he feels is necessary. But I know nothing of his wiring. I know nothing of why he is the way he is. I know nothing of why he cannot love me the way I want to love him. For love is a two-way street, and despite how much love I have to give, I cannot give it all unless he returns the favor. And it should not be a favor at all due to the father-and-son correlation.

I just want to go home and dream. Dream of that day when I leave this earth, knuckles stained in red from battling a violent swarm of insecurities. He will be there then. He is always there when I die. He is always there to see me through my final breath. I want him to savor the opportunity to share oxygen with me. Only to never grasp it in time.

I truly hope that comes to fruition. My scars would be so worthwhile then.

III

Oh, he's just not going to talk to me, huh? Oh, he thinks it's okay to just ignore me, huh? Oh, he thinks… he thinks… he thinks…

Ahhhhhhhh!

Finally out of the confines of that car. Able to breathe in all of my insanity within these walls, my favorite walls, the walls of my bedroom. I rest all of my secrets in these walls. My blood stains its cracks, ripples like the Red Sea throughout its crevices, only to bubble over when its route seemingly ends. It gurgles at the edge of the carpet, screams at the sight of cleaning supplies only I provide. It wants to sit there, as a reminder to the pain that I go through whenever my father is the focal point of my innermost thoughts.

I try to remove him. Really I do. I try to focus on the wonderful woman who gave birth to me. The goddess who walks the hallways of this home with a grace and dignity only the queens she descended from can attest to. I love my mother with everything I am.

I loathe my father with everything I am.

There he is again. Invading my glimpses of happiness with his unrelenting vile.

Why…

(I drive my hand into the wall)

Won't…

(I do it again)

He…

(I do it again)

Love…

(I do it again)

Me…

I love my father with everything I am.

There is a dent in the wall where my hand likes to punch. If he paid attention at all, he would question why such a thing is in my room. But how can you question what you do not know? He would view it as some sort of teenage angst. I respond this way because I have raging hormones and out-of-control emotions. Funny thing is that I am in complete and utter control. I know why I do these things. I know why I must bleed from my knuckles. I know why I must feel pain. I know why the outer edges of my hands must be rough and rugged, despite my penchant for painting.

I am provided with an adrenaline rush that is lacking due to his absence in my heart.

I love my father with everything I am.

My door opens as I pace back and forth. I pause to look who it is. And it is a goddess, checking in on me.

"Oh, Vinnie… not again…"

She wraps me in her arms, nestles me against her bosom and I am a child once again.

"You can't keep doing this to yourself."

Her tone says otherwise. Her tone tells me to scream at the top of my lungs until my deaf father hears my cries tearing through my adolescence with the fury of 1000 men at war with themselves.

"I worry about you, son. Why must you punish yourself for something that he does?"

"I just want him to see me."

"He sees you, just maybe not in the way that you would like."

"Are you defending him?"

"I just want you to focus on the things he does do for you."

Roof over my head. Cash in my pocket. Money for food. Gas. Electric… I don't see love anywhere on this list.

"What he does isn't enough. What I need you cannot purchase."

"And what is that?"

I lift my head from her bosom.

"You already know. You give it to me every day."

My mother smiles. It is warm and understanding. Our connection is one that my father and I will never reach. Yet, I continue to leave my arms outstretched. Hoping. Praying. Well, maybe not praying since that prayer is routinely sent back with a notice that reads, 'Your father doesn't seem to be responding.' Neither is my Father.

My mother, on the other hand, is the only reason I am still here. She fills my lungs with the oxygen necessary to continue with the melancholy existence of a 14-year-old boy who is too smart, too advanced for teachers and their ilk to ascertain. All I need are my books, my paintbrush, some paint and my mother. This is what sustains me, enables me to continue to blossom into a successful human being – with daddy issues.

I love my father with everything I am...

My mother looks my hand over. My right hand is noticeably more damaged than my left. I paint with my left so I am less likely to punch the wall with that hand. I am angry and disappointed, not stupid.

She smiles her heavenly smile. There is not a lot of strength behind her smile. Her beauty is evident. It is oddly painful to watch her smile. Yet, I cannot refrain from wanting to see her smile. There is just something about her smile...

She guides me towards my easel. There is a blank page sitting there, waiting. She puts the paintbrush in my hand, dabs the tip in paint. It is her favorite color – viridian green. I always keep a full cup of it for occasions like this. Moments when she reminds me of why I picked up a paintbrush in the first place. Our strokes are seamless, the imagery abstract. I save my abstract art for her. I have to be clearer with the average audience. But between us? Abstract is as concrete a language as any other. It is us in plain English. We know what it says. We know what it wants to say.

I love my mother with everything I am…
I loathe my father with everything I am…
She massages my hand. Her hands are soft, an extension of her calming demeanor. I love this woman. I do not know what I would do without her…

But I have to learn.

…to love my father with everything I am.

IV

If my father fell in the forest, with no one around, would the sound he made include his only son's name?

Mom loves the sound of me reading. I do not know what it is about hearing my voice reciting the words of another, but it soothes her. Maybe it is just the idea of my returning the favor from my time spent in her womb. The warmest place I have ever laid my head. My sensory memory is one of my greatest strengths, as I sift through daily reminders of a past my young mind can often forget. I am not meant to remember, and yet still, I do.

I lay my head on her stomach as I feel her falling asleep underneath. Her breaths lift my head ever so slightly, rhythmic in nature. I am where I belong. I drift back and forth in the consciousness of my younger self, for now, I reside within murky waters. I am neither child nor adult. But the choice to be one or the other needs to occur at some point. I actually prefer the vacillation between the two. It suits my propensity to go from James Baldwin's protégé to needy adolescent. Oh, you didn't think I realized I was needy, huh? But are my needs really all that difficult to ascertain? I don't think so. I never will.

I never will…

I will never leave her bosom. I will rest my head here for eternity. This place is where I belong. I belong here, with her, just not in this place. This place is dark, dreary, ugly. It pisses me off that I cannot use my immense vocabulary to describe it. That portion of the words at my disposal are surrounded in beauty.

Surrounded in her.

But this place erases all of those intellectual options. Its simplicity is its strength. Each room filled with its own insecurities. Too many people entering. Too much commotion. But commotion connotes life. So as annoying as it can be, it is ever so necessary. Knowing and understanding that life is prominent within these walls keep tears from falling down weathered cheeks.

Tamir Rice's family...

Amadou Diallo's family was not given...

Sean Bell's family was not given a chance to...

Oscar Grant's family was not given a chance to sit with him...

Sandra Bland's family was not given a chance to sit with her within similar walls...

Never got a chance to say goodbye to a loved one. Never got to properly choose their final words. Never got to leave a legacy not drowned in anger. Their families walk around with memories of them with smiles on their faces. Rice played with toys. Diallo worked hard to find a suitable life for him in the States. Bell was prime to marry his best friend, a woman prepared to share her life with him forever. Grant cherished his fatherhood. Bland's voice rose above the tragic state of her people with her activism – until her voice was quieted against her will.

All this death. All of this life in the past tense. Just breathe, mom.

Still wish you would have told me earlier so you did not have to go through this by yourself. I, your son, would have provided you with my underused shoulder to rest on, cry on, scream on. I know you sat in your bedroom, alone, time and again, and even on days when my father was there, he was unaware of your internal struggle. How do you love so loyally without it being returned in earnest?

It is ugly between these walls. It is painful between these walls. It is unfortunate between these walls. It is... inevitable between these walls. To be naïve of such things would damage my ability to handle it even more. The images, tears falling down the cheeks of people of all ages, screams raging through the hallways, knees buckling at the news. The news is rarely positive. This is not a place of survival. This is the place you go to come to grips with your mortality. The flesh is a depressing realization. To many, it is a slow grind towards the end. To others, it is a sprint, smacking right into a wall with no room to maneuver around it. It would be there no matter what.

I read too much.

When you consider yourself to be a connoisseur of Octavia Butler, Toni Morrison, Junot Diaz, Tim O'Brien, Langston Hughes and, of course, Baldwin, the mind becomes a place of rapid development, almost out of control growth. If this were a freeway, I would be arrested for speeding. Fourteen years is plenty of time to slap together an immaculate intellect, just have to spend the time cultivating it.

My father is not here. He is elsewhere, probably gaining financial stability, or something else that matters not. His presence is not necessary here anyway.

I wish he was here…

My head has not left her bosom. Her breaths are steady. But these walls continue to strangle, second by second, minute by minute, reminding us of the fleeting nature of this location. If my father were here, he would be able to tell you his final words. I do not think he would have anything profound to say. Something along the lines of him doing everything he could to provide for you and me.

"Mom? Mom? Mom?! Mom?! Mom??!! Mom??!!..."

Her bosom, no longer a safe haven for my resting head. Its ability to lift me up removed forever.

"Mom??!! Somebody! Anybody! Help!"

My father just fell in the forest, and his final words did not include his only son's name…

I hate hospitals.

V

The devil cannot stop scratching my throat. His talons sink deep into whatever flesh is available. He must be a man. There is no argument. There is plenty of argument as to whether God is man or woman. I lean towards the latter. But there is no argument as to whether the devil is man or woman. He is man, through and through. And I cannot get the pain of his claws that ravage every inch of my voice from defining who I am in this moment.

I cannot scream any longer. The pain is too definite, too sure. All that leaves my mouth is a crackle, like an elderly man whose bones submit to their history with each painful step. My face stained with streaks of moisture humans call crying. My eyes committed suicide hours ago. Tear ducts fell apart as the last images of my facial rivers posed for their final pictures. I am unaware of the presence of a photographer. I am unaware of whether or not I have been in this room alone, with her, all this time. It is a blur I do not wish to catch up to, converse with, learn from.

I have scared the nurses. They have not attempted to move me for some time now. In the beginning, they reacted with the knowledge that this was a simple mother and son relationship. They were sadly mistaken. This was an aggressive love affair severed at the most inappropriate time. This was where my scream started. This is when the devil looked to escape my throat. Clawing at my windpipe as nothing but silence was able to leave my mouth, yet, the pain on my face was enough to shatter any eardrum in the vicinity.

My face wrinkled. My brow furrowed. My lips chapped. Slobber drips. Spit cakes in the corners of my mouth. Eyes water to the point of dehydration. The veins in my neck protrude. But no sound. No sound can be released. The devil wins, which is ironic, since the devil is the angel of music, you would think he would want to hear the agony a severed love could produce. Nevertheless, he relegates me to unmitigated silence. One of the lost pains.

I am numb. The strength I possessed earlier is unavailable. My heart palpitates at a rate of concern. My hands quiver, like violence is in the air.

The door slams open.

My father steps in. His eyes land on the permanently resting body of his now-deceased wife. This image dwarfs all thoughts but one at a time. The first, he is now a widower. The second, he is now a single father. A man who lives to be in complete control now has none. It only took him four hours to arrive at this point...

"What... what happened?"

From somewhere, I found that strength I once had. The devil released me from his grasp. The crackle cracked under the pressure. I could scream again.

And the power of its echo through my body buoyed me in the direction of my father, flailing into his chest, swinging with no realistic target in sight.

"You happened! You happened! It was you!"

I scream with the power of 300 children whose mothers have spent eternity negotiating with God for any chance of returning to this earthly vessel.

"I didn't do anything, son. I didn't..."

He was unaware of the truth in that statement. His wife felt such a disconnection to him on a spiritual and emotional level she hid from him for nine months that she was fighting breast cancer. For nine months he walked in and out of their bedroom unknowingly watching as his wife was slowly passing away.

I did not notice or know that she was dying either. But our connection was based in her making sure I only saw the good in everything. She even tried to get me to see my father with a different eye, a different viewpoint. I was successful with everyone but him. I now wish I had been just as unsuccessful with her. Maybe I would have seen the pain she was in, the suffering she was going through. The blessing and the curse of black women – their strength. You can lean on them for as long as necessary, but when it comes time for them to lean elsewhere, they hesitate with the marksmanship of an abused child who finally pulls a gun out on their father.

"How could you not know?!"

"I didn't know. She never said anything. How could I –"

"You should have known!"

I stood next to her in this moment. I stood next to my mother, cold, lifeless, posing for a portrait only a sick freak would ever snap as a memory.

"Can I grieve, please?!"

"Sure. I already had a four-hour head start."

I leave. Slam the door behind me. Act like a stereotypical teenager in an increasingly typical scenario. Or, at least, I have convinced myself of this over the past four hours as a disgusting coping mechanism.

The door behind me would not allow me to go further. I return to the door only moments after exiting. I peer through the small window, set my sights on my father. He wobbles to my mother's bedside, noticeably shakes. His knees buckle. He lands in the same position in which he proposed. He stares up at his wife, my mother. Tears attack his cheeks at an unimaginable rate.

Never seen my father like this…

He paces back and forth. Distraught. Sick. I feel bodies behind me. Nurses hover. I turn to face them. I breathe deeply. They breathe deeply. We stare. They feel the pain on my face. It resonates. They stagger backwards a bit. They are worried, not wanting to upset the delicate balance of service and grief. They study my face to see if anything has changed in my stance from earlier in the day. It hasn't.

It has.

They notice my slight change in demeanor, rush through the alleviated tension into my mother's room, where they find my father, drenched in a puddle of his own tears, shirt unbuttoned, untucked, unlike anything I have ever witnessed.

Never seen my father like this…

I follow behind the nurses who finally begin the process of removing my mother from her machines, from her room, from this world, from us. My father fights this process. I wrap my arms around him from behind. He tries to escape my grasp. We fall to the floor. He screams at the top of his lungs as my mother is taken out of her room.

It is always difficult… to witness someone thoroughly recognize… that they are too late to do anything… about something they could have…

VI

Poor paintbrush. It feels so out of place. It wobbles, within an almost violent ricochet between my fingers. Quivers under the vibration of my shaky hand. The paint touches the surface of the formerly blank page, lacks all the precision it once possessed. I sit on my stool, decked out in the only attire I know now. Black short sleeve button-down collared shirt. Black loose-fitting slacks. Black socks. Black sneakers. Black laces. Black baseball cap, no logo.

I sit in front of this easel, paintbrush in hand, attempt to find my muse. My hands falter. My creativity wanes. I stare at my walls. Paintings splatter across every inch.

The one of the last time we went to the beach. Perfect blue sky. Clear blue water. I can still hear the sea rushing onto the sand only to rescind its flawed offer at God's command.

And the one of her sleeping that caught her by surprise. Not that I did it, but that I painted it from memory. Such detail derived from wanting to protect her while she slept, serving as her sole means of survival.

And the one of her standing, I on my knees, with my ear to her pregnant stomach, only I was the one she was pregnant with. A reminder as to where I am from, and where I have landed, and who is responsible for both locales. I am listening to our connection being formed over the course of nine months, a connection no umbilical cord could ever sever…

And the one…
And the one…
And the one…
My mother is dead…
The paintbrush shakes violently in my hand. I barely control it enough to place it in the cup of water, but not before splashing a mix of paint and water onto any

nearby item – including my shirt. I quickly take it off, toss it into the dirty clothes hamper and open my closet door. The closet is black. Not in color but in literalities. I had to look that word up, but apparently it is one.

Nine short sleeve button-down collared shirts. Nine black loose-fitting slacks. Nineteen pairs of black socks. Another pair of black sneakers. A backup pair of laces. An extra black baseball cap, no logo. Black boxers. But you don't need to know that.

I grab one of the short sleeve button-down collared shirts. I put it on. It fits. No surprise there. My clothes are the only things that fit. Nothing else – fits. A 14-year-old motherless black male with an absent, overly ambitious father and nowhere healthy to vent his frustrations. This is not a combination for someone that – fits.

Where I fit has been taken from me. I no longer have her bosom to rest my weary head. I can no longer listen to her breathe to soothe my angst. My heartbeat is out of sync without the synchronization of hers next to mine. I always knew I was alive simply because she was. What kind of son would I be to continue to live without her? How selfish would I be? She must be angry with me. The audacity to try to keep going. I go back and forth every day about whether or not I should just join her now, get it over with. But I have never been one for personal bodily harm…

My mother is dead…

My knees buckle under me. I collapse to the floor. Sprawled out, uncoordinated, pound on the carpet. Tears flood my face. Inaudibly, at first. I hold back any sound for as long as possible. Only sound heard is the heavy whisper of my fists hitting the carpet. I cannot stop crying. I try to turn off my memories. They clog my vision, carry me to a place where all I can do is surrender. Surrender to her death, and the emptiness it has caused.

My fight against inaudibility is officially a losing one. I cannot hold back any longer. I whimper. I wail. I bawl. I bellow. I scream… I mourn. Days – I think – have passed since she left this earth. Her funeral is on the horizon. No one will recognize me. This level of emotion makes one unrecognizable. Look into my eyes and fall into a darkness only fit for those who have lost the loves of their lives.

Only thing I knew how to do was be her son. My paintbrush even knows she is gone. It has lost its ability to function properly, used to working under the guidance of my mother. It is sort of funny; I feel the same way. I am unable to function properly without the guidance of my mother. She was the only one who could direct my tears in a different direction. I possess a certain level of strong sensitivity my mother could navigate to make sure I was in the proper emotional state. Without her, my emotional dexterity is off kilter.

It is quieting down. Whimpers stop. Wails halt. Bawls subside. Bellows silenced. Screams calm down… but mourning…

My mother is dead…

I lie on the floor. Face down. Arms sprawled out above my head. Breaths deep, and fluid, like someone who is patiently waiting for something better to come along…

I hear another heartbeat. I feel another cadence of breath. There is someone else in here. I slowly roll over to witness the sight of my father standing in my doorway. He just stares at me, my tear-stained cheeks announcing what has already transpired.

"Why are you crying?"

"Why aren't you?"

He continues to look at me, study me. He looks at me like he has never seen me before, as if I could not be his son. Not this emotional child, unable to function without his mother on this earth.

And he just… walks away. Walks away without once thinking about how many pieces of me he has broken and left in the middle of my bedroom floor. His exit brings the sound in my room back to the simplicity of my solo breaths. The calm pains me. His calm pains me. I do not think he has shed a tear since that first night. Since the night she left us to our own accord.

Silence, deafening. I have to do something about it. Screams are past their prime. I just need something for me at this point. There is only one place to go at this stage. A place filled with darkness. Darkness painted in red, ashy knuckles in between its crevices. Dripped and dropped in puddles of blood. Dents in walls, too familiar to fight back.

I stand up. Slow, methodical, with a purpose. Dust off my slacks. A little bit off my shirt. Prepare. Face flushed within the calm of my conscious decision to harm myself. Have not been to this place since my mother ---

My mother is dead...

My hand pounds against the wall. Slow at first. Paced, even. Slowly, the pain I feel is the pain I feel. The melanin in my brown-skinned hand fights the screeching red as it gushes with newfound energy down scarred knuckles and stretched out fingers. A new dent created. A new attack on myself. A new journey to self-destruction.

I use my father's bathroom to clean up the steady stream of blood flowing from my hand. I rinse it off, put together makeshift bandages, wrap them around my hand. It is well-done, if I say so myself.

I make eye contact with my father, as he watches me tend to my wounds, my pain.

"How much is that going to cost me?"

How much are sons going for nowadays?

VII

Such a blessed closet. So much black. So much beauty. Today calls for something different. A white short sleeve button-down collared shirt. White loose-fitting slacks. White socks. White sneakers. White laces. White baseball cap, no logo. Laid out on my bed. Attire so fitting for a viewing.

You are assuming that my mother is an angel, so the attire is appropriate. That is incorrect. White is depression. White is the prison-industrial complex. White is the school-to-prison pipeline. White is the destruction of human rights. White is oppression. White is slavery. White is racism. White is death. Are you shocked? Are you surprised? How could I place white in such light? Imagine how black must feel.

This shirt fits perfectly. One sleeve at a time. Five buttons. So do these slacks. One leg at a time. Zipper. One button. Comfortable socks. One foot at a time. Sneakers snug. One foot at a time. Laces clean. Double knots. Both sides. Baseball cap fitted. Perfect imagery.

My soul is splintered into thousands of pieces and not even the best surgeon with the most steady of hands and a surgical team of the best in all of their select fields could put it back together again not without the voice of my mother guiding them putting them in the right position to properly assemble a soul only she knows up close...

Run on sentence, run on...

Sentenced to an earthly existence sans my mother. Dressed in exactly the message I want to portray. I just hope people can understand my word choice, my style choice. Not trying to make some grand statement. People only question you when you go against the Eurocentric norm. Baldwin would be so proud of me in this moment.

"What are you wearing?"

My father wears tradition on his back like his slave first and last name were tailored for his lips. Black suit. Grey tie. Black shoes. Grey socks. Perfectly shaven. A crisp gentleman. Baldwin would put my father in such a properly structured sentence, dropping him to his knees in Uncle Tom anguish. Oh, the whole armor of God is on me today and She is just as fed up as I am.

"She would want you to be appropriate at this time. We are about to bury her. You look silly. You do not look like my son."

I stare at this oddity of a man. This traitor of gene pools. What does his son look like? I look like my mother's son, possibly the greatest visual representation I could foster. His approval is not necessary in this moment. Neither is his presence. Neither is mine. My feet start moving. Somehow, I end up out the door. Walking up the hill from our house. Someone calls my name.

"Vinnie? Vinnie?!"

Sounds like my father. Does not sound like my dad. My legs make my decision for me. One step at a time. No need for directions, this is natural progression. I am supposed to go this way, in this way. Time to walk in my truth. I will be saying goodbye to my mother's body soon. There is no way to prepare yourself for such an occasion, only time.

Footsteps behind me. Louder. Running – with a purpose. I do not want to turn my head around. I do not want to see my father in his house slave's Sunday's best. The footsteps slow, replaced by heavy breathing.

I hope it is my father…

"Look at me."

I know this voice. It is one of friendship, of knowing when to show up, of being there, of providing a shoulder, of walking in my truth. I turn around to engage.

"My dear friend."

"You walk too damn fast."

"You're just out of shape, sir."

"You need to learn slang."

"Colloquialisms?"

"Why you ruin everything?"

I smile. This burst of youthful exuberance comes at a time when my thoughts only surround that of the adult realm. I am dealing with things beyond my emotional scope. Am I intelligent enough to understand? Absolutely. But despite my academic prowess, I still cannot add more years of experience to my current 14. No book can substitute experience. I have experienced other worlds through my favorite writers' viewpoints but that is all that I can claim. To be a kid, on occasion, is a necessary reminder to slow down.

"You thinking about something overly deep, ain't you?"

This white boy makes me laugh.

"How can you tell?"

"You make facial expressions the rest of us don't know how to. Like you've been here before or something. When it happens, I have to fight the urge to slap the hell out of you."

"Fight the good fight."

"I hate you."

"I miss you too, Walter."

He wears a beat up white T-shirt, dirty blue jeans, busted sneakers and battle scars. He looks like he auditioned for The Sandlot or Stand By Me. A stereotypical rugged white boy, attractive to some, a threat to others. His experiences differ from mine. It is written in his outfit, on his skin. In his eyes. His tongue paints a different picture, but his eyes? Pain's locale.

"Where are you headed?"

Drop my eyes. Raise them again. Slightly smile. But I would not call it a smile. That would be disrespectful to happiness. Walter puts his arm around me.

"I'm going, too."

"You are?"

"I am now."

We walk. Nobody talks. Only about a mile remains in this trek. A car has not pulled up yet to reveal my father. It is a detail of this trip I thought would be added. He let me leave his house, on the way to his deceased wife's funeral, by myself. I may not be dressed like his son, but he is not dressed like my dad. He is forever my father. Biological necessity. Financial security. He fills a need but, does not satisfy mine.

VIII

It smells like brimstone. Hell swims in my nostrils, explodes onto my tongue, and spits out venom. I do not want to stain the pews of this church. It would be unbecoming.

I stand here, with Walter behind me, in the middle aisle of a church I have not entered in five years. It stopped being a place of frequent visits when my mother realized her husband was not going to love her as Christ loved the church. He loved her as Christ loved his cross – you hang in there out of love and destiny, but you will die here.

My mother did not die here. And yet, days later, we must revisit her death as this fresh occurrence. Something to sink our grieving hearts into. And by all of us, I mean me. My grief is the only one that matters. Unless these others are willing to reach my level – the level of a son losing his best friend, confidant, security and place of rest – then no, you may not claim grief. Not now. Not in my vicinity.

Walter stands by my side now. I do not know when he arrived there, but he is there, like he always is. Funny how someone with seemingly no redeeming qualities can be such an outlet at a time when I am burying my mind's focal point.

"Dude, this sucks."

"Yes, that it does."

"I'm sorry, man."

"Just something else we have in common now."

"I didn't want that."

"And yet..."

Time refuses to sit still...

The sanctuary is three-quarters full. Friends. Co-workers. Family members. Strangers. Each with their own reason for being here at this time. I just wish they would stop consoling me. Words can do nothing at this time. None of these others were there on my level while my mother was alive so how can they join me in grief? They could not join me in love so how can they join me in grief?

My eyes water. I hate this emotion. I hate that I cannot control it. It is the only way my body knows how to express itself. I wish there were another way. But there is not. I will spend the rest of my life trying to find another way.

I do not hear any of the words rendered during the service. I am sure they are nice. I sit here between my father, and his politically correct grief, and my friend, Walter, whose attire is just as renegade as my own.

The naked eye would deem my attire angelic. This beautiful black boy draped in light. But how these others look at me is what this color, this light, this white, deserves. Stared at in disgust, stared at with disdain, lost in this flood of black and grey. This light seems out of place in this darkness.

My skin crawls. The fake in the air stifles. I find myself watching as these others find it in their hearts to mourn. Their backstories each scream of negligence; showing their faces here now is just a means of clearing a conscience.

Oh, it's my turn...

I find myself being called to the microphone. The expectation is for me to say something about my mother. Seems like a simple enough task.

I step to the microphone and turn to the crowd. Draped in my socially incorrect garb, it isn't difficult to ascertain exactly why the others stare. Nevertheless, they all expect words to leave my mouth. For them to receive some level of understanding, of the one relationship my mother had that no one else could quite understand. This bond was something unseen before.

But even as paragraph length stacks of sentences with Baldwin-isms flanking every precisely put together turn of phrase crafted with a seamless literary quality barricade themselves behind one another expecting to be released into the awaiting ears of the others – I cannot speak.

There are no words. I am incapable of expressing myself in this moment. So, I stare into the audience, pick out one-by-one those who intrigue my eyesight. All the while hi-jacking the attention of those in attendance.

I'm so sorry... that I'm not sorry...

Angst fills a row with a divorced man on one end and a divorced woman on the other. It is palpable, the angst. It is clear that the angst is between them specifically. The angst is theirs. They know the angst all too well. It chokes their breaths as they attempt to mourn, but they cannot decide whether they are mourning my mother, or mourning the death that birthed the angst. Too bad they cannot go back and do it again. Too bad they would not know that they should try again anyway.

My mother tried to help them...

He has beaten her. Over and over. She stays still. Over and over. She refuses to move from beneath his iron fist to shelter. He uses her face as a launching pad for his insecurities. He marks his territory with black and blue bruises encapsulating the loathing of his mother, in her lack of a father. She never knew what the love of a man entailed. So she suffers a sick retribution for mistakes she never made.

My mother consoled her...

Muscular arms across his chest. He needs no seat. Just the vestibule. His jawline screams of past battles, both with himself and his demons. But he has won now. He has taken his innumerable mistakes in his youth and transformed them into a ministry, guiding young men of today away from the drugs, sex and violence that consumed his once frail psyche. I welcome his presence here, despite being unaware of his why.

My mother respected him…

An elderly woman sits solemnly, Baptist-church-goer hat adorns her petite head. Her eyes – fixate on me. That matters not. All that matters is that she has been here before, too many times, yet this, is still, her first time.

My mother honored her…

A civil rights activist who brought me non-fiction upon non-fiction books to add to my colossal collection of literature. She saw something in me. She saw herself. I welcome her presence here.

My mother adored her…

A young girl, innocence drips from her eyes as everything that reaches them is new. She stares at her mother, engulfs the image of her scowl, her inability to feel, and packs it, only to be used later when her attitude blossoms and she needs a reference point for her immediate demolition of souls. She had to get it from somewhere. That somewhere is here.

My mother prayed for her…

I burst from my post at the microphone and back into the pew. The crowd incapable of gathering the proper response to such awkward emotion. I am an emotional embarrassment of riches as I struggle to find my place among the two men in my life.

Tears dart down my cheeks. My father to my right. My Walter to my left.

I rest to the left…

My father, rigid. He sees nothing. Blind to emotional dexterity. His natural inclinations muffle the silent cries of parental instinct. He does not recognize his child in need. He will, though. One day… if it's the last thing I do…

Baldwin…

I stand at this, at this microphone, near the burial site where my mother will rest. Make eye contact with a hoard of strange spectators gathered for sport. My stomach gurgles, pushes through my esophagus, creates a bile word vomit to land on the laps of those who dare to watch me speak. I do not apologize for such things. The taste, one of decadent souls and rotten relationships.

I speak.

"'No one can possibly know what is about to happen: it is happening, each time, for the first time, for the only time'... James Baldwin."

The crowd hushed.

"'Love does not begin and end the way we seem to think it does. Love is a battle, love is a war; love is a growing up'... James Baldwin."

Does no one understand this grief of mine?

"'Love takes off masks that we fear we cannot live without and know we cannot live within... James Baldwin.'"

Their eyes feel so violent against my skin.

"'It was books that taught me that the things that tormented me most were the very things that connected me with all the people who were alive, or who had ever been alive... James Baldwin.'"

Tears in my eyes. So necessary. As is my anger. My voice betrays me, crackles in the pool of pain in my throat.

"'To be a Negro in this country and to be relatively conscious is to be in a rage almost all the time... James Baldwin.'"

Each time I say Baldwin's name, more and more of me is released into the air. I am relegated to a sounding board, a young man whose voice is no longer his own.

"'You know, it's not the world that was my oppressor, because what the world does to you, if the world does it to you long enough and effectively enough, you begin to do it to yourself... James Baldwin!'"

They are scared now. They should be. They do not know how to handle my emotion. So they sit still. Soak in my breakdown with a sponge-like quality.

"'Children have never been very good at listening to their elders, but they have never failed to imitate them!' James Baldwin!"

Screeching. Shrieking. Howling. Face flushed.

My mother is dead...

My father stands up. Fixes his suit jacket. Turns to his minions first. Half smiles. Walks in my direction. He matters not.

"'The world is before you and you need not take it or leave it as it was when you came in!' James Baldwin!"

My father attempts to grab me, wraps his arms around my waist. This is the closest thing to a hug he has ever given me...

I fight him at every step, my voice incapable of being muzzled. I feel like Samson when he got his strength back that one final time. No one could stop him. No one will stop me.

"'The most dangerous creation of any society is the man who has nothing to lose!' James Baldwin! 'The future is like heaven, everyone exalts it, but no one wants to go there now!' James Baldwin!"

Within our struggle, my father finds my ear and coarsely whispers into it.

"You have effectively ruined your mother's burial service. You have effectively ruined everything. You are effective. You are defective."

"'People who treat other people as less than human must not be surprised when the bread they have cast on the waters comes floating back to them, poisoned!' James Baldwin!"

Defective... defective... defective...

IX

It must pain him to sit back here without the distraction of driving. Without the immediate excuse of needing to watch the road that prevents him from making eye contact with his single fatherhood. Our limo driver took that away from him. Rid him of his ever-so-useful excuse. Now he must make eye contact with the one thing he has never attempted to understand.

I stare at his face. The muscular ridges of his jawline. His cautiously furrowed brow. His flared nostrils. His stern chin. All attributes he held back from me. He could not imagine giving me something that was so integral to what made him him. What gave him the ability to walk into any room and garner the respect of all those who entered, all those who stayed. His expressions were that of a man who beat pain into submission, hurdled obstacles with grace and dignity, who did not put his failures in the laps of others, rather he just refused to fail at all. Made it easier that way.

He fights an unnatural feeling now. That feeling of failure. He failed as a husband. A protector. A lover. He fails as a father, though the latter is not a psychological locale he will rest in just yet. It is still up to me to invite him to his inevitability. Do not worry. I am working on it.

"Are we almost there?"

Nothing. I knew this would happen but I still felt the need to question him in some way, even if it was of the small talk ilk. At least he could never say I did not try. I try. I have tried.

"Do you know why they call it a repast? Seems like a word with a lot of meaning behind it. Traditional. Historical, even."

He looks left. He looks right. He looks down. He looks around. He never looks at his son.

"I'm hungry."

That inhale-exhale was earth-shattering...

"Shut up. Just – shut your mouth. I do not want to hear you. I do not want to see you. I do not want to breathe you. I want to rid you of the half of you that is me so I can stop blaming myself for who you have become. For you are my fault – at least in part."

He looks at me now, with a sacred disdain only used for a certain kind of hatred. Derived from a place of love. One cannot hate something as strongly as something they once loved. That thin line is through and through. I do not return his eye contact. I wanted it only a moment prior but it is now unnecessary. He said what he said. I heard every word, every enunciation, every syllable.

The limo slows to a stop.

"Your answer."

He opens the door. Sunlight floods the interior, burns where he once sat. I sit there for a second, wait for the heat to evaporate my father's scorn. The seconds become minutes as the palpability of such an emotion proves itself steady. It will not dissipate by simply being patient. It will not fold simply by my own sheer will. It will need to be destroyed, brought to its knees before ever considering an attempt at its rebirth.

But first, I must exit.

Sunlight bounces off my pearly white garb, blinds onlookers as their black skin and attire absorbs every ounce of heat it can. They starve for what already nourishes me.

I enter the facility that holds all the remaining funeral goers as they await to partake in the repast. In normal surroundings, I would question the necessity to eat food following the burial of a loved one, but funerals are selfish occasions anyway. They are for the living. The loved one is dead and gone. Sometimes for over a week of time. The grieving begins well before we take the time to bury someone. Yet, we still gather together to celebrate a life. It is done only to be seen. We want others to know just how much we cared. How much devastation we are enduring. It is odd, in the least. It is scary, at the most. It is tradition, in the end.

Eyes find me. I have not forgotten what just transpired at the burial. I am aware of what I have done. Glares pierce my every step. I will not be alone again as long as we continue the celebration of my mother's life. I will be a target. This I accept.

I take my place in line. A few elders motion me to the front of the line. Tradition states that the family of the deceased eat first. I listen to tradition. My plate reflects all that is cultured about this occasion. Chicken. Mashed potatoes and gravy. Ham. Green beans. Collard greens. Buttered roll. A plate of celebration. It is supposed to replace the sadness of the day with the small talk of the hour. Here, at the repast, I am supposed to engage my fellow mourners in conversation that either further mourns my mother, or completely forgets she died in the first place. Either way, I am supposed to slowly start putting a smile on my face. My mourning ends with this meal. That is the only reason I could come up with for me to be eating right now.

Oh, and tradition.

I take a seat one spot down from my father. This was an odd selection on my part but necessary. I stare at my plate. Everything looks delicious. If only I were hungry. Only thing I starve for is understanding. Why was I still here and mother was gone? Why was I left here to deal with my father on my own? Why was this food in my face like it was going to satisfy any level of my grief?

Anger builds in me at a steady pace. Confusion chokes my sanity. I cannot eat this. I move my food back and forth. It mixes together into a farm boy's slop. Its aesthetic ruined.

"Anger builds in me at a steady pace. Confusion chokes my sanity. I cannot eat this. I move my food back and forth. It mixes together into a farm boy's slop. Its aesthetic ruined."

Eyes never left me. More eyes join in. My father moves his food around as if he did not hear me. He heard me. He listened. Intently. And what he heard was worrisome. But I doubt he is worried about the proper thing.

I must not partake in this conclusion of my grief. I must not. My grief is not over. Your grief might be over. Their grief might be over. But my grief is not over. You cannot tell me to eat this!

"I must not partake in this conclusion of my grief. I must not. My grief is not over. Your grief might be over. Their grief might be over. But my grief is not over. You cannot tell me to eat this!"

I realize I am standing. I have been standing for some time now. My mind and mouth no longer singular entities.

My plate. In my hand. Launched at the wall. Its remnants splatter amongst the shock of my action. I am not shocked at my actions. Nor am I surprised at the rising stench of my father's fury piercing my nostrils, his loathing soaked in his inability to pass me off to another person.

My mother is dead...

I am his problem now. This much is true.

X

Hate is love's ricochet. As humans, we would still know hate, even in the absence of love. Darkness came before the light. We have always known the darkness. The same cannot be said for the light. The light is a guest of darkness. And it has long overstayed its welcome.

Darkness looks back at me with the same cluelessness as it did during light's origination. It renamed itself in recent years. Thomas is what it is calling itself nowadays. And this is the most attention he has given me since my mother forced him to be a father. It did not last as long as she would have liked. She took her duty to the next level. Originally, she forced darkness into fatherhood with the promise that she would be around to help. She broke that promise recently. Took her last breath without warning. Leaving darkness and light alone to reconcile their function in each other's worlds. At the very least, we must find a way to get back to dusk and dawn. Staying in the midnight and noon hours will leave us forever separated, perpetually missing opportunities to reconnect with each other, to meet in the middle, to mix darkness with the light.

I am aware of how much darkness fills my light. I am half-darkness after all. I have lived at dawn for years now. Dragged my feet towards the light as darkness continued to pull at my waist. It was not a pull of jealousy. It was a pull of interference. A recognition that preventing me from seeing the light would leave me in purgatory, void of darkness or light. I would be nothing. A never-ending story.

Thomas has not stopped staring at me. I question whether I should seek his love. I fear for my psyche, what my emotional health would look like in his lathered in lotion yet calloused hands. I morph into lines on printed paper. Material on his desk at work. A creation to be studied, read over and over again. His overtime hours in the flesh. A pro bono assignment. All work, and no return. A project with no deadline. An issue with no clear resolution. A representation of his loss of control. My humanity dissipates. A son, no longer. Person is the past. Project is the future.

Nothing...

The limo stops. Darkness, or Thomas, remains. Tilts his head to the right. Rotates it back to his left. Back centered. Raises his chin. Fixes his coat. Slowly, exits the vehicle. I sit in what remains of his shadow. The door closes behind him just loudly enough to leave a lasting impression.

"Where to, young man?"

Limo driver, hush. I am trying to think. Never struggled with gathering my thoughts quite like this. Last time, maybe, five years old? I have to be coming up on a decade of knowing exactly what I want.

Nothing has changed...

I have nowhere to take my emotions. My shield is becoming one with the earth we buried her in. I could dig her up, hoard her remains until I no longer need its nutrients. But, no. That would be unbecoming. I just... I do not know where to go from here.

Return to the darkness before the darkness returns to you...

"It is getting dark outside, young man. What would you like to do?"

"Just take me down the street, thank you."

Gas given. Wheels rolling. We embark on such a necessary journey. So short in distance, long in relevance.

"Here, please."

We stop.

"Thank you, sir."

"Be careful, young man."

"I will."

"And... sorry for your loss."

"I appreciate the sentiment."

I exit facing the houses. As the limo departs, I turn towards the canyon behind me. And to my left is Walter. I smile. He holds a change of clothes for me.

"I thought you might need these."

"You would be right."

He hands me my garb. Black short sleeve button-down collared shirt. Black loose-fitting slacks. Black socks. Black sneakers. Black laces. Black baseball cap, no logo. Only thing that stays the same are my boxer-briefs. But you didn't need to know that.

I keep an extra outfit at Walter's house. The runaway ensemble.

I remove what will never again grace my skin. White short sleeve button-down collared shirt. White loose-fitting slacks. White socks. White sneakers. White laces. White baseball cap, no logo.

My black is nicely laid down on the sidewalk in front of the canyon. My white is tossed to the ground in a pile of forgotten. In complete disregard of my surroundings, stripped down to my undergarments, I dress in what is my reality. I must not forget the place where I found Baldwin. The place where I tackled intellectual immaturity.

"You got it?"

"You know I do."

"I can always count on you, Walter."

"Hey, I'm only here for the fireworks."

Walter reveals the slabs of wood. Plays with his lighter in his hand, his teeth foreshadow the brightness of the near future. I cannot help but to smile right back at him.

We carry the wood down into the canyon. Our past still where we left it. We place our future where the past has sat since last summer. We do not visit here as often as we once did, but when we do, it is as if we never left. We both understand when we need to return. Like today. This is much needed.

"Lighter or dropper?"

"I'll drop."

"Good. I wasn't allowing you near the flame anyway."

Walter hands me my white clothes. He initiates the flame. It smothers the wood in its heat. Smoke enters the air, floats ever so slowly towards my mother's current conversation with God.

"Drop 'em."

I place each white garment into the flame one by one. The flame grows, its light glistening off the teeth of Walter, who enjoys this. He likes fire. It is the one time being explosive is a good thing for him.

The fire scarfs down the garments, inherits their stories like a touch from Rogue's fingertips.

"Sit down with me, my dear friend."

"You're so gay --"

He looks to me. He knows I disapprove. I do not force him to read bell hooks for no reason.

"I'm sorry. My masculinity does not define me."

"That's better."

"I hate it when you make me be smart."

"Intelligence is not ugly. It is the most attractive thing a person can exude without seeing it."

"Wouldn't that be love?"

"An inquiry?"

"Dude, I'm already trying to backtrack and figure out what the hell 'exude' meant. Now you hit me with inquiry?"

"No apologies."

"Shit."

We breathe in the unhealthy toxins produced by our makeshift fire as if it is fresh air.

"So sorry for your loss, bro."

"I'm sorry for my loss, too. And thank you. For being there."

"Ain't nothing soft about losing --"

And there it is. The mask removes itself from Walter's unyielding exterior. This is the only place he feels vulnerable. And I am the only one invited to such a locale.

"I know you miss her."

"It never goes away, man. It never does. As much as you shake your head back and forth. As much as you cry. As much as you throw your fists into a wall. As much as you want to kill... It never goes away, man. I will die without a mother. That is the only thing I know to be true."

A black boy painter with James Baldwin tattooed to the brain and a white boy with tattooed scars on his skin sit amongst the flames. Friendship further connected by their joint disconnections from the only people they have ever known to truly love them – besides each other. I am thankful to be a part of this duo, of this bond, of the unexplainable. It is all we know now. It is all we want to know.

Walter puts his hand in his front pocket. Dives in with purpose. Yanks out a small, shiny object. The fire attacks it, shines light until it glistens in the night shine.

A box cutter. I cannot help but stare, for I have my own. But I assume that my reasons for ownership are different than Walter's.

"I wonder what it would be like to kill my father."

I assume correctly.

XI

I could not lie. I shall not lie. Lying would be wrong. Lying would be inappropriate. The truth is all that is necessary, in the here and now. So I speak only of my truth. For I, too, have thought about it. I thought about it, too. I thought about it, I have. I have thought about it.

I wonder what it would be like to kill Walter's father...

"I already know how I would do it."

He plays with the box cutter in his hands like a child prodigy at the seat of his piano. His fingers sing a song of routine, the eagerness familiar. They have done this dance before. The fire kisses the cutter, moisture engages its shine. It sure is beautiful.

"I would want him at his happiest, ya know? I would want him happy as hell. I'd want him – gleeful. Gay, in the good way. It would have to include his beers. His television. Probably a football game. He would laugh. He would be so damn comfortable. Then... I would end his smile. One smooth cut would do it. But not well enough that he would die without knowing it was me who did it. He would get his chance to look me in the eye. I would give that to him. It would be the last thing he would get from me."

I look my dear friend in his eye. Or, at least, I attempt to. But he will not engage me. To watch him deep in thought, surrounding the worst and best thing he could ever do for himself, somehow increases our connection. He is letting me watch him. He does not have to allow me in this space. I guess it is simply repayment for all the time he has spent in my own.

"Such a well-thought out entrance into the prison pipeline."

"So worth it."

"Would it be?"

"You mean to tell me that you haven't thought about offing your pops? Bullshit."

"Destruction can come in so many forms. Death is only one of many choices to pick from. To each their own."

Walter licks his box cutter, tastes every nook and cranny of its potential.

"Tastes like forever."

"So poetic of you."

"This is the only poetry I would write."

Walter allows the fire to kiss his box cutter one last time before placing it back in his pocket. Walter's hands, a steadying force. We look at each other. My curiosity beckons for more. But I will leave it alone for now. For now, I will be here as a sounding board for my friend, as he has been for me time and time again.

We walk away from the heat. Take steps towards the familiar angst that will find us in our homes. Being outside, being with each other, provides us an escape we truly treasure. I view him through a different light now. As the fire burns behind our backs, Walter takes his first steps into his new role. I do not know how much more his shoulder can handle. I have brought him so much of my pain when his is already so palpable. It might be selfish of me. But Walter always presents himself as someone incapable of letting pain get to him. Pain is just part of life.

Pain is life.

This walk is so familiar. It is second nature. Naturally, we do not use our words. Just steps in the right direction. I peek into the windows of the various homes on our street. I do not see anything of substance but I still picture these families, their operations, their quirks, their pain. Pain is no assumption in this case. Pain is everywhere. I assume.

Pain is life.

I smile at this notion, this realization. There is no real reason to be lonely within pain. No one person is feeling something that has not been felt before, that is not being felt right now. There is no emotion, no pain, singularly built for one person. We share pain. We take our own pieces of it but its essence is connected to all others who have witnessed or felt the same. Tears are recycled, passed on to the next generation to be used all over again. Our ancestors laugh when we place our pain within the realm of independence.

Front of my home. Its walls encapsulating my escape, and my destination. Walter stands at the top of his driveway. I do the same with mine. We stand there, breathing in sync. It takes a moment of preparation to return to the place of your torment. It takes everything in me not to rush Walter, tear his box cutter out of his pocket, and off his father. To alleviate Walter of his torment, and provide him with a place to rest his head for the remainder of his time in this world, the offer is written in stone. But I have a father, too. Or at least, there is a man in my home auditioning for the role. It is not going well.

Walter and I make eye contact for the last time, each at the door of our home. One final breath. Entrance. Doors closed. We will not know what the other needs until tomorrow. This is friendship.

XII

Silence is such a powerful language. I speak it fluently. Answers to questions do not always need to be expressed verbally. I can answer with my lips in a smile, smirk, frown. The slouch in my back, pace of my walk, body language. But my favorite is my eyes. My eyes answer questions in ways no other part of me can. It is truly unfortunate that my teachers are not as fluent in this language as I am. Their jobs depend on verbal responses from their students. They seek a sense of accomplishment. They need to know they are reaching their pupils. Hearing words is their means of doing so. Such an incorrect analysis.

Period 1...

Starting a day with a math class is supposedly a detriment to a student's education. I look at it differently. Starting my day with a math class gives me an excuse to not interact with anyone else the rest of the day. I simply blame it on a long recovery time from the painstakingly stagnant, conceptually inept consumption of math concepts that lack practical application.

Oh. And I am stupid amounts of good at it. That's probably what annoys me the most.

Ms. Williams worries about me. It is even worse on this day. She thinks I am incapable of being in her classroom with my mother no longer on this earth. She would be wrong. For my mother is still here, with me, at all times. Her inability to fathom such a connection is not my worry in this moment.

"Vinnie...?"

She waddles to where I sit as I attempt to get the rest that I could not attain the night before. She taps me on my shoulder, the pudge from her fingers push down into my skin with each tap.

Tap, tap, tap...

My head rises, such methodical prowess I possess. The class, in my grasp as Ms. Williams comes to the conclusion that awakening me from my slumber is more important than engaging the riff raff she has assembled in chairs befitting the back problems lingering in our not-too-distant futures.

"Vinnie…?"

My eyes open to the stares of my peers. They all fear me in their own way. Some for my intelligence, which, let's face it, dwarfs theirs into such immense darkness that it causes one to question even their completely correct answers. Some for my attire as it sends them nervous energy screaming with unpredictability. What could I do next? The irony of it all is that I do not really do anything at school. That is what scares them. Inactivity to mediocre human beings shrieks of mental frailty for I choose to refrain from joining them on their journey to the eastern shores of nothingness.

"Vinnie…?"

"Ms. Williams, please, just say what you need to say so I can get back to counting my sheep. They are frightened without me and I must care for them like they were my own."

"You count someone else's sheep when you sleep?"

"I mean, don't you?"

Have you ever trolled someone in mid-conversation? No? Witness its glory.

"I don't think so."

"I do not own sheep so how could I possibly count my own if I do not own them? Would that not defeat the purpose of defining the word 'own' within this context?"

Ms. Williams does not know how to handle such a riddle from such an adolescent man. I continue to play.

"Or is the intellect dripping from such a riddle too intricate of an ask for someone who simply deals with numbers all day in order to refrain from critical thinking?"

Ms. Williams is in a permanent state of pause. I should know since I put her there. I take one look at the whiteboard.

$5(2x + 6) = -4(-5 – 2x) + 3x$ ... *Why does she insist on providing me with literally no challenge?*

"10."

I rest my head back on the desk where it belongs.

"That is correct."

I know it is, or else I would not have said it.

I am sorry. I was a bit hard on Ms. Williams. I do not mean to devalue her ability to teach. I have just spent so much time learning on my own that time in classroom settings is almost disrespectful to my relationship with Baldwin.

"The paradox of education is precisely this; that as one begins to become conscious, one begins to examine the society in which he is being educated" - James Baldwin

And, of course, it takes away from my nap time. I sleep more now without my mother's bosom to rest my head. Rest and sleep are not the same thing. Sleep now is only an escape from the residual pain of her absence in the flesh.

Period 2...

English. A safe haven, of sorts. Math has already rendered me mute for the remainder of my day but being unable to speak has never prevented the greats from performing at the highest of levels.

Ms. Chasity: "Pen a poem. No parameters. As we begin our poetry unit, I want to see where you stand in relation to your ability to put together a poem using whatever literary devices you may remember from your past classes. Is that ok with you?"

Class: "Yep!" "Bruh." "Yessir!" "Yadada feel me?" "Naw."

I'm clearly not a part of this chorus but the assignment itself intrigues me. I decide to oblige Ms.

Chasity. I guess I can write a little something...

"To be 14 years old and conscious is to be in a constant presence of inferiority/So ahead of my time I could sedate my tongue and still be the loudest intellect in this lucid dream/They say age is nothing but a number/To me, it's more like a slip knot dancing with a 12-foot poplar tree/I'm swinging while standing on both feet/My afterthoughts defy gravity/The only asphyxiation that has made my acquaintance comes from a man I've known my whole life but never truly met/Looks like the only option I have left is to let my skin breathe ruby raptures/It's a self-inflicted symphony I have yet to harmonize but every instrument I've ever held in my hands has become an essential element/I am alchemist/Bending bass and woodwind to my will/I expect nothing short of samurai when 22-by-43 millimeter stainless steel become the bow to my string instrument flesh..."

Eh. I think it is okay but not my best work. The jaws rendered motionless in my wake would beg to differ but difference is what I live for, strive more, want more. But it was just a poem. You would think Langston Hughes was sitting in this chair by my side, whispering poetic excellence in my ears, but no, it was all me. And I will not apologize, though I am keenly aware that no apology would be necessary anyway. Preemptive strikes are a fave activity of mine.

Ms. Chasity: "Your work never ceases to amaze me, Vinnie. You truly are a special young man."

If only my father felt the same...

Period 3...

World History. This place elicits my wrath more than any other class. Why? Because it is allergic to the truth. It vomits inaccuracies with drunken precision. It saddens me, sickens me, just how much our Eurocentric education model has warped the minds of teachers into thinking their knowledge base is all-knowing. So I speak up

– often. Get into spats with our curators of education about what they deem to be the truth.

Sometimes, I just enter class early, ask what today's lesson is about, and if I come to the conclusion that it will be falsified information, I ask to be excused to the library for some independent study. If my "teacher" - she gets no name - thinks I should stay in class to defend my perspective, I either devise a way to get kicked out of class or remain to engage her in psychological warfare. The latter is my usual, the former occurs as residual to a previous night's shame wrapped around my father's neck.

"Christopher Columbus discovered America."

"No, he didn't."

"Yes, he did."

"No, he didn't. How do you discover land already occupied by a group of people?"

"He is the one -"

"Exactly. You can't. And he was lost anyway. He called Native Americans, Indians. He was a directionally challenged drunk who probably had a disease."

"Step outside, Vinnie."

Now, this is not currently happening. That was just a rehashing of something that may, or may not have happened already. I will let you come to your own conclusion as to whether I would have said something like that. Should not take you long.

At this moment, I do not have the energy to fight. I do not want to be bothered with this inferior distributor of incorrect information.

Five minutes left in class...

"Vinnie?"

We make eye contact. I do not utilize my vocal chords.

"Vinnie?"

They still do not seem to be working.

"Vinnie? I know you hear me."

I raise my hand.

"Why are you raising your hand when I am the one calling on you?"

I take my raised hand to my lips, pointer finger touches. My audience - or classmates, depending on your view - gasp. The international symbol for 'be quiet' has just been unleashed from the lips of an adolescent to the bruised ego of an improperly educated educator.

It feels so good to hear the orgasmic release of my 'shhhh…' I am sexy in this moment, at least, I think so.

Her white privilege sings a song of despair. I know the tune well. This is not her first audition.

"Get out of my classroom!"

The bell rings. I shrug. And, ironically, execute exactly what she has asked of me. Only with a slight change - I head to fourth period. She will tell her husband about this L she just took during their pillow talk on their unfluffed pillows purchased with her paltry teacher salary and his guitar-playing corner boy tips. No, I do not know if she is dating or married to a guitar-playing corner boy. But she just seems like she would be dating or married to a guitar-playing corner boy. So…

Period 4...

Ms. Scott. Far behind my mother, she is my favorite woman. She brings out the best in me. She had a chance by simply being my art teacher, but she took it and ran with it. She supports me in every way. Being here, in her presence, I welcome this.

"I know you have been away for awhile, Vinnie. Again, my condolences. Were you able to procure anything from your immense talent for us to lay our eyes on?"

Ms. Scott rests her eyes on me. I appreciate her for simple things. Like, using words such as 'procure' and 'immense' when speaking with me. That is a sign of respecting my intelligence, instead of running from it like the rest of my uneducated educators.

I take a rolled up piece of paper out of my backpack. I take off the rubber band and unroll it. I spread it out across the table, unveiling my piece.

Ms. Scott gasps.

I smile.

In front of her lies an HB pencil sketch of a black man in his late 20s being lynched in rural Mississippi and the heavens opening up as he takes his last breaths. Hence, the gasp.

"The detail... I don't know what to say."

I don't have anything to say either. Art speaks its own language. Why draw if you're going to need to explain yourself?

Oh.

And I drew it a year ago. Birthday present to an elderly black man who went to my church - he died of a heart attack before I could give it to him.

And I cried under the weight of that realization.

And its vibrancy almost killed Ms. Scott.

And...

Period 5...

Sign language. I like this class. I get a grade for saying the least, while communicating the most. Needless to say, I have an A.

Period 6...

Physical Education. I do not play a sport. I do have physical education with all of the athletes, however. This scheduling quirk has to do with my playground legend.

Yes, I am a playground legend. I know. All my gifts are becoming annoying. Think of it this way: How can a child with seemingly so many gifts and abilities still not have the ability to make his father see him? Yeah. Now, who's annoyed?

"Line up!"

Mr. Curtis wants all of the boys to prove their manhood by racing one another for 100 yards. My hands can't seem to leave my pockets. My care level is slightly above non-existent.

We line up. My pockets still house my hands.

"Ready! Set! Go!"

My peers take off.

"Stop!"

My peers are upset. I might know why.

"Man, Vinnie. Just race, dude. That's all coach Curtis wants."

"Is it?"

I make eye contact with Mr. Curtis. He looks sad. This is a new look for him. As the school year has progressed he has gone from anger to sadness in my lack of participation. I have my reasons. The main one being - wait - I will get to that soon. I have decided to line up properly.

"Ready! Set! Go!"

My peers and I take off running. My peers collectively decide to run slower than me, or, at least, that is what it seems like as I, in my usual all black ensemble, create space 10 yards long between myself and their dreams.

Oh. Now I remember the main reason why I don't participate - I embarrass easily. Oh no, not me. I don't embarrass easily. Let me rephrase. I embarrass *my peers* easily. Sorry. I misspoke. The trail of egos behind me at the end of this race is about 12 students long.

Mr. Curtis: "We need you!"

I need my mother. And Walter. And a version of my father I can love. No one else.

My hands return to my pockets as we transition to flag football. One of the girls puts my flag around my waist. I smirk, which is taken as some form of 'thank you'.

I am considered a neighborhood wild card. Here, I am in the mood to provide an example.

I stand at one end of the field. We are the receiving team. I was picked last. I am accidentally on this team. I am not wanted.

The ball gets kicked off. It bounces on the ground, over the head of our team captain and heads in my direction. I stare at the ball at it careens wildly towards me, my hands never leave my pockets.

That's a lie.

My hands leave my pockets, to catch this crazy football as it flies towards my face. I catch it. Mr. Curtis' interest grows. I smile.

First victim gets the Reggie Bush.

Second victim gets some Gale Sayers.

Third victim gets some Dante Hall.

Fourth victim gets some LeSean McCoy.

Fifth victim gets some Barry Sanders.

For those of you not following, I have buckled the knees of five of my classmates as they attempt to snatch my flag from my waist. No one has touched me. And no one touches me. I just touch down. Touchdown.

I drop the ball. Metaphorically, drop the mic. Girls bite their lips in my direction. I am attractive to them. This angers my peers. But they can't do anything about it, with, you know, their knees being in shambles and whatnot.

I am the best football player at my school and I do not play on the team. I think this might be the best thing about me.

School is out…

I walk home. I walk home faster. I run home. I run home faster. Backpack bounces up and down on my back. The tears start to flow before I reach my door, fly from my face like suicide raindrops.

I sprint through my front door, enter my room, toss my backpack on my bed.

I scream.

Cry. Laugh. Cry. Laugh.

Scream. Scream. Scream.

My peers do not deserve this. My teachers do not

deserve this. Their slights towards me are stories I have told myself. Nothing they have done requires me to respond to them in the manner in which I do. But...

I am allowed to say whatever I want until someone explains to me why my mother is not here anymore! Explain this to me! Someone! Please?! Please... please... please... explain this to me...

Father.

XIII

This easel is so unattractive. So much of its beauty has been eradicated within the constraints of memories I can no longer attempt to replicate. Each time I sat at that easel, whether with my mother or alone, it was a time filled with wonder. And glee. And happiness. And the unknown. Art provided an outlook for the supernatural to become normal. And now, it is just an empty space. An infuriatingly empty space.

Why was she taken from me?

Somehow, my hands wrap around the easel's neck. I squeeze, wrinkle the sheets like the aftermath of unprotected sex with strange... from what I hear. Violence overwhelms me. I tear at its blank pages with unbecoming rage. Scream at the top of Mt. Everest lungs. Stomp on its remnants like Kirk Franklin's motivation to make street gospel. Put my knees to its throat. Suffocate its ability to create magic like Johnson's AIDS announcement. Punch its lines like police guards through the center of the Selma bridge during one of God's darkest hours.

This easel, this easel represents a life no longer known, a person I no longer am. *My tears sound like they're being chopped and screwed.* I see you, Rudy Francisco. My cries ring of slave hymnals only making sound to renounce the pain, the inevitable setting of a sun that only darkens our skin, provides light only when oppression is looking for us.

I sit with my knees on what remains of the sacred in a backwards prayer. My easel is no longer. Crushed under the weight of a boy who defends himself with defense mechanisms created out of defense of an unknown enemy. I need an escape from this agony, from this realization that all that has provided me with outlet after outlet is severed, in this moment, at this time. But, somehow, I cannot let what has already happened dictate what will happen next. I know, I have seemingly lived my entire existence based on the past and the past has dictated my every step into the future. I must escape its grasp. I must relinquish its hold. And the only way to do such a thing is one final visit to the past. Don't judge me. This is going somewhere.

Hello, mother…

I knew I would land here. At the feet of my mother's grave, breathing deeply in a wind she now controls. Flowers fresh as her spirit holds them at an angle, shouldering all she left behind.

Her tombstone sits atop the earth. Her picture engraved in marble, my father spared no expense. It is one thing I give him credit for, though, his reasoning for doing so is still unknown to me. Love? Quite possibly. Image? Quite likely. Nevertheless, I am thankful that my mother was buried in a magical way, in a magical space, where our bond can meet in space, and time, at the edge of life and death. I know she is among the living, for thou art dead, as I am, among the dead, for thou art alive, we inch towards one another, the other striving for what the other already has left.

The wind, calm in its breeze, settles in around me. I am engulfed, one with it, and it soothes me. I take in a deep breath, breathe out as if it is for the first time. My heart palpitates in a familiar rhythm. I know this space, I know this air, I know this life, for only one can create such a thing in the dead of silence.

Hello, mother…

Your son is here with you now. I am unsettled, mother. It is unsettling. In this dark space, where I have settled. And I don't like it here. You were the only one who could take me out of my doldrums and place me back into reality. My rage is without warning now, lacks direction you provided. Only you. In a special way I still can't define. Has heaven defined it for you, yet? I am now reckless, with no guidance. I take out my anger on the innocent. I rip their energy to shreds, discarding the pieces until they no longer have the will to fight. I am good at it. I thrive in it. But I don't want to do this anymore, mother. But my fear of being hurt is real. It is palpable. You remember when you taught me that word? Palpable? Nevertheless, I am afraid of connecting to anyone. Anyone. Too many available exit slips. Too many opportunities to leave me alone. If our bond was not strong enough to keep you here, what bond will be? Nothing compares to us, and yet, God severed us. Mutilated us. Humiliated us for all eyes to gaze upon the wreckage, the ending. God ended us. She claims to only put on us what we can bear but how can I bear this? How can I set our love aside to allow someone else into my distorted view of this life? Especially... him? I have so many questions, mother. Can you – please – show me the light?

    I am still within the breeze, ears open to the possibility of conversation. I am patient, at this time. A weakness of mine in the real world but this place is one of magic. One where bodies lie to rest, and humans come to make sure they remain that way. Our society has a fascination with vampires and zombies and the undead because we yearn for the possibility of seeing our loved ones on this earth, once again, in any capacity. It is one of the most selfish aspects of humanity. We argue with God about decisions She makes when all of us are a decision She has to make. Some of us come earlier than expected. Some of us last longer than we should. Either way, we all reach the point of decision, and we never come back from what it is that God decides. Her legendary sense of humor shows itself most readily in this way. I find myself chuckling from time to time at just how foolish we are to be upset with an inevitability. God could tell us our day of reckoning at the very beginning, if She wants. But She wants us to live a life of reckless abandon, one not governed by the time Her decision has to come to pass. It would be wrong of a loving God to take that freedom from us. And this God everyone speaks of is a loving one, no?

Yes, I am a loving God. And I am loving having your mother here among the angels where she belongs...

To God: What does it feel like to be me?

I am not you. But you are me. And I represent the only being capable of reaching the heights of love you and your mother have reached.

To God: Why did you take her from me?

I am a jealous God. I wanted that kind of love all to myself.

To God: You didn't think to ask if I'd share?

I know you better than you know yourself, young man. Do you honestly think you would have shared?

To God: I see your point. But why produce the level of pain in me my mother's death produced? What is the endgame of erasing her from this earthly existence?

You are stronger than you think, Vinnie. In order for you to recognize that strength, I had to remove the security blanket you were taking too long to grow out of.

To God: That's bullshit.

It is that anger that must be corralled or you will choke on the bile of your own grief. Your mother is safe. Your mother is where she should be. But she cannot rest peacefully until she knows that you are going to be alright. And I do not know what to tell her.

To God: What happened to being all knowing?

You all are made in my image. My image is flawed, just as you are.

To God: That explains the whole white Jesus thing.

It does.

To God: You don't speak to me like I think you should.

I speak to you every day. You just struggle recognizing my presence. But you will soon understand just how much I am in your life.

To God: Thank you for her. She was the ultimate gift.

There are more gifts on the way...

XIV

My conversation with God pitted me against an upbringing filled with doubt, but knowing that God is open to such discussion, open to being vulnerable within Her own strength, open to entertaining my doubts, insecurities and rage, allows me the room to explore my spirituality without fear.

So much of religion is based on the robotic nature of its followers, when the purest form of religious belief systems are that of the individual. The individual builds their own spiritual rapport with the deity of their choosing for one cannot make it to heaven on the wings of another. You are not saved by association. So looking to carbon copy one another's spiritual journey is to do your beloved a disservice.

I now show the wind the utmost respect, for it represents my mother, in her newest form, and a God I am feverishly getting to know, even as I dissect Her actual existence. I do not think that I can continue to live the way in which I have been living, with acts of love only geared towards Walter.

It was not as if I dispersed love all about when my mother was alive, but the distribution of the love given to her, from me, could be spread among the masses. That love could make its way into the lives and homes of so many, if only I could harness it and put it to good use. I refuse to keep this kind of love to myself. Selfishness is unbecoming. I do not want to be regarded in such a light.

I seek change in this world. I truly do.

"You need to get back to your art thing."

Walter snaps me back into the present, with his own distinct form of simplicity. It always tickles me, and yet, he can be quite deep at times.

"Are you a fan?"

Walter looks at me with playful disdain.

"I don't like any other art, or artists, I'll just say that."

"I'm touched."

"Touch your paintbrush. Lonely thing probably misses you. Hard to deal with that fast of a break up. When your normal isn't normal anymore."

We sit in the silence of our dead mothers. It is a silence only we understand. But it is a silence nonetheless.

"I destroyed my easel."

"Then fix it."

I love Walter. He has to understand that there are no boundaries to this. That my love knows no ceilings, or rooftops. I do not fear the stares or glances of those who do not seek love in all its forms.

Those who do not seem to be getting love in the places they yearn for the most seem to be drawn to me. My mother, from my father. Walter, from his father. Relationships built in silence, or terror. I swim in the sadness of others, wash upon its shores, and save others from drowning. In the meantime, I never leave the water myself, always in position to save, or be saved. I am them, and they are I, so who better to know what is necessary to breathe.

"I do miss how it feels in my hand."

"Why destroy it in the first place?"

"Let's just say it was a crime of passion."

"I could see that."

"Without my mother, it just doesn't feel right."

The wind blows. But this is different. It feels like it was summoned, as if I had called its name, and wanted it here at this very moment. Then I realize that I had called its name, for its name is no longer 'wind'. Calling my mother's name was all the wind needed to blow. She controls it now. It is her paintbrush. Who am I to surrender my own when my mother could find hers within the pain of her departure?

"Mother…"

The wind again, shifts in a useful direction. It passes through my fingers with precision and grace.

Mother…

I, and the wind, hold hands. I, and my mother, hold hands. I feel where she would want me to go with my painting. I feel what is necessary for me to move forward with my work. I must not let it flounder in her absence. I must continue what we started.

Mother…

Destroying our canvas, our place of worship, was the action of a petulant child. I have consumed too much literature to behave as such.

How dare I?

Mother…

I will rectify this situation.

"You meditating or something?"

Walter has witnessed this trance of mine. It's cute; he almost looks worried. Knowing I can go to this place, hold hands with this wind, breathe in an angel who has left this earthly vessel, is a knowledge I can take with me, to sustain me as I take these tainted steps into an uncertain future.

"No meditation necessary. I just needed to have a conversation with my muse."

"I won't pretend to understand what that means. But did you at least get what you needed?"

"That I did, my dear friend. That I did."

"Good. That's all that matters. Let's get out of here. Staying too long at the cemetery turns beauty into fear fast as hell."

I smile at my friend. He is the one whose shoulder will be used the most in the coming days, months, years. I do not trust anyone else with my heart like I do Walter. He doesn't even try. It comes naturally to him, at least, when it comes to me. He doesn't have to think about it. When you love someone like Walter loves me, like I love Walter, thinking is a secondary consideration. It is an innate response to need. If, and when, he needs me I am there. If, and when, I need him he is there.

Love like this is rare, among males. I will hold his hand but will not kiss him, nor do I want to. I do not think he wants to kiss me, either, but if he did, I would smile and engage him. If that is how he wants to express his love for me, so be it. We must not put love in a box for patriarchy to turn into an expression that lacks diversity. Romantic love should not be the pinnacle of expression. Familial love, friendship, and such, should be held in the same esteem, with no barriers to how that love is expressed.

Our exit from the cemetery turns into a race home. I intermittently saunter and sprint, naturally faster than Walter. He tries to keep up, but to no avail. I humor him a bit, give him moments of possibility before crushing his hopes in the most loving of ways. This is nothing new to us. Walter is very aware of my capabilities and I feel him wondering why this friendship works. But he truly is my best friend. And I wouldn't change him, or us, for the world.

I am tired from running. The cemetery would seem like it was close by due to the vicinity of this and the latter sentence, but I promise, it was much further. Upon arrival onto our street, we run into an argument of sorts. An argument that Walter and I can help with.

"See, with Walter and Vinnie here, we can play two-on-two football with me as all-time quarterback."

This is Pinto. A fat kid with a strong arm and short legs. He can't play any position other than all-time quarterback because his running a route would seemingly take us to the brink of extinction.

"It don't matter to me. Whatever we do, whatever we play, I just know that I was sent here to save the day."

This is Velcrow. A tall, lanky kid who rivals me as an athlete. I am faster, by a hair, but due to his height and athleticism, he is widely regarded as better. This challenge excites me. I do not like to come (in) second. But you knew that already...

"Y'all gonna pick the same bullshit teams y'all always do. Screw it, I'm winning anyway."

This is Spencer. If you met him and Walter together, you would automatically think they were brothers. He has the same rugged exterior as Walter but lacks the heart beating in Walter's chest. Spencer is all aggression, all the time. It's hard to tell whether he actually likes us, or we actually like him, but nevertheless, he is one of us and as tough as they come.

Pinto. "Y'all know the deal. Spencer and Vinnie versus Velcrow and Walter."

Walter. "We never even said if we were playing or not."

A long pause engulfs the group. Walter wouldn't dare ruin the game with some excuse as to why he and I were not going to participate. Velcrow laughs a high-pitched laugh.

Velcrow. "Thought so, bro. We don't turn down football games around these parts. You know how we do."

Pinto. "Let's get it."

Spencer. "I wasn't playing earlier. An ass kickin' is comin'."

Velcrow. "You must have just met me the other day or something, bro. I don't take losses. Not in my DNA, fam."

Spencer gives me a long look. He knows I am a wild card, depending on my mood. I am the only one who can possibly give Velcrow a run for his money, if I so choose.

I choose…

Pinto. "Spencer and Vinnie, y'all get the ball first."

Velcrow. "Don't matter."

Spencer and I head down to the other end of the street to await the kickoff. Pinto rears back and launches a perfect spiral to our end of the street. As it is in the air, Spencer looks at me. I look at him. He nods in my direction. I smile, my utter glee catching him off guard.

I move under the ball and catch it. Spencer runs in front of me to block. Now, normally, I would want him to block Velcrow and let me just give Walter a quick move to break free. But I was in too good of a mood to not let Velcrow in on my shenanigans. I was going to take out all my joy on his knees and ankles.

I run behind Spencer to set up his block on Walter. As Velcrow makes his move to tag me from the side, I put on the brakes, side step him, disrespect his ankles and explode up the sideline, leaving him wailing in the wind. I swear my mother must have held him up for a second because he hit that Matrix something vicious. My explosion up the sideline turned into an egotistical jog as everyone watched me score.

Pinto. "Yo, that was just foul, yo. Why you do him like that Vinnie?"

Pinto laughs. Velcrow stares my way like, 'Don't worry, I got you.' I hit him with a smirk. This is going to be fun.

We switch sides of the street and Spencer can't stop smiling.

Spencer. "Next time you plan to embarrass Velcrow, at least let me watch."

"Deal."

Pinto. "Bombs away!"

He launches another perfect spiral. Both Velcrow and Walter look to catch it, making them both hesitate. The ball hits the pavement and bounces onto the sidewalk, out of bounds.

Velcrow. "What the hell would make you think it

was time for you to touch the rock?"

Walter. "I didn't know if your ankles would be up for running after what Vinnie did to them."

Pinto falls over laughing. This game is not going as planned for Velcrow. Embarrassment is not usually a hat he wears. But on this day, he is getting it from all angles.

Velcrow. "Just throw me the damn ball."

Pinto slowly gets up. I could go home, watch an episode of Master of None and still get back in time for him to reach his feet.

Pinto. "Ready... Set... Go!"

Pinto backpedals like a quarterback who is actually being rushed, despite no one in that role at the moment. Walter runs a deep crossing pattern and Velcrow attempts to run a deep post. As Velcrow moves into the latter half of his route, Pinto seems to be eyeing the Walter-Spencer matchup. I see this and make the reckless decision to leave Velcrow. That dude is wide open. Pinto can't see him, though. He has already made his decision that he is going to Walter.

The ball leaves Pinto's hands, heads in Walter's direction. Both Walter and Spencer see the ball, but they don't see me. I sneak up on both of them and snatch the ball out of the air. Startled, they both watch as Pinto attempts to tag me. I give him a slow but filthy move as punishment for his mistakes. All I hear in the background is Velcrow whining about how wide open he was.

Velcrow. "Throw me the damn ball!"

Pinto. "He was open, man. I swear he was."

Velcrow. "If I have nine people on me, you still throw me the ball. I'm Velcrow!"

I just smile.

Velcrow. "What you smiling at?"

"All love. It's not your fault that this is all you are."

Velcrow gets in my face now. Typical.

Velcrow. "What you say to me?"

"If you took away football, who would you be?"

Velcrow. "Definitely not you. I got a better relationship with my daddy and he's in jail."

The game stops in its tracks. All eyes are on me. I hold it together the best I can. But I can't lie, Velcrow's words actually caused a bit of damage.

Velcrow. "Oh you think we don't know? We have always known. You walk around like you're better than all of us. But them books ain't saving you from the same fate the rest of us got. I ain't gotta daddy. And your daddy don't want to be here. I wouldn't wanna raise you either. Too much damn work."

Velcrow stays in my face; breath smells like his grades. I have never really cared for this gentleman, but in order to find some level of competition in the athletic realm, we have always chosen to be on opposite teams in all sports simply for the challenge. We have never been on the same team. And we aren't on the same team now.

This easily could resort to violence. But I live a life of WWJBD: What Would James Baldwin Do? And Baldwin would not succumb to the adolescent urge to solve everything with fists. So, I just take the football from Pinto. Punt it over a nearby house that none of us live in. Piss off everyone. And head home smiling.

Walter smiles, too.

XV

My mother is dead...

But through me, and the wind, she still lives. And I must honor that. I must live as she would want me to. I must continue my journey through this earthly existence without a glitch, without an extended pause that hinders what it is like to be human. I must take what this world has given me and do what is necessary to create even the faintest bit of joy. It is what my mother would want. The wind told me as much.

I need to flash this smile of mine. This painful, subtle, awkwardly charming smile of mine. This, spreading of lips, shining of teeth, this opportunity to exhibit some level of joy.

I need to make eye contact. Without it looking strained, beaten or borrowed. Real eye contact that matters, that cares, that focuses, that provides undivided attention even in the slimmest of moments.

And I gotta stop fucking with my teachers, man. I know, I know, watch my language. I usually refrain from such lingo; it just seemed like an opportune time to unleash the beast, so to speak.

Period 1....

I no longer will use starting my school day off with math as an excuse to not interact with anyone else the rest of the day. I must find ways for this subject to ignite something in me. I must look deeper at its nuances, at its capabilities, to possibly find some sign, something to which I can broaden my horizons, inbue some sense of creativity within this space.

I must find me in this work.

I'm already good at it, so why keep it at such arm's length? Why push away good when it can be harnessed and used for my benefit? I must not engage with the world in a way that constantly puts my back against it. The wind finds that unbefitting a young man of my unique gifts. I shall not disappoint the wind. I cannot do such a thing.

Ms. Williams looks in my direction. She has the look of concern that always envelops her face whenever she looks in my direction. It is so commonplace, it can be regarded as routine at this point. But today is not the day for such a gaze. I practice this new smile I have been working on. You know, that smile that gives you an inkling as to how handsome I have a chance of being at a later age. That smile that soothes, that moves, that grooves. Well, maybe not those three exact things but you get the picture.

My smile takes her aback. This beautifully pudgy woman reacts as if her high school crush just flirted with her. It is quite entertaining to watch her so flustered. But I pull back my smile a bit, add a slight head nod, and that lets her know that she may proceed with teaching. She moves forward with the lesson now that she knows that I am fine.

She poses a question. I answer said question. She poses another question. I answer it. She poses another one. I look to answer but she politely asks for someone else to participate. I am almost embarrassed, almost ashamed. Teachers have spent so much time trying to drag participation out of me, I do not know how to react to a teacher telling me to do less of it. I cannot lie, in this moment, I smile to myself. I am proud of myself.

I am moving forward.

Period 2...

English. Ms. Chasity never received my wrath like the others, she just had to endure my lack of energy. But not today. She was going to get Rudy Francisco today.

Ms. Chasity notifies my classmates and I that we will be tackling narrative poetry today. I always have a story to tell so might as well tell it.

I stare at the clock on the wall. Its consistency is breathtaking. It continues to hold a conversation with the one thing we cannot get back - time.

I take a gander at the plants in the corner. It truly takes a village to grow - anything. Seed, soil, water, plants are a microcosm of classrooms. If only serving as an incubator for all of the pieces needed to put students in a proper position to ascertain their mental mind frame. I know, that was doing too much but, yo, look at the literary devices in that last sentence! I'll give you a moment to check it out... See? See? This English stuff ain't too bad.

At this point, I have broken three pencils. I am frustrated to no end. I know what kind of story I want to tell but I am telling it too strongly. I need to back off, back off the page and give it time to marinate. Finesse it a little bit. I just need to leave it be.

I need to treat this poem, like the world needs to treat me.

The pencil starts to move. I hope it does not break this time. I am flowing. Yes. That's the right diction. No, change that word. That's better. Watch your punctuation, Vinnie. It can be a death knell in the pacing of a piece. You want your reader to pause when you want them to pause, not when they are running out of breath. That is unbecoming of your pen prowess. Linger a bit here. Sit with this information. Now... hit them with a curveball. Shock. Awe. Peel back the emotional layers, one by one. There, you got them now. Now, all you have to do is raise your hand and wait to be called on.

I just want to be seen...

"Yes, Vinnie?"

"Would it be alright if I read mine aloud?"

Hushed silence. This volunteering for anything not painting related is going to take some getting used to. Both for me and for them.

"Why, yes, you may."

My classmates sit on the edge of their seats as if this was the first time they realized I actually have a decent speaking voice when I care to use it.

So I start reading. Somehow, this is what ended up on my paper:

The doctor told her to push but all she could do was cry/tears shed among the basement floors of a past too dark for light/a past built on the frail foundation of a bruised self-esteem,/stagnant within the confines of self-loathing/she never had a chance.

Her father introduced her to a world unfit for an 11-year-old imagination/touched here, touched there, touched anywhere her mother was too blind to see./She was his little woman/and little women complete womanly tasks, even if the man shares her bloodline/she didn't have a choice./One false move and her cheeks would match the color of her Barney blanket,/the only remnants of a childhood she never knew/her inner thighs vibrated amongst confusion/the anguish of her father sweating in between thrusts of disgust and/the curiosity in which her young body reacted she was conflicted./Maturing into a woman whose morality was beaten, innocence destroyed/and sense of self-worth funneled into a safe for no one to open again.

She's 22/petite with full breasts and a defense mechanism the Army would be jealous of./His name was Anthony/he spent seven months, four days and two hours attempting to remove her cloak of armor,/22 years in the making./She smiled, and he found his opening/charmed her panties onto an apartment floor only her bare feet had ever touched/made love to her as if love was present/swimming in tears unsalted for the first time/she wanted to keep this feeling/she deserved this feeling/she yearned for this feeling/and he knew it.

She spent more time on her knees begging for forgiveness than she did in prayer/she was never good enough./The kitchen, dirty/the bedroom, a mess/her sex, lackluster/all in an attempt to keep her isolated from a world/she never saw for more than 30 minutes at a time.

She was trapped/trapped beneath an iron fist that didn't hesitate to put her in her place./The second man she ever loved, loved her only when it fit his needs/and his needs were fleeting.

Five years, two months & three days later/she stood over his body/nine months pregnant with his first born/and nine seconds removed from alleviating this earth of her torment/he was gone./Blood-soaked sheets remained, combining with her sweat to make the river of her future/she'd go in it alone this time/her fractured psyche high off her immunity to love another man/it was over./She plead not guilty, put on probation, her water broke in triumph.

And now, she sits/not ready to give birth in fear her worst nightmare is realized:/"Please don't be a boy, please don't be a boy, please, just...don't"/She gives in to her destiny/a crying child falls into the hands of a doctor who is clueless as to what it is she has just done./In the doctor's hands lies the last chance a man will ever have to love her/we'll see how it goes...

I look up from my piece of paper, immediately run to get a box of tissues. I don't even know where to begin. So many eyes are watering. I hand the box to Ms. Chasity and give her a smile. Ms. Chasity takes the tissues from me, grabs one and dabs her eyes.

Someone else wrote this...

"Your mother would be proud of you."

I close my eyes. Take in a deep breath. It could be viewed as a sigh of relief to those on the outside looking in.

"I think I agree."

My mother wrote that poem...

Ms. Chasity gathers herself.

"Would anyone else like to read theirs?"

Whole class, in unison: "Hell naw!"

This makes me chuckle. Chuckle, indeed.

XVI

Period 3...

World History. I still do not like how much the truth is despised here. Nevertheless, my approach to broadening the horizons of those who find solitude in their inaccuracies - primarily my teacher - could be retooled. No use in constantly barking about what I find ails our education system, and the below-average intellect that runs amok within it, if I can never properly engage in conversation that might change a mind or two.

Being intelligent is only fun when you're winning.

I hold back my tongue from even mentally calling my teacher a minion. That sentiment alone has ridded any opportunity for possible respect to be created. She has no chance to reach me. I hate how she delivers her subject matter, the subject matter she delivers and the people whom she sets out to satisfy in delivering said subject matter.

But today is a new day. You can still teach a young dog new tricks. Even if that young dog might be the most stubborn pup of them all.

By the way, my World History teacher's name is Mrs. Ward. I know I refrained from naming her earlier, but that was out of utter disdain for her face. Her face is fine with me now. I can stand to look at it, if only because I have convinced myself that it would be much easier to look at her than to continually find new ways to rotate my neck in a direction that does not include her in my eyeline.

Apparently, God does have a sense of humor. Today, the day I am attempting to change my attitude towards my teachers and to give them at least a chance at educating me further than I have already educated myself, Mrs. Ward decides that she wants to tackle the controversial topic of apartheid South Africa.

She sends a sly smirk my way but I do not budge. I

actually decide that this would be a good time for me to raise my hand.

Hand is up.

"Yes, Vinnie? What am I doing wrong, now?"

"I'm just curious as to your view of apartheid South Africa from the perspective of a white woman in America. Not even in a sarcastic way, just in case you may have jumped to that conclusion. I am truly interested in hearing the opinion of someone so far removed from the topic."

My classmates' glares go from me to Mrs. Ward. She is somewhat stunned at this opportunity that has befallen her and is slow to react. She is used to going back and forth with me to no end but this calm creature before her who actually seems interested in her viewpoint is a creature she is not yet used to interacting with. I'd hate to say that this is actually more fun than my usual tactics with her but...

"Well, Vinnie, first and foremost, I don't think I should give my opinion in class."

"But we want to hear what you think, Mrs. Ward. Use this as a chance to truly give us your perspective. I mean, the only white women we really interact with are those of you who decide to teach in the inner-city, for whatever reason, so please do enlighten us. You're allowed to have an opinion, Mrs. Ward. This is America. There is no apartheid here."

"Can you let me teach, Vinnie?"

"By all means, Mrs. Ward. I am all ears."

I might have raised my hand to either ask or answer a question about 12 times that period. Mrs. Ward had to have gotten sick of me by the fourth one, but she knew that I could not be stopped. I am now both every teacher's joy and fear, dream and nightmare. I am a smart kid who knows he is smart. And once I decide that I want to be a challenge instead of a nuisance, the entire student-teacher dynamic changes and I am now a teacher's walking insecurity.

You cannot come into class unprepared anymore, Mrs. Ward.

"Vinnie?"

"Yes, Mrs. Ward?"

She stops to carefully choose her words, yet, she chooses something so simple, it still resonates: "Thank you."

I just smile the same smile I have recycled the past three periods. This period was going to be my biggest challenge no matter what kind of changes I was looking to make. It didn't go quite like I planned, but it was still an improvement.

I don't want to kill her and she seems like she doesn't want to kill me. I'll chalk that up as a win.

Period 4...

Art. My HB pencil sketch of a black man in his late 20s being lynched in rural Mississippi with the heavens opening up as he takes his last breaths is hanging up on the wall. It's like a white privilege shield for all to see.

Ms. Scott sees me. And it is immediate.

"What changed?"

"The wind."

"Makes perfect sense to me."

Ms. Scott smiles at me. I smile back at her. She senses the difference in my smile. The calm, the love, the freedom, her eyes tell me this. She knows how to communicate with me. We speak like artists speak. It's just what we do. If anyone understands who I am in this moment, it is Ms. Scott.

I head to my seat.

"Vinnie?"

"Yes, Ms. Scott?"

"I have something I want to talk to you about."

"Now?"

"Not yet. But soon."

"Sounds good, Ms. Scott."

Whenever Ms. Scott says she needs to speak to me about something, it either has to do with my mother, or art, or both. My two favorite subjects. This puts yet another smile on my face. I am starting to get used to this whole smiling thing.

I get up to open a window. Need a little wind in here.

Period 5...

Sign language. I participate with earnest. Engage in the silence. Learn a few new signs. Truly enjoy myself. Word has spread that I seem to be a different person. I keep getting leper's stares. I'll take it, though. I am enjoying this sense of unpredictability. As we well know, I take pleasure in the oddest of things.

Jhene...

One of our counselors speaks with our teacher. Conversation is fast. Conversation is necessary. I cannot keep my eyes off them. Or...

Jhene...

Our teacher signs to us the most beautiful phrase she has ever produced. 'Class, we have a new student joining us. Please welcome...' Our teacher does not have a sign for her name. I do not think one would be available to her even if she wanted to. There is no sign that could properly put into perspective the beautiful being before us.

"Jhene," the being says.

No taller than 5-foot-1. One hundred pounds might be a stretch. Short haircut, Halle Berry circa 1991. Shy eyes. A baggy long sleeve shirt. Beat up jeans with organized holes in them. Dirty black and white Chuck Taylors. A bag with pins and stickers tossed about its outside, it touches her right knee as it hangs. Avril Lavigne splashed with melanin. Her lips full, but not wide. Her smile, effortless, but I might be guessing. I don't think she has smiled yet. That might just be me.

She looks my direction. I cannot escape her eye contact. I am entranced by her piercing brown eyes. She flashes a slight smile, a strategic move. Her smile is indeed, effortless. This beautiful girl before me is everything...

She has me.

Period 6...

I'm pretty sure I went to class. I'm pretty sure I enjoyed it. And I'm pretty sure...

Jhene...

XVII

It would be about my father…

It is all I can think about. It always comes back to him. It is never without him. All about him. Forever about him.

But it needs to be. And that's what makes Ms. Scott's request so powerful. She wants me to put on another art showcase. But…

It would be about my father…

She knows what it means to make this request. She understands where my mind goes in order to paint. I center all thoughts, feelings, pain, joy, frustration and happiness into whatever it is I am painting. I become one with the subject. It is all encompassing. It is its own form of method acting. I remove all other considerations from my existence. There is no room for anything else. I must be all in, all the time, crafting piece after piece in hand and in mind.

But this will be about my father…

A subject so thoroughly aggressive, I worry it will crush me below the weight of its uncertainties. He could just be himself and alter the very stroke of my paintbrush, smudge progress with unconstitutional wrath. How dare he destroy the possibility of this attempt at perfection? See, I haven't even started yet and… and… and…

It would be about my father…

Where would my mom go? She would need a place to rest within my psyche while my focus moves elsewhere. I would put my love for her on hold, as to not disrespect the paintbrush with excess energy. Oh this doesn't sound right at all… it is almost unfathomable to think of not centering my paintbrush around her light. Painting - about my father, within my father, without my father, for my father, against my father, through my father - requires a starting point of darkness. An abyss of emotional silence. A disgusting pit of pure angst and volatility. Yet, I would not be able to shy away from such things. If I am to accept this endeavor, respond with my truth, balance the delicate with the decadent, I must create a space where my hatred for my father does not overwhelm the love for my art.

But this will be about my father…

I don't know. I don't know. I don't know. Maybe I shouldn't? Maybe I should just leave this request next to my mother's grave. Let it rest in perpetuity. But it isn't a requirement. But I won't be getting a grade. But it is simply because Ms. Scott asked. But the ask is not simple in the least. But she knows that. But she knew that before she asked me. But I think she wanted me to challenge myself. But I am not emotionally equipped to do this. But what if I am? But… but… but…

But this will be about my father…

This work will be more than just painting. I will tell the story of a splintered bond, severed at the sight of an umbilical cord. Or was it when I said my first word? My mother would know the answer to that question, but she's not here…

My mother is dead…

But this will be about my father…

But my mother is dead…

But this will be about my father…

To embark on this journey with only the wind to guide me is my first trek into young adulthood. This quest could be therapeutic. It could damage me to a point of no return. I am putting all of my emotional strength behind a man who has not cried since the night his wife passed away. A man whose capacity for emotion is limitless in its nothingness. A man whose presence, voice, breath and being I have loathed for years now, despite the unequivocal urge to hug him, hold him and kiss him, like a son would do a father he loved, a father who was here, in flesh and soul.

But we are talking about my father...

The imagery is so profound. I'm witnessing each stroke of the paintbrush as his rigid features announce themselves onto the page. His inability to smile makes him an easier target for my photographic memory. I could use a picture of him, if I so choose, but closing my eyes will encapsulate the pain, flood the page with its rage, calm it within its beauty. It will be some of my best work. It will struggle to procure the love my mother once provided so effortlessly. Now, I must journey to this unknown space, where only my father and I reside, with the sole purpose of recreating our treacherous journey together, but maybe this time, with a look towards a future where such disturbing anger is no longer present, nor useful.

I haven't dipped my paintbrush into a molecule of paint, and yet my mind is flooded with bright colors and fluorescent lighting. The freshness of the material abounds as I recreate visual stimuli, mentally producing my art before it becomes my reality. This process, done over and over and over again, flushes out all of mediocrity's toxins making me less and less susceptible to its commonality.

But the bright colors and fluorescent lighting elicit laughter. For I know that darkness will touch the page well before light does. There will be no shortchanging the journey. There will be no turning back against the pain. The paintbrush knows no lie, and speaks only for that which is true. It would look back at me with a scowl knowing the insincerity of my strokes. My father must work for the opportunity to be seen in the light. He must first deal with his darkness, my darkness, the darkness. It is only fitting. It is only right. It is only just. And I must not hide from doing so.

Ah, this back and forth has my stomach rumbling. I am hungry for what is at stake like steak at the feet of a starved hyena, as he cackles at the night sky, high off the moon's palpable energy. It is oddly satisfying to know that this project will either give me what I have wanted since my entrance onto this earth, or it will sever forever the last inkling of hope that my father will one day act like the man responsible for half of my DNA. With each and every stroke of my paintbrush, I will push him further away or draw him closer, both options will satisfy me. I have lived this long with him as a distant figure within my existence, a few more years won't hurt.

But we are talking about my father...
So we are talking about me...
Oh.

XVIII

I'm sorry, mom...

But this has to come down. This one, too. And this one. And that one. And this one. And that one. This one, too. And that one. And that one. And that one.

Rolled up pieces of paper. All wrapped in rubber bands. Neatly placed under my bed. Each a painting I cherish. Each painted with love. Each painted with, or for, my mother.

But they can't be here now. Not in this moment. They can't be here. It will only distract me from the place I need to go to create this new era. My paintbrush can sense fraudulence. I must not give it a reason to mistrust me. It will know if I am painting from a place of unconditional love. It will know if I am painting from the place in which my mother resides. So I must remove her memory, for now.

I'm sorry, mom...

I think she would understand. I think she would want this. I think she would appreciate the steps I am taking to produce the art Ms. Scott has asked for. This art that will showcase the explosive energy shared by myself and my father. An energy like no other. A literal representation of the thin line between love and hate. This inconsequential line that elicits such varying consequences. I must provide this art balance. I cannot cheat this art. It will know if it is being cheated. So it must start within the darkness. The darkness of him. The darkness of I. The darkness of we. So no mother for a little while. Just a little while. Just.

I'm sorry, mom. Please forgive me...

Day One…

I sit at my easel. Paintbrush in hand. I stare at its bristles. Sly smile displayed across my lips. Nothing hangs from my walls. All remnants of past work are tucked beneath my bed, serving only as a memory to what I am capable of with my paintbrush in hand. This space is clear. Anticipates the creation of a new present. A new frontier, galloping through his darkness, my darkness, our darkness. Looking for a place to rest our weary heads, our weary relationship, on some semblance of solid ground. But until then, I paint.

Regal strokes. Black. White. Grey. Ingrained darkness. Feeds off my longing for acceptance. *Stroke.* Places his fatherhood - or lack thereof - at center stage. *Stroke.* It must be drawn with all its faults, dangers, and despair. *Stroke.* The scene starts to manifest itself. *Stroke.* His image walks with its head held high. *Stroke.* My image walks, in the opposite direction, with my head hung low. *Stroke*. All that remains between us, is space for the wind to blow. *Stroke*.

My strokes increase in speed and proficiency. Painting is always a slow crescendo, gradual, methodical, in its pursuit of perfection. I never see what it is I am painting until about the midway point. Then I get excited. Then it becomes real. Then it becomes an all-consuming sprint to the finish line. Something my mother would warn against. But she is not here in this space right now. I am alone, to fend for my own artistic self. It is only right. I cannot be disrespectful to the process, my process. I know she understands.

Day Two...

Steps away from completion. This image is so real, and clear to me. A father and son headed in two distinct and opposite directions with nothing to bring them back to the middle except for their apparently shared love of one woman, one mother, one wife. Her stellar reincarnation as the wind notwithstanding, her powers seen as mere mortal within the chasm that is this father and son debacle. The irony in his head being held high and mine being held low, when he is the one who is indeed failing at his task of being a father, brings this piece its narrative talking points. It will cause those in attendance to question it, to question us, to question him, and he will have to respond in kind as to why such an image could be procured from this supposedly loved mind of mine. Oh, it will be glorious to witness, I promise you that. To see his face as he recognizes the narrative being displayed in front of him is indeed one of his shadow parenting. His only talent he would rather not have shown to the masses, rather kept buried beneath the sheets his wife slowly died under.

But this is about love, right?

This is about a reconfiguration. I did not leave the splendidly missing arms of my mother, place my person at the feet of this man, without considering the possibility of true love, here. There are some things in life that deserve never. This is not one of them. This takes work ethic, definitely, and an almost destructive naivety to believe that this man is capable of what I want from him. But I refuse to take defeat without a lengthy fight that may even last the length of my days. My patience wanes at the speed of silence so we have time. I have already waited 14 years so a little more will not hurt.

Stroke. Almost there. *Stroke*. A little less handsome. *Stroke*. Do not give away his humanity. *Stroke*. Make them all believers. *Stroke*. Bring them into your hell. *Stroke.* Before placing them among the light of heaven. *Stroke.* It is lonely here. *Stroke*. But I love it here. *Stroke*. I belong here. *Stroke*. I am strong here. *Stroke*.

This piece is complete. And I did not lose my mind, yet.

Success.

Day Twelve…

I can't stop crying. (Don't I have homework to do?) Painting no. 6. (Did I go to school today?) Mother withdrawals. Her absence buries me with each passing minute. I do not want her here but she keeps fighting me.

Fighting to return to her rightful place, as my spiritual liaison, confidant. I can hear her screams but the wind is not welcome here. It swirls around this house like a tornado with no place to land but it is not welcome here. It would be disrespectful to the process that is before me. The final piece on a journey to anorexic bliss.

I do not remember my last meal. I do not remember the last time I smiled. All I see is paint, and more paint. Pain, and more pain. Suffering, and more suffering. Yet, love and more love.

Painting no. 6. It is not derived from memory. For it has not happened yet. This is the painting that pains me the most. It is the one where he loves me. This is the painting where he stands by my side, wraps his arm around my shoulder, and loves me. Supports me. Encourages me. Cries with me. Laughs with me. Fathers with me. Fathers his son. This is the painting worth all of the heartache. This is the painting worth all of the anguish. This is the painting that will set me free. This is the painting…

That is blank.

A naked canvas, grins at its own ineptitude. It struggles to fathom just how irrelevant it is, in this moment. It must be accomplished at some point, but how? When it is sitting there, with only lies to derive its conversation. It speaks in lost languages, no longer in use. Retired rhetoric scholars deem it unnecessary to pass down to the servant and peasant industries. Its attempts at communication futile at its best, dangerous, at its worst. The most important piece from this showcase is the one I cannot produce. I wonder if Baldwin ever ran into a chapter he could not write. Or a book he could not finish. Or a thought he could not relay on paper. Of course not. Baldwin is literary perfection. He could not have suffered at the hands of his own talent, could he?

Of course he did. He was human after all…

I close my eyes. I rest my arms by my sides and

breathe deeply. My breaths, resemble sighs to the naked ear. But they are natural to me. I transform into a highly meditative state. Remove all thoughts from my psyche. If one presents itself, I simply acknowledge it, then let it go.

How could you leave your mother's love? Let it go.
How could you ever love your father? Let it go.
How could he ever love you? Let it go.
How could you ever not think? Let it go.
Who do you think you are? Let it go.
You are not worthy of his love. Let it go.
Why must this be so difficult? Let it go.
Pain is so beautiful... Leave it be.

My eyes slowly open. My arm slowly rises up and grabs the paintbrush from its resting place. I place the paintbrush in the cup of water. I shake it dry, yet still moist. I dip it into a cup of red paint. I stare at it as it drips like blood, contemplates whether it is a sign of life given or life taken. I use this brush. I use this color. I paint a distant future, where love and family find a space within hyper-masculinity. Where showcasing love for one another will not elicit stares normally relegated to the eye contact bestowed upon women. I paint in love. I paint in blood. I paint in the destruction of patriarchal norms. I paint in pedicure. I paint in softball. I paint in WNBA. I paint in reality show. I paint in soap opera. I paint in pink. I paint in kisses. I paint in hugs. I paint in the divine feminine. I paint in me.

I paint in… him.
I paint.
Jhene…

XIX

Tonight is the night.

Ms. Scott opens the auditorium for this one. This one is special. The community is all invited. She pulled out all the stops for this one. She wants to make sure I understand just how much my work differs from all others. How much I stand out. How much I am unlike anything this community has ever seen. That I am an entity all my own. That I am...

...My father's son.

I invited him earlier in the week. I invited him later in the week. I invited him over and over. Sometimes he looked like he heard me. Other times he looked like I was a nuisance. All I know is that he knows of this night. He knows of its importance. He knows how I looked when I asked him to come. He saw my eyes, yearning, begging, for his approval, acceptance, presence. So he'll be here. I know he will. He has to be.

Sixty minutes. Six 10-minute reveals of each painting. A question and answer period. All centered around me and a talent others can view on their own. It is much easier to include me in such a viewing, but I am not truly necessary. Within art, if you cannot come to your own conclusions as to what is being spoken to you, then your eyes should lay upon something a little less complex. For this is not for the simple at heart. This is for those who recognize their humanity in others. Recognize that pain knows no single address but can reside in locales that even the most joyous and spiritually healthy people alive cannot prevent from entering.

Ms. Scott reads to the audience an introduction as to why we are all here and who I am. You would think I was her child the way she beams at the mere mention of my name. Her support is beautiful. She is the most genuine person I know remaining on this earth. I am thankful for her. I truly am. And in this moment, she presents me to a world that I have mostly hidden from. A world where judgment is possible, and judgment is free. I have only lived in its space for short periods of time with limited amounts of people. But that ends as soon as I step on stage…

Vinnie Smith.

The applause is deafening. This must be what a standing ovation feels like. It rumbles through my chest, vibrates my rib cage, shakes my core and rests in my fingertips. I must not let them see just how nervous I am. But I am 14 years old after all, despite my lifelong journey to prove otherwise. This is new to me. This kind of attention is not something I am used to. And this is the first time I have ever presented any of my artwork without…

My mother…

This realization hits as all eyes rest on me, the audience patiently waits to hear what I have to say about Painting No. 1.

"It's simple, really…"

The applause is real…

Painting No. 2.

"I guess this would…"

The applause is genuine…

Painting No. 3.

"At this point, my father…"

The applause is muted…

Painting No. 4.

"I just want him here…"

The applause is heartfelt…

Painting No. 5.

"I believe in what's possible even when it isn't…"

The applause is worrisome…

Painting No. 6.

"I could not use blood, so red was my only option…"

The applause is… no more.

Stunned silence. Mouths agape. Tears shed.
Handkerchiefs defeated. Tissue crumbles. Hands held.
Strangers hug me from afar, with no real contact. I am felt
in this room. This room full of people, who in my natural
state, I would toss aside as meaningless collections of
breaths and blood, shower me with love I have not felt in
quite some time. The slow reconvening of applause upon
completion of the night resonates with me. It picks me up
in its collective hands and tells me that I matter. That my
work matters. That my feelings matter. That I am not alone.
That I am one with humanity. That humanity feels my pain.
Understands my pain. Accepts my pain. I have never felt
this level of acceptance for just being me. And all I did was
present my truth in the best way I know how. Through
painting, pain and perseverance.

As the crowd dissipates and congratulations
bestowed upon me, I smile. And within my acceptance of
the praise and adulation that this night has brought my way,
I search the room.

Where is he?

I saw Walter as soon as I stepped on stage. He came
in jeans and a T-shirt. A smart move considering I would
not have recognized him in any other get up.

I even saw Jhene. She attempted to hide behind her
petite frame but her aura radiated above and beyond her
and our spirits touched in mid-air, embraced, then came
back down to earth.

No, that did not happen. But her presence is
something I did not expect. I know this is a school event
but it was not mandatory for students. The majority of the
students in the room were either dragged here by parents or
sat with and around their favorite teacher. Jhene simply sat
in the back, by herself, eyes on me, seemingly at her own
will. There is something there…

Where is he?

"Did he come?"

Ms. Scott? Walter? Anybody? Can anybody answer me?

My search continues, ignores all of the many faces that attempt to congratulate me on this powerful and amazing endeavor I just succeeded in accomplishing but my mind is no longer in that space of deferred happiness. I am in the beginning stages of mourning, of death, of depression, of anxiety, and I am a frequent flier within this space. I know it well.

And its cause is common. Its cause is why we are here in the first place, for I do not produce what I produced tonight without the consistency of this cause. The consistency of his absence.

I stare at the auditorium door. No one enters. Only leave. I stare until my limbs begin to move in its direction. I am sure that Walter and Ms. Scott call my name as I begin my journey outside but I cannot hear them in this moment. I am no longer present. All I see is the exit and the one place I hope my father will be because I am petrified of what will come of me if he is not.

I barge through the exit door. It flails behind me, swings back and forth.

"Dad?... Dad?!... Father?... Father?!"

Nothing. No one. He is not here.

"No, no, no, no, no, no..."

I shake my head violently. Flustered. Angry. Disappointed. Anxious. Furious. I sprint onto campus. Find myself headed into a direction of solitude. A place I have visited on multiple occasions but never really understood just how relevant it would come to be.

The boys' bathroom.

I push open the door. Slam it behind me. Check to see how dry the floor is. Then I slide down the wall as my tears fall in unison.

How could I let this happen? How could I? How could I resist my mother's love for so long? How could I place his existence above hers? The parent I need is gone. The parent that is here is gone... Fuck this process. Fuck my process. No art is worth this. He is not worth this. He will never love me like she does. He will never hold me like she does. He will never understand me like she does. He will never support me like she does. He will never know just how much pain he has put me through...

So I must do what I need to do to ease the pain within the pain...

I must leave the status quo behind forever...

I must become one with my skin... one with my veins... one with my blood... One...

Where is my box cutter?

XX

This is new. Distinct. Powerful, even. To know
what twirls from finger to finger can possibly alter the
trajectory of your skin. Mind. Life. Liberty. Halt the pursuit
of your impossible happiness. Only fools take that journey.
It is moot in this earthly vessel. Selfish to even think
otherwise. Happiness resides where darkness does not. And
darkness is everywhere, that happiness is not. For
happiness is light, and darkness usurps light at every turn.
Like this box cutter, for instance.
On its own, it seeks no harm. It may remain sharp
but it has no means of causing any damage unless someone
comes for it, calls for it, summons its powers onto flesh and
screams its name. It is beautiful in that sense. Its power
derived from another, yet strengthens its muse tenfold with
just a gentle move from left to right. Or is it right to left?
Oh what ecstasy...
Baldwin would be ashamed of me, right now.
Ashamed of my giving up, giving in. Playing the victim.
Baldwin, as gay as he was black, was stronger than any
man to slang his thang. He cautioned his people against the
wrongs of the world, provided direction in interacting with
our oppressors and used literary and oratory skills to leave
a legacy of intelligence and might surpassed by only a
select few to walk the earth. He is my role model. He is my
intellectual stallion. And I am failing him, in this moment.
For this box cutter is seducing me. It licks its lips,
douses its shiny exterior with liquid love, swallows its
purpose and spits up insecurities like the bile they are. It is
feeding off my lack of control in this moment, hungry for a
taste of my veins for it knows not of the poison that runs
through them. It is only curious about the carnage it can
inflict on a teenage black male vacillating between option
'black' and option 'white'. We all know the stereotypes. To
cut is a white person's ailment. Mental health is a white

community problem. That just isn't us. We figure it out. We find a way. We tough it out. We man the fuck up.

Fuck you.

I have swam in my black skin since birth and this is the closest thing to freedom I have ever felt. To approach death like the bitch that it is and slap the shit out of him. And I apologize for the profanity but this is no time for childish vocabulary Nazi-ism. This is life or death, left or right, slice or no slice, blood or no blood. The sanctity of the moment washed away in the palm of my father's absence. He had the utter audacity to not be present when it was him who placed me here. It was him. It was all about him. Each stroke, whether through anger, love or whatever word means both, it was all for him. And he could not find it in his darkness to show up. He could not find it in the wind the show up. He could not find it in life to show up. He could not find it in death to show up.

Maybe I need to kill myself and arise again like the Phoenix to burn his aura to ashes. Light fire to his financial security. Obliterate his job status. Nuke his narcissism. Bury my mother further into the ground for him to no longer see her. I must cause him pain. I must create his loss. I must accomplish what my mother attempted to do in dying.

I want to humanize you, dad...

Would it work if he were left alone? What is a big house if you are the only one in it? What is working hard when there is no one there to share it with? What is bragging when there are no ears to listen to you? Would solitude finally break him? His bed is empty now and it has done nothing to change his darkness. Darkness continues to win within him, he is one without light, one within night, and it is frightening to ascertain the depths he is willing (or unwillingly) able to go to not feel, touch, absorb, heal his own fatherhood. The only job in his life that truly matters, does not. And this box cutter is here to further accelerate a cautionary tale. One where a son's cries should be heard, listened to, dealt with, with a sense of immediacy, in tune with the quickness in which you released yourself into a womb to create him in the first place.

I am crying now...

Ugh, slobber. Spit flails. Babies jealous of my oral freedom. Eyes drenched in past, present and future sorrow. Sorrow. Sorry. I am. Sorry. For ever going against the grain. Sir Baldwin, I am not the protégé you have thought me to be. I am not worthy of calling you my spiritual father. For. I. Am. Truly. Considering placing this. Here. Box cutter. Against my. Very. Skin. Oh, it sounds. So very. Sweet. To my ears. And. To think. This was. Never. My. Intention. Oh no. No. No. No, it was. Not. It was. Not. This. This moment. On this. Here floor. Among flushed. Defecation. And urine. The irony of this place. And its wonder. And its decidedly. Disgusting. Usage. This box cutter. Is. Decidedly. Disgusting. In its. Seduction. Of.

Me.

I run my finger against its edges. It does not cut. But it does create a precursor against my skin. Teasing it with its capabilities. It calls out for it like Amsterdam Red Light District window shopping. It is erotic in nature, bliss in nurture. It is getting harder and harder to say no to its constant yearning. I can hear its loins palpitating with a sharpness all its own. It is sexy in this moment. A sexually deviant partner for which I am not strong enough to avoid much longer.

My legs shake. The hair on my arms stick up like hundreds of black men at the sound of police sirens. I tap the box cutter against the hardwood floor. It tap dances to a rhythm of silent screams from the vocal chords of men whose emotional outcries were muted by the very women who asked to hear them in the first place.

It craves my skin at this time, and Baldwin can do nothing about it. All he can do is hope I pull through this maze of emotions better in the long run. But even the greats have to take a step back every once in awhile to delve into decadence to get reminded of just how fragile this humanity of ours is.

I know pain. My knuckles, still stained with the memories of the force it takes to dent my bedroom walls repeatedly. But I do not know a pain quite like this one. This one is intimate, eloquent, passionate. It is a pain subtle in its execution, explosive in its response. It is like taking drugs for the first time, only to find out that you have been hooked on drugs all along.

But black men don't cut...

I can hear my father's ego slither into my eardrums with his stereotypical jargon about what a man is, about what a black man is. To cut in the black community is to succumb to the white man's way of coping. Almost like we succumbed to the white man's religious beliefs, but no one likes to talk about that. Or to his education system. Or to his aesthetic. Or to his criticism of the arts. Or to his hypocrisy. Naw, we have enough hypocrisy on our own to not need his. Do not tell me how I am supposed to handle my pain when you are the one who hurt me in the first place. You do not get to select my bandages when you are the one who made me bleed. It does not work that way. It will not work that way. It will work how I want it to work.

And now, I want this box cutter to please me. I want it to make love to my insecurities and blanket my dreams with thoughts of irrefutable bliss. I want it to take turns enticing my ego with its violence, destroy my self-esteem and leave it on the basement floor in shambles, only to be gobbled back up when I come to. I want this ecstasy to drip from my lips with rabid flow, Nile River mo'. Drown me in its waves of complications. I want to feel like Stockholm Syndrome. I want to yearn for its rapture, despite my capture. I want it to save me. I want it to love me. I want to be one with its intricacies, an enemy with a pass for entry.

I want it to be a father I can control…

I cannot control my tears. I cannot control my fears. I cannot say no any longer. I place the box cutter to my wrist. Tap dance an interlude against my skin. And slowly, cut.

Oh it hurts… but it hurts properly. It is what I have wanted all my life. Blood drips in opposite directions, stains the bathroom floor with its colorful texture. It writes my name in colored ink. Cursive. The writing of creatives. Creatively dispersed among this concrete floor, it opens its mouth for more but I am not ready to supply it. Right now, all I want to do is bask in the ambiance that is the scent of my own blood. And wait for a father who will never reach me in time…

XXI

Walter is so beautiful…

"Damnit, Vinnie. That isn't what we're supposed to use the box cutters for."

Walter wraps wads of paper towels and toilet tissue around his arms and brings his collection to me. Without any real sense of what he is doing, he attempts to create makeshift bandages for my bloodstained wrists. As he continues to soothe my wounds, I remain in a state of bewilderment. This new form of bliss washes over my soul and psyche, all-consuming my youth with its adult consequences. I am high off death, in this moment.

The taste of coal frolics amongst my taste buds as darkness fills my lungs with smoke. I am hungry for more but I am too tired to continue. If every trip down this narrow lane is such as this, I will need to be selective in its usage. For this could turn addiction, and I do not want to be the town drunk who drinks his own blood. My intellect would disapprove of such a thing. And Walter might try to kill me for impersonating his father.

My wrists are clean, now. Walter worked some type of magic and it is as if I have never placed a sharp, miniature object against my skin at any juncture of my existence. I am clean. I am pure. I am still wet from the water buried underneath the paper towels Walter used to clean me up. He is always here to clean me up, despite being his own hell of a mess. It is amazing how some of the most hurt people can be the most loving and caring people. I know the saying is, 'hurt people, hurt people'. And for the most part, that remains true. But 'hurt people, help people' could be the proper retort to such phrasing as my pain is felt by those who feel it, too. We are our own elite club of broken, and entry into our ranks takes a particular brand of hopelessness.

I rest in Walter's arms, now. He holds me. My head rests against his chest as he rocks me back and forth in an irregular rhythm. The white boy in him unable to keep a beat. But I am happy to sing this song with him. He is the only one who understands my melody, now.

My mother is dead... And this is the closest to her I have felt since she left me.

"I hope this doesn't become your norm, man. The janitor is going to be pissed off all the time."

"At least my mess tells a story."

"I don't think he's trying to read this."

"Why? Are my words not worthy?"

"Blood ain't pretty. And it's a bitch to clean up."

Walter has a point. I guess I can try to be more considerate of others as I go further and further down this rabbit hole of mine. Or maybe I can just give the janitor a heads up that his work is going to get a little bit harder, thanks to me. Either way, it's the consideration that counts, no? That's what this lesson is trying to teach me?

"We really need to leave soon before somebody finds us and flips the hell out."

Walter tries to get up, while pulling me up with him. At first, I am of no help. But as much as he has done for me at this time, it would be wrong of me to continue to allow him to carry me. So I aid him in our return to our feet. Dust myself off. Stare at my blood as it dies against the hardwood floor of the boys' bathroom at the school I attend five days a week. I foresee this bathroom being a new home away from home. I can only afford to pay my rent in blood, but my humanity can produce plenty of that on a regular basis, so payment is no concern of mine.

I straighten up and stare at my friend. He stares back at me.

"What?"

"Thank you, Walter."

"No problem, man. Just don't make this a hobby."

"Cutting?"

"Me saving you. I'll keep doing it. But I need to save myself first."

"I am aware. Safety first."

"Yeah, whatever."

Walter opens the door and leads me into the hallway.

"He really didn't show up tonight?"

"Yeah, man. Sorry."

I take in this information as if it is all new to me.

"He should be kicking himself. He missed one hell of a show."

Walter half-smiles and starts to put his arm around me. But someone beats him to it. A girl sprints into my arms and holds me in a lengthy embrace. Her head against my chest, her scent reaches my nostrils and envelops my senses with her ecstasy.

Jhene...

She releases me. Barely looks up to smile at me. Turns to Walter. Slightly smiles at him. Then sprints down the hallway until she is out of sight. Her arrival just as swift as her exit.

"What was that?"

I just smile at Walter. Jhene's mere presence tonight speaks volumes as to the conversation our spirits continue to have. We have not had one legitimate conversation yet, but it seems as if we are getting to know each other through other channels, other means, other aspects of life's ricochets. I enjoy our spiritual tango. I just wonder at times would she be able to take in the complete scope of who I am. I cannot imagine the damage I could inflict upon her existence with my mere presence. But something tells me that she lives for such danger. We will see where she stands at a later date. In the meantime, this hallway is not going to exit itself.

The walk home is peaceful. We don't say much.

Much isn't necessary. We just need each other's presence. We would be each other's shadows if we could. We are the only people we trust to stand behind us, or beside us, for long stretches of time. It would only be right. Funny thing is, I trust Walter as my shadow more than I trust my own. And I am sure he would say the same thing. Our brotherhood is built on a foundation of shared pain. But oh the love that has risen from the concrete is something I will never, ever, take for granted. He is my other half. And I am his.

We reach my home. My father's car is not in the driveway. He is more than likely still at work. The place that steals him from me and provides him with every excuse he needs to not be present. They pay him in dollars and status. I pay them back with my sanity.

"Do you know what you're going to say to him when you see him?"

"No real reason to discuss it. If I told him that him missing my showcase tonight led to me cutting my skin with a box cutter for the first time, he would be worried about whether or not the blood landed on my clothes he bought. It's no use."

"Fathers…"

"Fathers."

We hug. I hold Walter in my arms. We don't hug like homies hug. We don't add elements to our hugs that signal that we are still men while engaged in this embrace. We don't symbolize our masculinity with frivolous additions to a stereotypically feminine activity. We hug like we love each other, which we do. We hug like we care for one another, which we do. We hug like bell hooks is in our libraries, which she is. We hug like James Baldwin would hug us if he wasn't so ashamed of what I just did in the boys' bathroom of the school I attend five days a week.

"I love you, Walter."

"I love you, too, Vinnie."

103

"Thank you for being there for me tonight. In all ways."

"Always, in all ways."

I take his hand in mine. And kiss it.

"Bro…"

I give him a look of playful disdain.

"I'm sorry."

Walter squeezes my hand, half-smiles then heads next door to face his own demons. Once he reaches his doorstep, we turn back to look at one another one last time. And enter our homes simultaneously, as one.

It's quiet in here. The silence screams to be interrupted, but only my breathing and the flick of a few light switches are able to oblige. This place is haunted. Nothing gay here. Nothing hopeful here. This is where my energy goes to die.

I sprint into my room. Slam the door. Scramble out of my clothes. Open a drawer. Grab a black t-shirt and black sweats. I put them on. I hop into bed. Pull the covers over me. Lay on my side. Face the wall. And I cry.

And I cry.

And I cry.

And I cry.

And I… rub my left arm with my right hand. Reminisce. The scars already show. This new frontier will need to be protected. I will need to find a way, find some time to keep it between me, Walter and the janitor. No one else can know. No one else can know of this self-inflicted pain. This shoddy excuse of an escape. This is mine.

So I cry.

And I cry.

And I cry.

And I… listen.

I wipe my tears. Deal with my last few sniffles.

My father is home…

I do not look away from this here wall. It is my

comfort in this time of need. My body shakes beneath my blanket. The hairs on my arms stick up. I am nervous. I am scared of what I might be capable of in this moment of conflict. Fury. Rage. Sadness. Disappointment. An emotional cocktail. Explosive, indeed.

My bedroom door opens slightly. I feel his shadow. It is gross. Icky. Grotesque. His breath, calculated, methodical, full of ego, pride, and narcissism.

I hear a familiar sound. A pseudo-apology in the making. He places a wad of hush money on my dresser. This is supposed to surprise me in the morning with how much he cares about me. If only he knew how much his money was a slap in my face. A hug would mean so much more. A kiss would mean so much more. His presence would mean so much more. Each of his dollars make no sense. Each of his dollars depreciate in value every time he uses them to squelch my angst.

But I will take them this time. If only…

…to afford these scars.

XXII

It's Saturday morning. I wake up to new scars upon my skin. They are welcomed additions to life's complications. And a wad of money, wrapped in guilt, sits on my dresser, awaiting my decision on what I will do with it. My father never asks what I do with his money. It is such a frivolous part of his life that he can throw it around with ease, not even need to check in on its usage, and still take pride in its delivery.

The homeless community thanks him for his contributions…

My father exists in a world of tax write-offs. I am his cash cow. As long as I depend on him, as long as he claims me as his dependent, then I am worth the hassle of having to feed, clothe and house. If only he knew of his anonymous charitable donations to street dwellers, he would have even more to discuss during tax time. I am running a non-profit organization right under his nose. I do not profit from anything my father thinks he gives me. I return it to the streets where it belongs. They are more than thankful for him there.

I rub my left arm with my right hand. A motion that is seemingly becoming second nature. My way of understanding what it is that I have done. Or that I may continue to do. The ridges of its already scabbing domain ripple under my fingertips. I can feel its scales, tingling. It is too public. I must not elicit questions from those that surround me. I do not want to become a topic of discussion. This is not a conversation I want to have. I must cover up my perceived sins.

That's what this trip is for.

Headed to the mall. Need to pick up some long-sleeve shirts. Need some reassurance that my already frayed reputation remains relatively in tact. Do not need to produce anymore ammunition for my naysayers, anymore anger within my father. This is an unwanted pregnancy that cannot afford an abortion. It must be kept hidden from the masses for as long as humanly possible. Aside from those that are truly in the know. And that only includes Walter and the janitor.

Poor janitor…

I left so much of my identity on that floor of the boys' bathroom in the school that I attend five days a week. Left a past of weakness, replaced it with a present of strength, a future of promise. What I severed from my body were my soul's outtakes, parts of my story that did not need to make the final cut. I did not make the final cut. I rough drafted my skin. Put it on notice for future drafts to come. I will revise, edit and proofread my story, until my skin screams, and Amazon makes a killing off the audiobook. Scripted pain, freestyled angst. To be a fly on the wall when the higher-ups at my school realize that one of their students may have tried to kill themselves. And it was the most troubled of them all. How would they swallow such failure to recognize the depths of his despair? Were they not supposed to be teaching him? How can you teach the self-taught? The well-read? My sleep patterns register a higher IQ level than the most woke teachers around. Bow to my intellect, and hear me roar…

I'm sorry. I took a step back. I still see my teachers and fellow classmates in a positive light. After seeing my mother, talking to God, talking to Walter and the outpouring of love and support that I was shown last night, I do not have any ill will towards any of those people. They are at least trying. They are attempting to engage with me in the only manner they know how. And I don't make it easy on them. But they keep coming back for more. Keep wanting to provide me with whatever it is that they feel I am lacking. I wish they didn't know how much I was lacking. But it is clearly written all over my face. I don't have to say a word.

I walk to the bus stop by myself. Decked out in my usual attire, all that will change after I reach my destination is that my black short sleeve shirt will turn into a black long sleeve shirt. Same brand who took all my money during my transformation makes black long sleeve shirts, so I figured I might as well keep up with the trend, make it easy on all of us. I trust their garments will work in my favor. No need to change now.

I give the bus driver a tip before I find my seat. She is a black woman, around her early 40s, and she never forgets to smile at me whenever she sees me. She grew up with my mother and would have attended her funeral but could not take off work. Having three kids to feed alone on a bus driver's salary is a good enough reason for me. I saw her leave a card on my mother's gravestone so I know she hasn't forgotten about her. Sometimes, work beckons. It sure does call out to my father a lot, so I know its voice.

I find a seat in the back, stare out the window. I silently pray no one decides to sit next to me. I especially abhor those who wreak of feces and have the audacity to snuggle in next to me. I do not bother you with my life's flames so do not bother me with your life's fumes. It is only right.

I manage to get through the entire bus ride without sitting next to anyone. This is a feat in itself and provides me with positive energy to see this trip through. I tell the bus driver, "Thank you" and continue into the mall.

Surprise! I hate it here.

Majority of the people at the mall are not there to actually purchase anything. It is amazing that the businesses actually make a profit. There is just a bunch of gawking, hoping and praying, that the next check will come along and leave enough disposable income for the middle and lower classes to engage in capitalism the way the one-percent begs us to. Ninety-nine percent of Americans continue to make the same people rich, over and over again. Without fail. Capitalism at its finest. And its finest is relatively disgusting.

I reach my store of choice. I am sure someone greeted me but I am in no position to engage in small talk. I simply want to grab 10 long sleeve black collared shirts, that aren't dressy. I want to spend my father's money, not look like him.

They have eight larges. I grab two extra-larges with plans to just roll up the cuffs. Making another trip to the mall just to get two more of the right size isn't something I want to do. So we will make do. And maybe this will get me to start washing clothes a little more regularly so I don't even have to use the extra larges. They will be my back-ups.

My father could fit these…

I purchase my items. I take off my shirt right there in the store, amid glances from those working as well as customers, and swap it out for one of my new shirts. I do not plan on wearing a short sleeve shirt anytime soon. Not with what my wrist and upper arm could look like in the coming weeks. I'm not wishing for that to be. But it could be.

It will be…

I decide that I do not want to take the bus home. The air is pure, the sun is still out, if barely, and the streets always provide me with stories to tell and material to create my art. It is unencumbered, free and magical out here where prostitutes frolic, old men drag their feet one more step towards death and old women reminisce about their former skin, before age ravaged their youth and spit them onto the curb, never to be seen again.

A particular old woman catches my eye. She sits in an alley, covered by a single dirty blanket, wool fabric. Her skin dangles from beneath her eyes, sprints down her cheeks and hangs there for dear life. Her eyebrows furrow, borderline unite and her neck sings a swan song both mythical and surreal. Everything about her screams old, except, her eyes. Piercing. Gorgeous. And grey. Her eyes rewrite her backstory in hieroglyphics. Paint a different picture filled with past beauty and male jaws dropped. Women recognized her as the only true competition but she walked to her own beat, never settling for the subpar, you had to work to be in her company. And work they did. Her place on this here sidewalk cannot be explained, for every privilege was bestowed upon her. She keeps this secret to herself, only whispering through blinks. She was beautiful once. And once was enough.

  I kneel down next to her. She does not understand, nor know what to do with my presence. So she shakes her head back and forth. I do not take this as a 'no' but as a 'don't know'. I smile at her, despite us being in completely different places within the same interaction. I reach into my pocket, take out what remains of my wad of money, and place it next to her blanket. She flinches at first, before she recognizes what it is I am leaving her. There has to be at least 300 dollars wrapped in that rubberband. Her eyes blink rapidly, a thank you of sorts. Her body fluid in the language of gratitude. I take this in stride. I do not need to hear her words. I only need to know her reaction for my future records. When I look back on my time on this earth and know that I provided someone with something they did not have. As I am someone forever searching for things I do not have.

  My mother is dead…
  Jhene…
  I loathe my father with everything I am…
  I miss Walter…

  I stand here, on Walter's porch. Listen. Grapple with what my ears tell me. Pain skirts my truth. I wish these were lies. So much damage being done. Lamps break. Tables fold. Glass shatters. Cheeks smack. Clocks tick. Clocks tock.

I cannot move my limbs.

I can only imagine if Walter can. As his beating takes place. In the heat of the night. He fights back. Aimless. No match for a match made in hell. A father with no restraint. A father with no checks nor balances. His father, Rick. Drunk off drink. Drunk off power. Drunk off insecurities. Drunk off his own filth. His demands bounce off the walls. Screams at the tops of lungs. Anger gallops into the air and sits. It is ugly here.

And I cannot move my limbs.

The music pierces eardrums. Yet I cannot turn away. It begs for an audience. I oblige within hesitance. High notes scorch earth. My other half splits in two. Fight is what he does not have left. I could not have left. Amidst the silence of it all. There is nothing left to listen to. He is through. This is through. I am through. Acting as if I am not jealous of the intimacy of rage. It is still interaction either way. Oh, how I would kiss the knuckles of my father as they swung and landed against parts of me he has never touched.

I long to be touched...

My father pulls up in his car. I stare in his direction, await his exit from his vehicle. He gets out. Straightens himself up. Grabs his briefcase. Finds his way to me. Eye contact. If just for a moment. He releases. Walks inside. Slams the door behind him.

If only he drank...

XXIII

"Here."

Walter hands me a house key.

"Next time you hear me getting my ass whooped, come get me."

I take the key and put it in my pocket. I stare at Walter. His bruises from last night stand out against his white skin. He does not attempt to hide them. They are simply visual aids to his life's presentation.

I continue to look at him. Study him. He starts to get uncomfortable. Does not understand my particular level of interest. I attempt to explain, though I know there is no way for me to say this without it sounding weird, at the least, inconsiderate, at the most.

"I just wish my father would touch me, too."

Walter shoves one of his bruised arms into my face.

"Is this what you want? If this is what you want, I will happily trade your skin for mine. Any day. Just say the word."

"But there is passion there, is there not? There is a certain type of intimacy it takes to –"

"– Do not twist this in your weird ass head into something good. Nothing good comes of what happened to me last night. Someone has to clean up the mess afterwards. That someone is me. I get beat and I have to clean up the mess. It's sick. That's what it is. It's sick. This is not some dramatic hug gone wrong. This is pure violence. And it's real. There is no fantasy. Just punches and pushes, man. Just punches and pushes."

There is a long pause between us. I do not know how to respond. All I did last night was dream about what I would need to do to get my father to react with passion. For him to become so enraged that he would need to touch me. I know that if he would just touch me, he would feel on my skin the remnants of a long lost love. A love only he has the power to reconcile. I just want him to love me. Even if that love is covered in rage, covered in anger. I would still have his undivided attention. It would mean everything to me. It is not as if I am not already scarred. Scars can be sacrificed. Proof can be sacrificed. I can be sacrificed. I just need to know it is possible.

"I'm going to walk to school by myself today, man. I need to think."

Walter begins the 10-minute stroll to school without me. I watch him leave as I contemplate just how much I may have hurt my best friend's feelings by speaking my truth. I am not worried that we will not bounce back from this but with Walter, and his father, there are unknown complexities just like there are with my father and I. It is why we can connect on such a high plain. We know no one can understand our particular cocktails of love and hate for the men who are supposed to raise us. We even give each other the benefit of the doubt when one misinterprets a piece of information given by the other. This may have been my moment of misinterpretation. I may have made this about me when it was about comforting Walter. I should have approached it differently. But I know I will have a chance to make it up to him. And all will be good again.

I still crave the violence…

Lunch time. Walter stands near me but does not say a word. Keeps his head down. I get the silent treatment. And deservedly so. But at least he is still near me, where I can see him, and still know that he is alive.

Trevor, a future skinhead white supremacist Nazi domestic terrorist, bumps into Walter. It's purposeful. Vicious. And right on time.

"Hey! Watch where you're going, man…"

I perk up. Walter adjusts his backpack, which is easy because there is barely anything in it. School and Walter are not exactly clicking their heels in holy matrimony. He just uses the facility as an escape from his reality. His schooling comes from conversations with me – and the books I force him to read and discuss with me.

Trevor. "What you going to do about it, punk? I'll fucking slay you."

Walter. "You really don't want that problem, man. Especially not today."

Trevor stares at Walter for a little while, his army of cronies – about four deep – stand in alignment behind him, ready to pounce at any moment. Trevor does not want it with Walter. And his cronies are unaware of just how much they don't want it with me, either.

Trevor. "I see daddy put his hands on you again. The ugly son of the neighborhood drunk. Dipshit. Dipped in shit. Can smell his shit breath all over you."

Trevor hits the ground. I just hit him. Right hand. His right jaw. Perfectly centered. It was a masterpiece of facial destruction. And Trevor still has not recovered.

His cronies jump in. Walter lays one of them out with a right cross. Wrestles with another. I kick one in the chest, knock the wind out of him. Then I toy with another one. He tries to hit me, at least three times, misses get progressively worse as I determine how I plan to end this. I explode through his nose with a straight shot. Lay him clear out.

This truly is not the day to come for me and Walter when we did not send for you.

Walter throws the last kid over his shoulder and slams him to the ground. The two of us look like action heroes as Trevor and his minions all writhe in pain on the ground with me and Walter standing over them. Other students walk by, stare at the carnage. Trevor tries to pick on everybody, so him getting help from other students that aren't his cronies, just ain't gonna happen.

A couple of kids get licks in while Trevor is on the ground. This makes both me and Walter chuckle. We smile at each other. All is right in the world again. My best friend knows I have his back. Always, in all ways.

"Principal's office! Now!"

Guess it's time to pay the piper.

XXIV

Principal Washington. "Where did you get those bruises, Walter?"

Walter looks to me. I look back at him. My eyes tell him to tell the truth. Walter doesn't listen.

Walter. "I mean, I did just get in a fight."

Principal Washington. "So those boys did that to you? That's why you fought them."

Walter. "Yeah, you could say that."

Principal Washington turns to me.

"I'd expect this from him but not from you."

"That's proof you don't know me that well, then. For I am him, and he is me. We are the same. Only separated by melanin and messed up fathers."

Principal Washington leans back in her chair. She cannot quite ascertain what would prompt us to leave so much carnage on her blacktop.

"You guys beat up five kids by yourselves."

Walter. "Sounds like we won."

Principal Washington. "All you won is a suspension."

Walter. "Even trade. Them boys now know not to come for us unless we send for them."

See? Same person.

Principal Washington. "Well, I will need to call your parents to come get you."

Walter. "Parent."

"Parent."

Principal Washington looks upon both of our faces. This is the first time she recognizes our shared pain, first time she understands exactly what brings us together, and why I would start a fight on Walter's behalf. She looks like she might even provide us some leniency on our punishment. But I understand there are protocols involved in this. She has to do what she has to do.

Principal Washington looks through some paperwork. She takes out the sheet she was looking for, picks up the phone and dials a number. I can hear the faint sound of the phone ringing. I wonder who she called first.

Ring. Ring. Ring.

Principal Washington's look of surprise at no one answering is almost comical. She slowly hangs up.

"No one was home."

Walter. "No, he's home. But around this time…"

Walter looks to me. The truth of his home life seconds away from leaving his tongue.

Walter. "…Around this time he's usually napping. Long nights, long mornings."

Principal Washington nods in understanding – she doesn't understand. I do. It doesn't take nighttime for the neighborhood drunk to begin his daily intoxication routine. At least at this time, he hasn't started drooling yet.

Or punching.

Or slamming.

Or cursing.

Or grabbing.

Naw. Not yet. Just sleeping.

"Let's try your father, Vinnie."

A sly smile spreads across my face. This woman has no idea what she is talking about. My teachers have a better sense of what they are dealing with when it comes to me. Higher-ups like Principal Washington only see me in small dosages. And her most recent dosages have included celebrating my art. She is apparently under the impression that I live a privileged existence sans any emotional or mental issues. Oh, how wrong can she be…

Ring. Ring. Ring.

Principal Washington. "I will try again later. It went to voicemail."

"It will always go to voicemail."

Principal Washington leans forward, elbows on desk, a power pose for those with perceived power.

"I need for both of you to walk home. And call the school as soon as you get there so we know that you are safe and at home. Your suspensions start now."

Walter gets up and I follow him out. Once we exit the office doors, we turn and smile at one another. This whole situation deserves a good laugh.

"Hey, at least we got in trouble together."

"This is all your fault."

We laugh.

"How is it my fault?"

"You're the one who clocked Trevor first. I wasn't even trying to go there with the dude. You're so damn violent."

"I am not violent. I just felt like…"

In unison.

"He shouldn't come for us if we didn't send for him."

More laughter. Who knew that getting into a fight could bring two people together so much? I guess it only works when you are fighting on the same team. Getting into a fight, and turning a loved one into an enemy, has the opposite effect. Thankfully, Walter is my loved one. And I love him. And getting suspended, a couple of days after being praised and lauded for my paintings, is further proof that it is Walter over everything. He is my other half.

We walk home. Laugh and giggle like we just got on honor roll or something. We do not look like two boys headed to our decrepit household existences, in the middle of the day, due to fighting. What we do look like, is us.

"Thanks for having my back, man."

"Anytime. You know I love you."

"I love you too, man."

"And look at you… Saying I love you back without

an ounce of a pause. Ain't you just the most beautiful white boy in the whole wide world."

I laugh. He playfully punches me in the shoulder.

"See, you always ruining it. Don't ask me to be all in my feelings and shit and then chastise me for it."

"Did you just say, 'chastise'?!"

"Damn right I did. And I used it correctly. That word is gangster. I like it. So damnit, I'm gonna use it."

"Vocabulary assassin!"

"Murking cats, one word at a time."

"Oh snap, son!"

"We have problems."

"Yeah, yeah we do."

Silence. We have arrived at the footsteps of our homes.

"See you later?"

"Yeah, see you later."

Food. Nap. Box cutter. Naw, no box cutter. *Another nap. Nighttime.*

Let's go see what Walter is up to…

Tomorrow.

XXV

Pops is already gone. That job he has seems to need him to be there at a certain hour, each day. They require a particular level of loyalty. I guess when they are the ones providing your paychecks, they have the right to ask for it. I just have his blood running through my veins, so maybe that isn't enough to ask for the same type of loyalty. I am still working on what I would be able to ask him for that he would actually be willing to give me. It is somewhere on the tip of my tongue. I will find it. I will speak it into existence. One day.

James Baldwin.

His book, *Notes Of A Native Son*, lies across my chest, open to the second paragraph of the first essay of Part One, Everybody's Protest Novel. *Uncle Tom's Cabin* is in Baldwin's sights in this particular essay, and though the subject matter is powerful and necessary, particularly at the time in which his book was written, I focus simply on his sentence structure, use of the underrated comma and his ability to make his humanity jump off the page and slap the reader clear across their cheek.

"Miss Ophelia, as we may suppose, was speaking for the author; her exclamation is the moral, neatly framed, and incontestable like those improving mottoes sometimes found hanging on the walls of furnished rooms. And, like these mottoes, before which one invariably flinches, recognizing an insupportable, almost an indecent glibness, she and St. Clare are terribly in earnest. Neither of them questions the medieval morality from which their dialogue springs: black, white, the devil, the next world – posing its alternatives between heaven and the flames – were realities for them as, of course, they were for their creator. They spurned and were terrified of the darkness, strived mightily for the light; and considered from this aspect, Miss Ophelia's exclamation, like Mrs. Stowe's novel, achieves a

bright, almost a lurid significance, like the light from a fire which consumes a witch."

Do you understand now? Without even having knowledge of *Uncle Tom's Cabin* – or the paragraph that precedes this one, for that matter – you see the striking reasons why his prose ropes you in, wraps its passionate precision around the reader's neck and suffocates you until you die – with a smile on your face. I consume paragraphs like this on a regular basis. I have read Baldwin practically every day since I was eight years old. That is six years of study. I have a master's degree in James Baldwin. Sat with a dictionary next to me, looked up every word that made no sense. And at eight years old, even the definitions themselves made no sense. But I kept coming back. Kept coming back to his words. Kept coming back to his intelligence. Kept coming back to his love. I would bring short passages to my mother and see if she could decipher them. Both for me and for herself. She almost always could. But even she would sometimes struggle with Baldwin's need to pause and insert yet another idea to think about while the reader is already dealing with the primary subject of the sentence. He would just keep loading and loading more and more intellectual stimulation into each sentence until you were forced to just consume it or choke on its strength.

I loved it. I loved him. I love it. I love him. He is where I go when I need to reconfigure my mental space, gather myself for the stretch run of whatever race it is that I am running. And as I sit here, lying on my bed, with a book of his that I have read at least six times, suspended from school for the very first time in my life, it is only right to bury myself in all that is him. He is my company.

Until I check on Walter...

I am a little fearful of what will come of Walter on this day of suspension. Weekends are a favorite of his father's to turn Walter into his victim, and a day of suspension is reminiscent of a weekend's stillness. Weekends seem like they are full of all of this energy but it is really just empty silence until humans decide to fill them with their errands, eating and engagements. Otherwise, there is nothing for a weekend to do but to twiddle its thumbs until the real work of the week siphons its attention away.

Pardon me. I have been wanting to use the word 'siphon' for some time now. And it just happened. Right here. Right at almost the end of that last paragraph. I am psyched right now.

Where did this blood come from?

See, Walter wakes up every morning and convinces himself that today is the day that he will not kill his father. He doesn't need to convince himself that he needs to kill his father. He already thinks so. He knows he needs to kill his father. His job every morning is to convince himself that today is not the day. Then make sure that tomorrow is not the day. Or the next day. Or the day after that. Until eventually, the day his father dies, will not be at the hands of Walter. And he won't feel like he failed.

Where did this blood come from?

See, Walter has all these issues he needs to come to grips with. He doesn't tackle or handle his issues with the same earnest and gusto that I do. I am his role model after all.

Where did this blood come from?

I have the emotional capacity to deal with the everyday trials and tribulations of a teenage boy living with his estranged, muted, emotionally stunted father or violent, alcoholic father. I do. I truly do. I have all the tools at my disposal.

Where did this blood come from?

I like to keep my books crisp and honorable looking.

Where did this blood come from?

I don't, like, use my books as some sort of disturbing coaster or anything like that.

Where did this blood come from?

But I do have multiple copies of certain books.

Where did this blood come from?

In case something were to happen to one of them.

Where did this blood come from?

I will always have a spare.

Where did this blood come from?

Almost like we have a spare arm.

Where did this blood come from?

You know? Like, two of them.

Where did this blood come from?

In case.

Where did this blood come from?

Something were to happen.

Where did this blood come from?

Or, like, we have two wrists…

Oh. That's where it's coming from.

I need to apologize to Baldwin. I have stained his pages with my filth. But I swear, Walter is the one you need to be worried about…

XXVI

It is, like, breakfast. It nourishes me. Starts my day with the proper nutrients. Pair it with my reading of Baldwin, and it is a spiritual experience. A high. Yes, a high. Dazed ecstasy. No one knows this feeling like I do. I cannot share it with another. I will not share it with another. I must not share it with another.

Jhene...

My skin tingles. The copy of Baldwin's *Notes Of A Native Son*, ruined, sticky, infested. Its sentences underlined by red marks more suitable for a bathroom floor or sink. Instead, I sunk into a place of uninhibited passion for my own pain. An addiction, of sorts. An addiction I have no plans on rectifying. It is much too soon. I have not hit my prime yet. I am still relishing in its profound deliciousness. I am here for a reason. I am but a student to its delicacies. This pain is delectable. And no one can inflict pain on oneself like oneself. They don't call it self-help for no reason.

The sun is setting. I have not seen Walter since we came home from school early yesterday. And, you know, Walter is the one we have to worry about. I have all the tools I need at the ready. I can handle all my teenage angst, anxiety and frustrations. You see that, don't you? Yeah, you see it.

Walter is the one who needs some guidance. Needs some help. I am here to help him. I am here to provide that guidance. I am his friend. I am his loved one. I am... sitting here. I am not there to help him. I am not there to provide guidance. I am not his friend. I am not his loved one. I am... still sitting here. Why am I still sitting here? Why am I so selfish? Why am I not sharing this glee I feel with my very best friend in the whole wide world? Why can I not rise up from these ashes and find my friend?

I have a key to his house! I will arrive in gleeful splendor! I will hug him! I will kiss him! I will love him! I will be there for him! What am I waiting for? Let's go!

But first, of course, I must rinse off my box cutter. It needs to be brand spanking new before I embark on my journey... next door. So close, yet so far away. I cannot hear Walter's heartbeat in this moment. I want to hear Walter's heartbeat in this moment. I want to sing its rhythm. I want to sing its praises. I want to dance to its pitter patter.

But damn this box cutter...

Just, just taking a little longer than expected to clean off this box cutter. This box cutter is trying to prevent me from leaving. It needs to stop. It really does. It needs to. It needs to let me go. It needs to let me go see my friend. It needs to let me figure this out. Figure this in. I need to go.

Finally...

Front door. Exit. Outside. Deep breath. Take steps in the right direction. Almost there.

Darkness...

Darkness befalls my being. I do not hear the beautiful melody of my best friend's heart. I instead hear the screams of my best friend's soul.

Why did my box cutter keep me inside so long?

I have been too drenched in my bedazzled high of ecstasy and pain to recognize his calls for help, his calls for me. I am now here to answer them.

Why am I walking so slow?

I actually want to do this. I actually want to get there. I actually want to be by his side. I do not understand this lackluster performance in which my limbs are currently undertaking. Now. Go. You fully realized calf muscles.

Thank you.

I take out the key that was bestowed upon me by my very best friend Walter, who needs my help, needs help, and I am the one readily capable of providing it.

I look at it for a second. I guess to make sure it is the correct key. It is. And I intend to use it. As my friend needs me. And I need him. But he needs me more. Because he is Walter. And I am Vinnie. I am the one equipped to handle all of our teenage angst, anger and hardships. It is me. I am the one.

Door is open...

Bang. Crash. Slap. Slap. Bang. Crash. Slap. Slap.

Rick. "Why are you in trouble again?!"

Walter. "I was defending you!"

"I don't need no defending from you, you little shit!"

"Get off me, you drunk!"

"Oh, I'm a drunk now?"

"I hate you!"

I stand there. Unable to move. This is the first time I have ever seen with my own two eyes a father put his hands on his son. A Rick put his hands on a Walter.

My father would never do that...

Walter sees me. His eyes scream for help. But I do not know how to answer him. My high is gone. All that remains is a 14-year-old boy watching in horror as my best friend gets beat up by his drunk father, and I am powerless to do anything about it.

"Kill him, Vinnie! Kill him!"

I cannot move. All I can do is watch. I am a spectator in this domestic violence sport. I do not want any part of it. This isn't Trevor on the blacktop. This is real. And that's a father. That's a man who should be providing.

Rick sees me.

"Kill him, Vinnie! Kill him! Kill him like we talked about!"

Rick. "Oh you want some of this too?!"

Rick tosses Walter to the side. He hits a table and falls to the floor. Rick takes heavy, long steps in my direction.

Wait...
Rick gets closer.
Wait... in my direction?
I finally snap out of my trance and take off.
"Run, Vinnie! Run!"
I sprint through the front door. Rick's footsteps deafening in my ears. I run towards my house. And in the driveway sits my father's car. And standing near my doorway is the one they call Thomas. The one I call my father.
Rick. "Bring your ass here, boy!"
I run into my father's arms. He quickly figures out what is going on. He holds me in one arm. And turns his attention to Rick.
"You better take your ass back in that house, Rick. You do not want this problem."
Rick stops in his tracks. Drooling. Spitting. Sweating. Disgusting. And heads slowly back into his own disturbing walls he calls home.
My father takes me into both of his arms.
Is this a hug?
"Are you ok? Are you alright? Did he hurt you?"
This feels like a hug...
Is this a hug?
It feels like a hug...
Oh my God...
My father is hugging me!
My father is hugging me!
My father... loves me...
Thank you, Rick.

XXVII

I wrap my arms around him. I do not plan to let go. I breathe in his scent. I have not been this close to him since my infancy, and even then, I am not sure. He hugs me. Holds me. Makes sure that I am alright.

This is a father…

There is so much worry on his face. So much concern. And it isn't for him. It isn't for his own well-being. There is an unselfishness in this embrace. He would not be here if I did not need him to be. And I need him to be. So he is here. Hugging me. Holding me. Making sure that I am alright.

This is my father…

Oh, how long have I awaited this moment? His scent envelops me. He smells like hard work, urgency and masculinity. He smells prehistoric. He smells stereotypical. He smells manly. He smells stern. He smells court house. He smells law degree. He smells widower. He smells single father.

He smells… human.

I sense his humanity for the very first time as I continue to snuggle into his rigid chest, pectoral muscles clenched as he steadies himself to counter my aggressive embrace. This man is strong. I can feel his sacrifices. I can feel his choices. I can feel all that he is, that is not me.

I can feel our differences. I can feel why everything is awry. I can feel his zodiac. I can feel his Capricorn. My senses, ravaged by this intimacy. I know it will not last forever, but forever, in me, it will last.

"Let's go inside."

The words leave his tongue in the most caring of tones. I listen with utter glee. I am smitten by this man. This father in sheep's clothing. I hope he gives me a piggyback ride before the end of the night. I bet he has a pony waiting for me somewhere. Maybe in the backyard.

That would seem to be the only place that makes any sense. Unless it is in the garage. But that would make the garage stink. And he works out in the garage so he would hate that. But maybe he is willing to sacrifice the funky pony because he wants to make me happy? I wouldn't have thought that doable only a few minutes ago but now that I am in his arms, anything is possible…

We walk inside but I still have not let go of him. He is slightly annoyed, slightly amused by this. I slowly release the embrace. This is one of the hardest things I have ever had to do. I do not know what would need to happen in order to get him to embrace me like that again. What would need to occur to make a man like my father hold me in his arms again? Do I always have to be in what could be viewed as danger in order to elicit a reaction in him the way tonight did? I do not know the answers to these questions but their potential terrify me.

But I will be embraced by any means necessary. And I mean that. Any means. I will do whatever it takes to get this feeling again. And again. And again.

I finally let him go. I don't know what I am exactly letting go of in this moment, I just hope it isn't more than just his body. I look him in his eyes. He gives me a half smile – which might as well be the largest smile in the world.

"Are you going to be okay, son?"

"Yes, father."

"I'm going to get some rest. It's been a long day. See you in the morning."

He walks into his room and lightly closes the door. I am in awe. Struggle with this newfound emotion.

"I love you."

It is too late for him to hear me. It took too long for the words to leave my mouth. I just wonder what it would mean for that hug, that embrace, to grow into something magical. Something beautiful. Something therapeutic.

Something that heals my wounds and drops my box cutter in the gutter, never to be seen again. Something healing. Something worthwhile.

My father hugged me…

My mother has to be smiling. Her two men, love in the room. Her exit finally having the results she sought prior to her energy transferring to the wind. I have wanted to love him like this for so long. I only hated him because I thought he hated me. It was my only means of response. I know of nothing else. He showed no sign of wanting to be in my life at the level, in the capacity that I wanted, needed him to be. He would not show up. Or, he would show up, and it would be as if he was not there. All flesh, no follow through. He would envelop rooms with his disconnect, announce to the world – and to me – that he was only there as a misconstrued obligation he convinced himself to fulfill, against his will, if you will.

I find myself walking to my bedroom. A slow stroll. My fear is leaving this moment here, alone, to dwell on its realness. It may not want to return again. It may have already overstayed its welcome. I fear that leaving it be, to reconfigure itself into my usual reality, is the easy thing for this moment to do – and that it actually wants to. There is so much work to do if this moment wants to indeed linger. It would not be able to sit alone and rest on its morals. It would need to be watered, and watered again, to near drowning. Morning, afternoon, evening dives into its roots, sprouting from the depths in which it came. That hug, that embrace we shared, that eye contact, that half-smile, that calm exit, that "I love you", that time, that space, that energy, that…

My father hugged me…

I sit on my bed now. I question how real this is. I wonder how I will sleep. I have never slept in a world where my father hugs me. I only remember my slumber in a world where my father despises me, where I am defective, where I disappoint, where I do not suffice, where I am burden, where I am not what he would have wanted in a son. I know a world where my fists puncture walls, my knuckles glisten from the pain, where my wrists dance the delicate tight rope of pleasure and pain, suicide and life, here and there. This new world, this new possibility, this new frontier, is not something I can grab a handle on, sink my teeth in, grasp, understand, fathom. He is new. And, I, am new. I am. I truly am. I am a boy with a father. A boy in love with a man, this man, the man who is half of me. I am not ashamed of this love. This love is thorough, is it not? This is the love we have all wished for, prayed for, hoped for, screamed for, cried for...

This is love...
My father hugged me...
...

...

...
Where did this blood come from?

XXVIII

Where did this blood come from?
I still cut. I still cut with regularity. Its high is
inescapable. It is a feeling I cannot get anywhere else. I
thought my father's embrace would mark the end of my
journey into the bliss that is *drip, drip*. It marked a turning
point, yes, but that moment lingered in that room, and
slowly rotted its inevitable death. It isn't that my father
reverted back to his old ways, he just didn't grasp the
moment as the launching pad to father-son exhilaration like
I did. It was as if I knew it was coming, did not want to lose
the momentum of my seismic high, and cut anyway. That
night might have been the best yet. I was equally buoyed by
the titanic glee of our embrace, and the cataclysmic high of
blade to skin. It was what losing my virginity will feel like
in 689 days…
     Jhene…
     I am still on suspension. Blessing of having a father
who works, a suspension is practically a vacation, and if
you can convince someone to join you, it can truly have its
perks.
     And my, oh my, is Jhene such a perk.
     She stays in this running rotation of baggy clothes,
and impeccably understated makeup. She makes the rest of
the girls at school feel so inadequate by comparison. She is
Avril Lavigne with Aaliyah's melanin. She speaks to me
only when she feels it is necessary for me to hear her
words. And that is a skill not too many can master. But she
has mastered my needs, my wants, and given me reason to
get out of the house. She is not one to let school schedules
hinder her travels, so she finds time to ditch school and
meet me at the canyon for casual canoodling and
conversation. I imagine doing things with her that I will
never do with Walter. I love Walter, but I can be *in love*
with Jhene, and that's what society wants from me, is it

not? To allow this petite girl to fondle my adolescence in her pop rock hands and birth a sense of masculine pride long dormant underneath bell hooks' inquiries, Baldwin's sentence structure and bedazzled dreams? To play on the ingrained faulty logic of what entails homosexuality is one of my favorite pastimes.

We sit next to one another in the deepest part of the canyon, furthest away from the street, furthest away from onlookers, furthest away from naysayers. She nestles into my arm in a way only she can. It's almost in the motion of a cat licking its milk, only without the tongue. Just, adorable, for some odd reason. I can't really explain what makes her so beautiful…

I'll explain later…

I rub my arm. Slightly, only noticeable if you're paying attention. And Jhene always pays attention.

"Will you show me?"

She says it with such delicacy. She is a delicacy. I completely believe that she is not lying.

"Why?"

"I dunno. Just 'cause."

She smiles. She needs no other reasons for her request to be satisfied.

I pull up my sleeves, reveal my wrists, upper arm, and all its glory. Nick here. Nick there. Nicks everywhere. I'm nicked up. Devastating artwork. Beautiful. A renegade tattoo artist with no guidance, no end in sight.

She takes my arm in her hands and examines it closely. Almost too closely. I can feel her deep breaths, the oxygen leaves her lungs, only to tickle my arm.

"What are you doing?"

She kisses one of my scars. Two. Three. Four. Five. Six. Seven. Eight. Nine. Ten. She leaves no scar unturned. She kisses them each differently. She switches styles, as if each has a different story to tell and she wants to respect their story, pay homage to whatever it is that it took for them to land in their proper place on my skin.

"Just catching up on your past."

She kisses my arm again. I am beginning to really like this.

"It tastes like darkness – and self-loathing."

She kisses my arm again. This is the best one yet. She truly takes her time. I have never engaged in such ecstasy with another person. This must be why the world makes so many mistakes.

"I've tasted them before. Feels different coming from another. But the tinge is still there."

My voice works again.

"You cut?"

Jhene looks at me longingly, the deepest eye contact I have ever felt. She melts me. I am melting. I cannot seem to quite put a handle on what is transpiring, at the moment. But it is a moment I am relishing. I do not have control over any of this. And that is perfectly fine with me.

Jhene kisses me. On the lips. Softly. Gingerly. At first. Adds micro levels of aggression to each step, reveling in her teacher status, as I, her pupil, figure out this tango for which I have never participated in before. I told you, if Walter ever wanted to kiss me, I would have kissed him back because I love him. But this right here, though…

Jhene…

We are all out tongue swapping, lip locking, tonsil dancing, hands rubbing through each other's hair, or lack thereof. Deliciously ravenous. Sheesh… This. Shit. Right. Here.

We stop. Sexy in its abruptness.

I take out my box cutter like it's a pack of cigarettes. We stare at it. Together. She takes it in her hands. Holds it close to her face. Examines it like seeing a long-lost friend for the first time in decades.

"I know the pain well."

Let me tell you about this girl I know...

*I have never met a girl who puts my heart into a
pitter patter every time she graces my presence sends my
loins into a spiral with no come down in sight oh my oh my
does this girl create quite a conundrum for my attempt to
live a conundrum free existence for her ability to turn my
feelings into her own personal bloodbath willingly
cleansing herself and myself with her blood and my blood
angry at the emotional Tetris of it all pieces working in
unison to create soul arithmetic where one plus one equals
two more opportunities to showcase a love like no other
teenager has ever showcased before my own painting
showcases hold no candle to the light she shows me when
she walks into a room with her Avril Lavigne get up and
her Aaliyah swagger they'd both be proud of the initial
daggers she shot through my heart on that crazy day when
she walked into my classroom and they announced she was
here to stay and she never once told me that she was a thief
of hearts she just did it on her own like the gangsta that she
is and I haven't been mad at her ever since for that thievery
is just what the doctor ordered in the form of a girl who
perfectly fits my idiosyncrasies to a tilt never any judgment
we never wilt under the pressures of societal measures only
we measure up to the expectations one another has
bestowed upon no one for we live a life sans expectation
only exhilaration of perspiration as we further solidify my
addiction to the love pill she forced me to swallow I do not
wallow in past hiccups and missteps for every missed step
led me to her and I will not allow her to suffer in silence
any longer for we suffer loudly in unison as she wiggles her
way in as my new best friend a role filled by someone for
the first time for this is the first time I have ever locked lips
with someone over and over again just for the fun of it just
for the love of it just for the feel of it and it feels oh so good
adding to my new highs attempting to move past my
father's embrace and the high of the cut for she is cut from*

a different cloth as am I and I represent a guy she has not seen in the flesh for she has always been too much of a mess for any boy to want to clean up too much work for the lazy I am in love with the crazy in love with her crazy in love with the possibility of massaging her soul with my impeccable vocabulary I hope I know enough words to describe her properly she stays on my mind streaming consciousness of the feminine divine the divine feminine is nothing to challenge she is my heart's challenge and it must beat over and over again to supply me with the life necessary to impact hers the way she has impacted mine...

For she is mine. At this moment, at this time. I must breathe now...

Jhene...

XXIX

Jhene holds my hand every step from the canyon to my home. I offer – over and over – to walk her home. She questions – over and over – what home really is. Her home is different, depending on mood and mission. I have no idea what this actually means, but the beauty in which she delivers this information suffices. I worry about her and her petite frame getting home safely, but I trust her judgment, and do not pressure her. She wants us to treasure this moment, this time we just shared in blood and beauty. I could not have asked for much more.

As she lets go of my hand, she skips around the corner and out of sight. I watch her, as her aura follows her, protects her from the unknown dangers that could be lurking outside of my view. I take a long, deep breath. A cool breeze passes through me, calms me, speaks to me. I no longer feel scared. The wind is here, now. The wind is everywhere.

I enter my home. My father is here, somewhere. In what mood? I do not know. I do know that I would like to update him on a few things. I would like to tell him a few things about myself. I would like to engage in conversation, son to father, child to parent.

We have to talk...

Not too much conversation has transpired between us since he hugged me. It is not as if he seems to still hate my presence. But further acknowledgement of our relationship, or lack thereof, has not happened. I would like it to. We need to take advantage of the space that hug gave us, before it evaporates into thin air, never to be utilized. That was my concern then. It is still my concern now, as the strength of that hug continues to dwindle with each passing day.

I sit at the kitchen table. No real reason for being here. Yes, I have a reason for being here. This table is shouting distance from my father's bedroom. An impenetrable locale I have not seen with my own two eyes since…

My mother is dead…

And even then, I did not go in there often. My mother and I spent most of our time either in the kitchen or in my room where we could interact and discuss all things painting without any distraction, disruption – or fear.

There is something sitting on the tip of my tongue. Words, perhaps. Sitting there wondering if they will be used this evening. If they will be spoken into existence, to be acknowledged or ignored, seen or not seen, understood or misconstrued. They are words, after all. There is not much you can do with them.

There is plenty you can do with them…

They are going backwards now, the words. They have left the tip of my tongue and headed south. No, they are not stopping at my throat to rest. They are barreling down to my stomach, diaphragm, somewhere, anywhere, screams are made. For this will not be whispered. Apparently, it will be shouted. It will be heard. It will be – necessary.

Blurt it out. "Her name is Jhene!" Shake, rattle, and roll the hinges of doors. My voice finds a bass it has never found before. I sit in my chair and wait. I wait for any movement, any sign of life coming from inside my father's bedroom. For a time, there is nothing. Then…

I hear the doorknob turn. Its slow, deliberate, like most of what my father does. And now, the door is open. He takes a couple of steps out of the doorway until he reaches my plain view.

"Did you say something, son?"

I did.

"I said… her name is Jhene."

"Whose name?"

"The girl I am steadily falling in what I think is love

with."

My father grins a grin only pompous people successfully execute.

"Love is not something you are capable of at your age. You cannot fathom what it entails, what it gives and what it takes. I do not doubt you like this, girl – Jhene – but love it is not. It cannot be."

"Can we talk about this further?"

"We are."

Do not push him away, Vinnie...

My father gets comfortable in a chair, a few feet away from me. It is still, at first, as neither of us – at least I know I can't – remember the last time we sat like this, so purposefully.

"So why do you think you're in love?"

"Why do you think I am not?"

"I mean, are you providing her with something?"

"My company, understanding, companionship and friendship. I lend her an ear and she takes it. It's beautiful."

"That did not answer my question. I said are you providing her with something?" Yes. I am. "I ask because women only deal with a man if he is providing something. Something tangible. Something she can hold. Only reason to keep us around."

"Are you speaking from experience or hyperbole?"

My father chuckles.

"Experience."

"Explain."

My father looks at me with intent. I stare back at him, not backing down from my question now that I have his attention.

He gets up and grabs a cup out of the cupboard. He places it on the counter. He walks over to the refrigerator, opens it and grabs a gallon of water. He opens the top, pours himself a glass, takes a long gulp and places the glass back on the counter. He looks back at me, quickly realizes I have not left the place of our eye contact, and therefore, I have not left this conversation. It will continue. And he will participate in its journey, its completion.

"Your mother never loved me. She loved you. She only loved me because I was taking care of you."

"I beg to differ."

My father, surprised at my response, adjusts himself in his chair. He gets comfortable. He is here, now.

"How could you say she did not love you when she took care of and nurtured the one thing you did not have time for?... Me."

"I was not necessary. I did not need to be there like that. She had my money and this house. You had my money and this house. I provided. I am a provider. There was nothing else for me to do. Nobody could come between the two of you anyway, and you know that."

"Did it ever occur to you that our closeness was out of necessity? That we had no choice? Our love had room for you. You never attempted to occupy the space."

My father clears his throat. That does not mean I have given him permission to speak.

"My mother's love for you was palpable. It is why she – over and over again – tried to convince me that how you loved me was good enough. That I shouldn't expect anymore from you than what I was getting. The whole 'roof over my head, food in my stomach' argument. She still saw you as worthy of love. I never saw you as loveable. You never noticed or cared that either one of us felt that way."

"No woman has ever loved me."

"I beg to differ–"

"Close your mouth and listen."

My father is visibly frustrated. I do not want to hold back but I do not want to lose him, now, in this moment, either. So, I adhere to his request – for now.

He clears his throat.

"I can't be emotional about these things. It's not how a man operates. A man has tasks to complete, duties to uphold and that is it. And I did mine. I am doing mine. If I did not love you, I would have put you out the moment we buried your mother. But you're still here. And I am still here.

"All I ever wanted to do was love your mother. But it is really – difficult – to ascertain love when you have not seen it with your own two eyes. My father – your grandfather – left us when I was 12 years old. Did you know that?"

I did not.

"He tried. He tried to provide for us the best he could. But he couldn't take my mother constantly berating his every move, making him feel less than, as if he wasn't doing anything right. Whatever he brought through the door was never enough. I watched this go on for years. Until he was gone. And here I am, in a position to provide for a family, to do the one thing that my father could not. I told myself that I would always provide for my family. I would never put myself in a position where my wife could find reason to ever question me or my ability to provide. I provide."

He does provide.

"But who taught you how to love?"

"What kind of question is that?"

"Who taught you how to love? You keep saying you provided but all that is is monetary, tangible, like you said. But you have not once mentioned anything else you have provided. Nothing that, maybe, we cannot see… So, who taught you how to love, father?"

My father takes this in for a moment, partially due to him possibly coming to grips with the fact his son has the audacity to ask him such a question.

"I tried to have a relationship with my mother. But she just saw me as another version of my father. So, I worked as hard as I could to obliterate any semblance or sign of his reflection on my face or behavior."

"But who taught you how to love?"

"My father provided. My mother didn't think it was enough. He left us. And she turned her attention to me. I fought back by being better than all of them, at everything."

"But who taught you how to love?"

"Stop asking me that. I've answered your damn question."

"But who taught you how to love, father?"

My father is breaking. And I am the one with the hammer.

"Nobody. Nobody taught me how to love."

"So then… how can you tell me how to love Jhene? Or how to love my mother? Or how to love you? Or how to love Walter? When you were never taught what it looks like?"

My father finishes his glass of water, every gulp audible, aggressive. He does not want to be here. But he knows that he cannot leave.

"The only real love I can say I have ever witnessed is you and your mother. Unconditional. Constant."

"That's–"

"–And I hated you because of it."

Now, I am the one adjusting in my seat. I do not know if I am comfortable or not.

"You needed tough love. Your mother – the sweetest woman I have ever known – made you sweet. Soft. Sensitive. Someone had to be there to provide you with something else, another outlook, another way of being."

"But why?"

"Why what?"

"Why did you think that was necessary? Why couldn't I just be how I was, how I am, and you still love me?"

My father chuckles again.

"At one point, I thought you were gay."

He is not getting away from me.

"Would that have made it easier to accept me? Would that have been the reason you used for why I am the way I am?"

"I don't know."

"I have loved two men in my life – Walter, and you."

"So, you are gay?"

"No. You just attach love to either women or gay men."

"That's how I was raised."

"That's how you were conditioned."

I would just like to thank bell hooks at this time...

"Conditioned, huh? You know, I practically raised myself when my father left."

"You provided."

"I provided."

"For yourself."

"For myself."

"And now, you equate all your worth on your ability to provide."

My father looks at me. And this is the first time he looks at me, looks at me. He studies me. His cloak of armor falls slowly to his side. His guard finally comes down. He is vulnerable, now. He is a man, now. He is human, now.

He is my father, now.

"Why'd she... why'd she leave me... why'd she leave me... to raise a boy, I do not understand?... You know it all. Can you tell me that?"

"If she hadn't left, we wouldn't be having this conversation."

My father's entire persona is at its end. I may have finally killed it.

"Men don't cry."

"Why not?"

"We just don't."

"And how has that worked for you so far?"

"I can't be your mother."

"I just need you to be my father."

"You got an answer for everything?"

"Yes. Now, hug me."

"No."

"Hug me."

"I said, 'no'." Sniffles.

"Hug me, father."

"No." Sniffles some more.

"It makes the crying easier."

"I'm not crying."

He is crying. And he is hugging me. And I am hugging him. And I am crying, too. We are crying, two. Too.

XXX

It was not me who spoke to my father on this night. It was literature. It was bell hooks. It was James Baldwin. It was hours upon hours of reading, studying, engaging in worlds and people far beyond my supposed mental capacity. I created a new capacity. I have slaughtered societal norms. I have defeated psychological barriers. I have come face to face with brilliance and made it my permanent domain.

My mother is dead...

And finally, my father is alive. And well. And resting his head upon my shoulder. In tears. In fear. In stereotype. In status quo. His mask peeled back, revealing a skeletal frame lacking emotional muscle. Yes, he provides. But in emotional strength, he is frail, miniscule, weak. I am strong in this arena. Do not laugh at me. I am serious. I bench press emotions. I scale the highest mountains of emotion. I silence all lambs of emotion. I rule my emotions with an iron thumb.

Do not laugh at me...

If I was so emotionally unstable, how could I rest the blade of a box cutter against my skin, pierce it, fall into its psychedelic glee, and lie my fears out to pasture? It takes an emotionally stable person to recognize that such a high exists, and that it exists for my pleasure – and pain.

I am stable enough to hold up this man before me. This man who fell beneath the weight of my questioning, the weight of my prodding, the weight of my scope. He could no longer fight the inevitable sinking of his machismo. My father is crying on my shoulder. Weeping rivers of tears onto my now drenched shirt. Baldwin would be proud of my execution. bell hooks would applaud the murder of my father's masculinity through my own femininity. Feminists rejoice! For I have slain yet another dragon of patriarchal norms and brought it to its knees.

He will not stop crying. I would say this is unbecoming but that would be – unbecoming. I have wanted these tears to fall for years. Only at my mother's deathbed had I ever seen an inkling of emotion come from my father, though, I still believe, his tears that night were not for my mother but for himself. Capricorns are notoriously heartless, emotionally selfish, bleeding only for themselves. I question whether he is capable of truly showing emotion for another. Though now, in this moment, my opinion may be altering. He will not stop crying. And I will not stop providing a shoulder for him to shed his tears.

We cannot tell men not to cry, especially once they begin. We have no idea how long they have been holding it in.

"How did you do this to me?"

"I didn't do anything. You have wanted to do this forever. You just didn't think it would be received well. And well, it has been received."

My father wipes his nose. Snot, spit and tears mix to create a sort of cocktail of physical properties only beings in touch with their emotions can concoct. My father has not touched this side of himself since his father walked out on him and his family – or so I assume. Keep touching, father. Keep caressing your inner child until your inner child perks his little head up and reclaims its place within your psyche. Ease your furrowed brow of its permanence. Re-introduce yourself to your smile, to happiness, to glee, to joy. Oh, to be gay! Shout this feeling. Scream this feeling. Rejoice in this feeling.

"This is unbecoming."

"You're becoming."

My father stares at me. His lack of conversation with me over the years still makes him question and wonder how I formulate such poetry in a heartbeat. Yet, he takes solace in knowing he does not have to dumb down his conversation with me because more than likely, I am familiar with whatever vocabulary he decides to use.

"I am going to bed. Good night, son."

"It was, wasn't it?"

He walks slowly to his bedroom door, still cleaning himself up. He opens it, closes it behind him, softly. I sit there, fathoming the only question necessary at this time – where do we go from here? That I do not know. But my father is no longer the tailored Neanderthal he once was in my adolescent dreams. He cried on my shoulder. He hugged me. He held me. He fell into my arms. He needed me. As I have always seemed to need him. He gave himself to me and I received him with open arms.

It's still early. The night is still young. It is quiet in this home. The only sound is that of an ego crushing beneath the high heeled femininity of my masculinity. I can smell the remnants. It wreaks of pent up angst, 2 am workouts and promiscuity – if I knew what that smelled like.

I get the sense my senses need attention. I walk to my room, open and close the door at a speed faster than my father but not fast to the average eye. My father will be my latest project, my latest conquest. I turned a rugged white boy into a reader of bell hooks, the least I could do is introduce the emotionless man who puts clothes on my back and food on my table to an outlook on life no one thought necessary to show him. I would be honored to spread this knowledge, this life-affirming revelation, of understanding that masculine energy is only at its strongest when led by the feminine. I do not mince words. Masculine is dangerous, at its heart, perturbed, at its base.

Where did this come from?

I sit down, body and mind in auto-pilot. The past few times I have landed here, on this bed, at this hour, in this silence, the same thing has occurred. I feel like this will happen again. Now. As I continue to have the sense that my senses need attention. I recognize this as intuition. It knows best.

Where did this...come from?

It would seem like I wouldn't need to go here anymore. Not with my father having finally broken before my eyes and all. But he has a way of not producing consistent results. So, until that moment happens, I will continue to insist on my own consistency. I will not break stride. I will not break my mold. I will not fold until it is absolutely necessary for me to start from scratch. Until then...

Where did this blood come from?

Ah. Yes. Here we are.

XXXI

Knock. Knock.

My father is at work. I am still on suspension. We never have visitors. This is weird. Nevertheless, someone is at our door, and I am the only person available to answer it. So, I guess I will answer it.

With a swing of the door, I stop in my tracks. This guest is not at all who I was expecting. You could have given me 10 guesses and I do not think I would have landed here – on her.

My father's mother.

She stands at our door with a light travel bag in hand. Five-foot-two, strong features and a caramel complexion with memories of better days. She was pretty, once. But years of anger and frustration have placed her beauty somewhere between yesterday and never again. She will not be mistaken for grandmother of the year, but our relationship has always been one of an awkward understanding. She knew from the moment she met me that I was not like other boys, and especially not like my father. At another place and time, she would have tried to rectify me, put me in my proper place within her perceived sense of masculinity, but by the time she would have had the inclination to do so, she was already tired – of living.

"Grandma Smith. Is my father expecting you?"

"Verbally? No. But he knew I was coming. That's been in the air for a while now. Grab my bag."

I take her travel bag from her and lead her into the house. She walks slow, with a forced energy as if she is angry she can no longer walk at the speed of her past. Watching someone whose entire persona is built off perceived strength fight their inevitable weakness is an experience – almost like watching my father cry.

"Is he at work?"

"Yes, he is."

"Why are you here? Shouldn't you be at school?"

"I got suspended."

"You? Suspended? What'd you do?"

"Got in a fight. Two against five."

"Were you in the two or the five?"

"The two."

"You win?"

"You could say that."

"Good. That's all you should say. The only losses this family takes are death – and divorce."

She finds a seat. I sit near her. She stares at me. Her smile looks like she practiced it in the mirror on the way here because she didn't know what hers looked like anymore. Every complication she has ever dealt with sings from her skin, notes hitting the air only to shatter all glass around them. She fights her age with every breath, disappointed in how much closer she is to death than to birth. But her assuredness distorts her eventual ending. She carries herself with the gusto of the one person on earth who would test death and pass. My father's mother is a shout out to every woman who ever dared a man to handle her and then did everything in their power to make sure he couldn't – then blamed him for it.

"Vinnie. Talk to me."

"What would you like to know?"

"A little bit about you would be a good start. And don't hold back on the details."

"Um, I still read a lot. Play sports but nothing organized. Uh, I paint regularly – like my mom…"

My voice trails off. We make eye contact. My father's mother did not attend my mother's funeral. I am unaware of her reasoning but I did not question it at the time. I was too busy burying my best friend.

My mother is dead…

"Why didn't you come to my mother's funeral, Grandma Smith?"

She looks at me, forces that smile of hers.

"That's actually part of why I am here. Part of why I need to speak to my son."

"You can tell me."

"I will. When your father gets here. You should both hear it together."

We sit in silence, our energies battling for control of the room. I am not my complete self around my father's mother. I tend to hold back on the intricacies of I for her eye always seems to foster judgment from the smallest seed. I am fascinated by what her reasoning could be for such an unexpected visit. I for sure understand why she would want to wait for her son prior to telling me anything about why she is here. But unless she has a means of passing the time, her son getting here is going to take a while, so hopefully she has some energy on reserve.

Or.

"Vinnie. I'm going to sleep."

"Ok, Grandma Smith."

"What do you call your other Grandma?"

"I don't."

"Then just call me Grandma. Saying the Smith makes it feel like I'm someone else."

"I can do that."

"Thank you."

If she only knew that 'My Father's Mother' is actually my preferred name for her. Grandma feels intimate. This relationship lacks intimacy. It might contain empathy. Maybe even a little sympathy. But intimacy it does not. I will oblige, though. I seem to have more time to appreciate the little things than she does.

"Is the guest room still the guest room?"

"Yes, ma'am."

"Can you wake me up when my son gets here?"

"Yes, ma'am."

Ma'am gives her the respect she deserves while still allowing me space to rebel. Fitting, in this moment.

She walks into the guest room with her particular stride and closes the door behind her. I now sit here, by myself, like this morning intended.

I now sit here, by myself, in my room, like this morning intended.

I now sit here, by myself, in my room, with my box cutter, like this morning intended.

The breakfast of champions.

Where did this blood come from?

My father's mother had it right. Now is a time to rest.

Where did this blood come from?

And to sit in whatever it is that causes your bliss.

Where did this blood come from?

There's no rest like the rest of champions.

Where did this blood come from?

Oh. I know where it came from. And now I must...

Wake up!

At least an hour or so has passed. I have not washed off my box cutter, as it sits in plain sight with nothing to guard it from the scrutiny of eyes that are not ready to be laid upon it. I quickly pick it up and walk to the restroom. Still no sign of my father and the guest bedroom door is still closed. Looks like the coast is clear.

I clean off the box cutter. It's so refreshing, and renewed, once it is clean. Such dirt, filth and anxiousness cover its edges when it feasts upon my flesh, but it is so beautiful again once it is clean. That doesn't mean I will refrain from its scuzzy alter ego. But it does give me something to look forward to once the venture into that scuzzy realm is complete.

I walk into the living room just as the front door opens. It is my father. He gives me his half-smile, I give him mine.

"Son."

"Father."

"My mother is here, isn't she?"

"Yes. But how did you know?"

"She knew I knew, huh?"

"Yes."

He places his briefcase down on the kitchen floor. "Is she taking her nap?"

"Yes."

"She give you marching orders for when to wake her up?"

"Yes."

"Figured. Based on my arrival?"

"Yes."

He takes his coat off and throws it on one of the kitchen table chairs. Begins rolling up his sleeves. He is searching for a certain level of comfort.

"You know her well…"

"I do. Almost too well. We spent a lot of time together, her and I. Good, bad and in-between."

"She said she has something to tell you. Tell us."

"Then let's wake her up and see what it is. Do you mind?"

"I don't."

I walk to the guest room and slowly open the door. My father's mother sleeps soundly, still fully dressed, except for her cotton socks. I walk over to her and lightly shake her to wake her up. She doesn't move. I try again, but a little harder. She still doesn't move. I start to get a little worried. I try again, but a little bit harder. She still doesn't move. I am officially scared now.

I shake her as hard as I can. She swings her arm at me, barely missing my chin.

"Boy, why are you shaking me so hard?"

"I've been here five minutes. You wouldn't wake up to light shakes, so I had to shake you like a salt shaker."

"That explains so much about me."

That explains so much about her.

"I've always been a lot. That doesn't change in my sleep."

"Being a lot seems to be a family trait."

I offer my hand to my father's mother and she takes it. We work together in bringing her to her feet. As she gathers herself, she looks at me, with intent in her eyes.

"He's here, isn't he?"

"I followed your orders."

"That you did. But orders sound so negative…"

I half-smile.

Slightly under her breath. "…Our relationship is negative."

She isn't lying. She isn't telling the truth. There is just an indifference there. A 'cool if it is', 'cool if it isn't' sentiment that resonates within our interactions with one another. It is very much an extension of my relationship with my father.

I do not want what they have…

We enter the living room. My father awaits. He slightly perks up at the sight of his mother. She smiles. He smiles. Smith smiles. They tell their own stories.

"Mother."

"Thomas."

I bring my father's mother to a seat at the kitchen table. She sits down, gets comfortable.

Thomas. "I hear you have something you need to tell me."

"I do. To the both of you, but yes, mainly to you."

My father gets comfortable. I get comfortable. She is already comfortable. But this, is uncomfortable.

My father's mother. "We have never sugar-coated. I barely had sugar in the house when you were growing up so it makes sense. We cut to the chase around here. No holds barred. Borderline ruthless efficiency… I came here for a couple of reasons. The first. Is. To apologize."

She now has my full attention. My father's as well. This is not a word that has frequented my father's mother's vocabulary.

My father. "For what?"

"I'm getting there."

She adjusts in her seat. Clears her throat. This is all new for her.

"I raised you how I thought you should be raised. I raised you how I thought a man should be raised. With ruthless efficiency. With a push towards independence. I wanted you to be independent. To stand on your own two feet. To be solid. Standing in a white man's world as a black man, you had to be solid. And that's what I tried to do. I didn't know I was doing it wrong… I drove your father away. I told you and him how to be men. I was never taught how to be a man. One, I'm not one. Two, I'd never seen one… I thought being in his ear, being hard on him, showing him, at least, what I saw as, tough love, was all he needed to thrive, blossom, and grow. But no. I beat that man into the ground. He was never enough. I never let him just be enough. And he tried and tried. I know he did. Didn't know it then, but I figured that out. I know he tried. And I put his spirit in my hands. And I crushed it. Destroyed his confidence. Destroyed his manhood. And then when he left, I turned my attention to you."

She looks directly into my father's eyes. They share a moment, an intimate conversation between mother and son. I know this intimacy well, only mine was always in direct correlation with love. This, this was different. But the intimacy was still there. And one of the world's most underrated requirements to learn anything is intimacy.

"You turned out great, on whatever paper the world judges you on. But the one… what do they call it?… feminine energy in your childhood, who was to show you sensitivity, and – empathy – and all those things that us women are supposedly innately understanding of – which I find to be a crock of bull – did not show up for you in that way. And you've brought it here. To this boy. This sensitive, beautiful, intelligent boy… Annette is dead, yet she's still raising him for you."

Grandma Smith.

"So, there's my apology for my part in why you are the way you are… And to tell you – both – that I'm sick. And I'm dying. And I don't know how much longer I got."

Grandma Smith.

My father. "I don't understand."

"I won't be here much longer, Thomas. I needed to say sorry before I left you to it. Though I practically left you already. But you get what I'm saying."

My father walks to his mother's chair, kneels in front of her, holds her hands in his hands.

My father. "Mother, what can I do to provide you with what you need?"

It always comes back to providing…

"Love Vinnie better than I loved you…"

They both turn to me. The two most difficult people I know, are now looking to me for answers.

Grandma Smith.

XXXII

There's a stillness in the room. My father and his mother – stare at me, eyes coinciding with a shared past. Their wants are similar, if their tactics differ. His mother wants order. He wants order. And, in order for me, to be one with them, I must adhere to order, or, provide order. What I cannot do is defy order, and that is literally the explanation of my existence.

I hold their stares. Both fighting back tears. Their collective pride seems to be winning this round. It is getting slightly uncomfortable. Remove the slightly. It is in full bloom, now. The longing in their eyes suffocates. I cannot breathe. Two Capricorns grasp at the heart strings of my Cancer, wanting my in touch emotions to touch them, fill them with beats of splendor, engage them in the cadence of love's melody. They think I know these things innately, simply because I cry.

If only they knew...

This responsibility irks me. I cannot pinpoint the foundation of this annoyance, but it is there, and it is prevalent. I rotate my head slightly to the side, analyze these two adults in front of me, and it hits me. I am irked by their adulthood. I am irked by their need to learn from me when I should be the one learning from them. The gaze they place in my orbit, longing to hear what I have to say about these emotions that I continue to try to bring to the surface within them, and our interactions with one another.

My father holds his mother's hands in his, a show of affection probably years apart from its last occurrence. I am thankful for the recognition that these two Capricorns are capable of such affection, of such longing for someone else to help them. She needs his help. He needs her help. They need help. And they are holding hands with the one person who could possibly provide it.

Yet their eyes are on me...

A son. A grandson. A boy. A teenager. A child. All the prerequisites for immaturity grace my life's resume.

Yet their eyes are on me...

I did not see myself being in this place today. I did not wake up this morning with the expectation that I would be called upon by two adult Capricorns to cure their emotional cancer with my Cancer. They are both infected. Infected with the inability to feel for others.

Yet their eyes are on me...

They seem ready for their chemo. It will feel as if it is harming more than helping. Their emotional hairs will fall out, almost scalping them, tearing at their emotional flesh, looking for a new beginning, a new place for their emotional health to begin to exercise. It takes workouts. It takes tears. It takes opening up. It takes embarrassing yourself, to yourself. It takes pain. It takes pressure. It takes everything they have not been, to be everything they want to be. As they stare at me, pondering my next move with the interest of children waiting to see if their parent will go to the restaurant of their choosing.

"Son."

"Vinnie."

Their eyes are on me...

As I exit. I just, leave. I leave them both there, still holding each other's hands, watching as their emotional savior walks away without a word. I do not want to save them at this time. I do want them to save themselves. They have not put in enough work on their own to have earned my input. They have not shown any sense of work ethic to better themselves as people. It would be unfair to jump in, rescue them, provide their lifeline, when they do not know yet what it means to sink. I have sunk. I live in a sunken place. Dark. Spacious. Violently silent. Crisp. Uninterrupted. I am its only resident. Its only survivor. And until I am ready, I am to be its only resident.

For now...

Door lightly closes behind me. Breathe in the air of night. Deep and full. My legs begin to move. I have no control over them in this moment. I am being taken somewhere. Subconsciously. I will arrive at the destination of my legs' choosing. I do not have a say in this sudden trip. All I can do is follow.

I seem to be headed to the canyon. A place of serenity. A place of solitude. A place of peace. Organic in all its activity, it seems only right that I am being taken there by my body. There, I can reconnect my mind, body and spirit so they are again one. I have reassembled myself there countless times before. It has proven its worth to me. It is a place I can trust. And, the people there…

Jhene…

I smile a smile only reserved for her. She smiles back. I reach my arms out to give her a hug. She walks into my arms. We embrace. I hold her tightly, place my chin on top of her head. She rests her head on my chest. I lightly rock her side to side. My eyes, closed. I take this in, this affection. This girl puts me in a place of oxygen. She is breath in flesh. The air I seek, the air I breathe. She was sent to me to hold. Nothing else belongs in my arms but her. She is where I am to love. She is energy. She is soul. She is ecstasy. She is blood and beauty. She is…

Jhene…

"I just felt like I should come, ya know? You didn't have to call or anything. I just… knew."

"My spirit summoned you. It is the only conversation necessary. Words are supplemental mechanisms. If the soul cannot converse with another, then that conversation remains a meaningless, bottomless pit of constipated progress."

"You had me at 'supplemental mechanisms…'"

She looks up at me. I look down at her. She longs for the eye contact, even within the darkness of night. I feel like I am disrespecting her greatness by looking down upon her. Feels too much like gender roles. But it can also be read as shaming her petite frame, so I will refrain from convicting myself in the court of chauvinism. I have served as judge in this arena far too many times to not receive the benefit of the doubt. I am bell hooks approved after all.

She, again, speaks.

"Why don't we spend all of our days like this? With me in your arms? There is so much pain in your arms, on your arms, that I know they can withstand the pain I might bring to them, I might bring with me..."

Just looking at her look at me is everything. She sees through every layer of my onion. When peeled, I am nothing but a boy. A boy who wears his pain under his sleeves. A boy in black – who is black. A boy with darkness held in the confines of his intellect. A boy fighting crippling insecurities. A boy who leaves his father and grandmother when they need him. A boy in constant mourning.

My mother is dead...

But the girl in my arms is alive. And I plan to love her until that is no longer the case. I am aware of my 14-year-old naivete in terms of love. I do not know where I am. I do not know what I am doing. I do know I want to live in this space with her. I want to learn with her. I want to make all my mistakes with her. I want to learn forgiveness with her. I want to grow into a man with her. I want to share oxygen with her.

I want to bleed with her...

I slowly release her from my arms. It is almost painful to proceed with such an action. Never letting go is such a metaphorical concept but sometimes, you truly do not want to. I imagine Rose Dawson felt the same when she let Jack float to the bottom of the ocean. But walking around with a frozen corpse that looks strikingly like Leonardo DiCaprio would not have been a good look.

But I digress.

I put my hand beneath her chin. Her eyes glisten in the darkness as she knows what is to come. I kiss her softly, her lips perfect matches to my own. She stands on the tips of her toes to meet me. Adds passion to the connection. This is her kiss now. I am just a participant. A willing one. Her only one…

"Y'all are disgusting."

We stop kissing just in time to start laughing. Embarrassment covers her face, but I stand tall. We have been interrupted by the only person I would not mind being interrupted by.

"Shut up, Walter."

"Hey, y'all are the ones in the dark giving each other mono."

"Jealousy doesn't look good on you, sir."

"Jealousy? Naw, I'm good. Y'all can live that life. I'll stick to this one I'm living."

"And how is that life going, my friend?"

Walter pauses. We are well aware of where that pause came from.

"It's going… I don't really want to talk about it, right now. We have company."

Walter motions to Jhene. I sense he still does not trust her presence. Finds her connection to me to be random, too quick to be real. He has never felt such a thing so it does not resonate as real to him.

Jhene looks in Walter's direction. He catches her looking but does not provide her with any eye contact. I see this happening. And prepare myself. For something magical. For Jhene is magic. She is black girl magic. And her spells know no boundaries.

Walter tries to refuse this sudden attention. Jhene slowly walks towards him, swallows him in her line of sight. He cannot look away now. She has him. She invades his space, and, simply, hugs him. Fully. Completely. Wraps her petite arms around his waist and holds him tight. Walter stares at me, with this little black girl wrapped around him, as black girl magic envelops him. Walter leans on his faux exterior. He wants to remain strong in light of the love being given to him. He does not want to fold. He does not want to succumb to the magic. But the magic is the magic. It is thorough. And pure. And all encompassing.

And. This black girl. And. Her black girl magic. Makes this. Rugged white boy. Cry.

And it is magic. For she is. Magical.

XXXIII

Tears stain Walter's cheeks, black girl magic still wrapped around his waist. I keep my distance, sly smile across my face. I witness this exchange of emotion, this disruption of norms. A petite black girl – history on her back, dripped from ancestral lips – uses her magic on a scruffy white boy, in the days of Donald Trump, in front of a black male who loves them both in an interchangeable way that breaks the neck of the status quo, usurps the cracked throat of traditional masculinity, and somehow suppresses the oppressive skin tone of one of its participants. This is unadulterated beauty in a way unseen in this decadent society in which we live. I am so happy to scream in the face of societal norms that have never tasted normal on my lips. It has always tasted like the manic state of darkness from which it came.

I approach Walter, still muted by the tears he never wanted to fall. I wrap them both in my arms. I hug them. Jhene hugs Walter. Walter, trapped between four black arms. Police would arrest such an action if seen. But it is just us. Just the two people in my life who understand how I want to love, be loved, give love, receive love.

But I have to learn to love my father with everything I am...

I pull back from our hug. This releases Jhene from around Walter's waist, her black girl magic spell having done its duty. Walter stands there, in the fallout of the magic, dazed, confused, unclear as to his next move. I grab his hand in mine. I grab Jhene's hand in my other hand. Jhene grabs Walter's other hand. We stand in a circle, hand in hand. I smile. Jhene smiles. Walter doesn't.

"Y'all are my family. Through and through. And together, we can make it through anything. I can make it through anything."

I squeeze each hand with the requisite amount of strength necessary to prove my point. They each reciprocate.

Walter. "What did you do to me?"

Jhene. "Me?"

"Yes, you."

"I don't know. It's something that comes naturally."

I smile.

Walter. "What you smiling about?"

"It's magic."

"It's too much, that's what it is. I did not give myself permission to cry, especially in front of a stranger."

Jhene. "Am I really all that strange? Even after all this time?"

"You can't use the phrase 'all this time'. I can. I have been friends with this dude 'all this time'. You can't say the same."

"Well, one day, I hope I do get to say the same. I don't plan on going anywhere."

"I guess I'll be the one to leave then."

"Only if you choose to."

There is an awkward silence. It feels like I am in the middle of something that I do not want to be in the middle of. I have never had competition for my affection before. My mother and Walter were completely separate aspects of my life, so when she was alive, I had ample time to satisfy my love for both her and Walter. They never ran into each other. Never caused the other to question my love. But this could be different. This is different. Jhene enters much of the space Walter resides in. Only Walter is not used to the company. Jhene is both used to the solitude, yet open to the company. It makes Walter twitchy. And makes me not know what to do.

Walter. "I'll catch up with you later, man."

"Love you, Walter!"

"Yeah, yeah, whatever."

I continue to hold Jhene's hand as we watch Walter head home.

"Shouldn't you be headed home, too?"

"Yeah, but I came for more than what has already happened."

"What else is there?"

Jhene takes out a shiny object from inside her pocket. It is a box cutter. She places it in her palm.

"Isn't it pretty?"

"What is it for?"

"It is for more…"

She squeezes her hand around it, the slight pain from its sharp edges tickles her palm with an adolescent violence she knows all too well.

"What do you get out of the pain?"

"I get… to control it, for once. I get to get out of the hands of another."

"What do you mean?"

"I learned what my body was capable of before I was old enough to realize that my body was the most sought after commodity known to man. I learned how to heal from bruises fast enough for my skin to look relatively the same on Friday as it did on Monday, as if Saturday and Sunday never happened. This, box cutter. This, cutting. It is a pain I feel on my own. It is at my own discretion. It is under my control. You get it? You get why that pain can be so real for a girl whose life had to be seen as make believe in order for her to live it?"

Speechless.

"Would it mean more to you for you to control my pain, as well? For you to know what it feels like to make a male succumb to the violence you've suffered for so long?"

"As tempting as that sounds, I'd much rather us suffer in unison. Duets have always been my favorite form of music."

Where did all this blood come from?

I stand at the doorstep of my home, Jhene long gone into the darkness of a life she is only beginning to share with me. Our shared darkness waters the soil of our burgeoning love. It is beautiful in its sadness. But it is us. And it is perfect.

I open the door slowly. As I enter, it is dark. No sign of life. My father's bedroom door is closed. So is the guest room. Adulthood is no longer alive and well within the open spaces of this home. It is confined behind closed doors. Exactly where it should be. And I should be in bed. Rest is the only thing missing from my now. Jhene already led me in my nightly ritual so it will not be necessary this evening. All I have left to do is quiet my thoughts. When they are loud, I cannot rest.

Shhhhhh...

I hope they have room to love me tomorrow...

My alarm is such a terrible appliance. Annoyance at its finest. It does its job, but nonetheless, it irks me.

I am in no rush to get up. Today is the last day of my suspension. A Friday. I should be celebrating but that would mean that I miss attending school. I still haven't decided if that is actually how I feel. I cannot differentiate between missing actual school or missing the consistency of having something to do that just so happens to be school. It isn't that easy of a choice, especially when I spend most of my time at home, by myself.

There is commotion outside of my room, a sound I am not accustomed to hearing at this time of the morning. My father is usually gone by now...

I peak my head out my bedroom window to find my father and his mother – *Grandma Smith* – talking over breakfast. I can't remember the last time someone cooked breakfast in this house that wasn't me.

My mother is dead...

My father sees me peeking.

"Vinnie! Brush them teeth then get out here for breakfast. We got things to do."

We? What the fuck is 'we'?

I brush my teeth. But I ain't happy doing it.

I leave the bathroom to join my father and grandma, a trio I did not think was possible just yesterday.

"Good morning, son."

"Good morning, father."

Grandma Smith nods in my direction. I nod back.

"We have eggs, bacon, sausage, potatoes and toast. If there is anything you don't eat, I'll eat it. All my favorites are out here."

I have no idea what is happening here.

"Um, thank you. I'll take a little bit of everything."

"Good. You're going to need your energy."

"For?"

"Well, you've noticed I'm still here, right?"

"Yes. But for what? You never miss work…"

Grandma Smith. "Well, he's missing today."

Father. "Yes, I am missing today. And I am spending the day with you."

Is that what the fuck 'we' is?

XXXIV

What the fuck is 'we'?
Profanity-laced stunned silence. Utter disbelief.
Dream come true...
Did my father really just say that he took off work simply to spend the day with me? He does know that I'm me, right? That I'm Vinnie, the son he has done everything possible to distance himself from, even after...
My mother is dead...
This can't be. This man masquerading as my workaholic father woke up and made breakfast on his day off. This has to be a dream.
A dream come true...
What if this is real? What if he really is here and here for me?... Naw, I don't believe it. That would be too easy. Nope. Naw. Not going for it. He's gotta do better than that. I'm not falling for that. That's that bullshit, yo. Playing with my emotions and shit. Naw, son. I'm good off that, bruh. Not feelin' that at all.
Yes, this is still me. I am still here, just hiding behind the son I think my father wishes he had. Maybe that's the kid he thinks he took a day off to hang out with.
"I'm on salary so it's not like I'm missing out on money. Vinnie, why do you look like you saw a ghost?"
I did. And it spoke. Using your voice.
Grandma Smith. "Your father and I had a long talk. This is something you both want. And have wanted. Right, Vinnie?"
This coma I'm in right now is quite comfortable.
"Uh, yeah. Yeah, I do. Did. Do."
That was real coherent, Vinnie. Do better.
"Is there anywhere you'd really like to go?"
This is a loaded question. There are so many places that I have wanted to go with my father over the past 2,920 days or so. But who's counting?

My father. "Anywhere you want to go is on the table. The world is your oyster. That's the saying, right?"

Who is this guy? He's all jovial and shit. I don't know if I can handle all this happiness. He needs to grow some balls and man up –

Oh no...

I will not. I worked to pull him in the direction of self-defined masculinity for too long to let this moment get away from me with my own secretions of toxic masculinity and patriarchy. My father wants to take me wherever I want to go as a showing of love and affection. I will adhere to his request and provide him with an answer as to where I would like to go. If we are going to do this, we are going to do it right, and under my terms.

"I do know where I'd like to go."

I have my father and my grandma's undivided attention. Grandma's usual demeanor remains but this happy-go-lucky father of mine is still taking some getting used to.

"I'd like to go to the bookstore."

Grandma chuckles a bit. My father clears his throat a bit. I take pride in this a bit.

My father. "I was expecting a little different answer."

"Why were you expecting an answer at all?"

Awkward silence. This is a key moment. If we get through this, we can make it through the rest of the day. I just wish this air wasn't so still right now. It's like we've all stopped breathing or something.

My father looks to Grandma Smith. She nods slightly. He understands now what he must do.

"You know what? The bookstore sounds like a great idea. I haven't read a good book in a long time. Maybe you can help me pick one out, son? How's that sound?"

"Oh, that's definitely the plan, father. I have some very specific literature for you to dive into. Learn a thing

169

or two."

My father nods, unaware of the bombarding of bell hooks and James Baldwin headed his way. Might even throw in some Roxane Gay just to mess with him. But I don't think he's ready for Roxane. I don't think anybody is truly ready for Roxane. Yeah, no Roxane. Not yet.

"You can get dressed as soon as you finish eating. So as soon as you're ready, we'll head out. That work for you?"

"Yes, sir."

"Good. Looking forward to seeing what you recommend."

I recommend all of the literature I have read during the 14 years I have spent on this planet, which has shaped me into the intellectually stimulating vocabulary monster that you see before you. Do you think these sights and sounds you encounter through every interaction with me were not specifically crafted over time to master the art of communicating with lesser beings than I? I didn't think so. So yes dear father, I will recommend to you some literature. I just hope you are ready for some reading that will challenge everything you ever thought to be true, and that includes this conversation.

Grandma Smith. "I'm going to get some rest while you all are gone."

"Ok, mother. We won't be gone too long."

Yes, we will. It takes awhile to get through the mandatory chapters I will be assigning you to read in the comfort of the bookstore.

See, I understand that my father broke down emotionally in front of me for the first time. I understand that he seemed to be responsive to my grandmother's needs when she needed him. And I understand that he took a day off to spend it with me when work is all he has ever truly cared about. I understand all that. But it takes more than just a small sample size of moments to replace an almost decade-long quest for him to see me. And see me for the boy I am, and not the boy he wishes me to be. There is still time ahead of us, for him to figure out how to be a father to an enigma such as I. I will be receptive to such things, but I must be cautious. This is my heart at stake, and he has not done well in the past with it in his hands. I must protect it. For it is the only heart I have.

XXXV

I am questioning. I still question. A state of shock is where I sit. A head scratcher of an occurrence. It is daytime, during the week, and my father is with me, purposefully. Fully. Attempting, a type of love I might be able to. Recognize. If only. I. Believed him. I do not believe him. And. That is what keeps me. Stationary.

This shoe drop will be powerful. I wait on it. I simply... wait on it. It has to drop soon. For this cannot be. This cannot be my current truth. Can it? Is this real? I, I, I'm so used to asking and not getting. So used to yearning but falling flat. I deflect. I don't accept, things, for what, they are. I linger in space, and time, sifting through facts and lies, looking for that almighty discernment.

Passenger seat cruising. Window perusing. Dewey dewdrops consider moist cheeks. Muggy. Hugs my spirit. For comfort.

A perfect day for reading...

I consider the possibilities. Of my father engaging my world. For the first time. A world filled with Baldwin. Morrison. Diaz. hooks. Butler. Alexander. Ward. Whitehead. Oh. My. God. Do I love literature! I don't just love literature. I love authors. I love points of view. I love consistency. I love expectation. I love nuance. I love their norm. And I hate norm. But I love their norm. Sentence structure deconstructed. Vocabulary stealth assassins. A literate iteration of alliteration. World views shattered. Obliterated bleak outcomes. Plot points point in opposite directions. Metaphor buoyancy. Simple similes. Lyrical lines elicit lukewarm's antonym.

My. Father. Is. Not. Ready.

Breathe... and neither am I...

Am I ready to share?

I have lived such an intimate existence, sans my father. All the while, I yearned for his attention, his love, his slight smile of congratulations. It was so much easier to loathe him with my mother alive, for our love was strong enough to deem my father's love unnecessary while still providing the space for his entry if he ever decided to accompany us.

But now he is here, willing, open, trying to figure this out. Trying to figure me out. Opening my book to the first page and reading to comprehend, not to rebut. But. I am petrified of the possibilities. I am still wary of giving him the space I have reserved for him in my heart for all of these years. And like any relationship, the first date has to go well. We are on ours now. And he better try to impress me. My love is no cheap thrill.

We pull into the parking lot, find a spot. It takes me some time before I exit the vehicle. I am still finding myself within this reality. Intimacy is not a language I speak with my father –yet–, but the local bookstore and I – Essential Books & Such – tickle each other's fancy. Its couches know my derriere, prints remain as unofficial reservations are placed. I am one with the bookshelves, a frequent flier who respects what they carry on the regular basis. And now, I must introduce my father to its aisles, its smells, its pages, its comfort, its collection of words.

I must introduce him to me...

We walk up to the bookstore. My father smiles at me as he adjusts his dress shirt. I half-smile in return. I am half-here. I hope my father senses my skepticism. But I doubt it. He is about to read some literature, but he still needs to learn how to read me, as well. And I am the most difficult piece he will ever have to read. There is no back cover. No table of contents. No choose your own adventure option. No summarized version on Google. Just, me. And I must be read from front to back. Thoroughly consumed over time, with no real ending in sight. There are volumes to this. I am an epic. 'War & Peace' ain't got nothin' on me.

My father. "This place is quaint. I like it. Makes me feel comfortable. Is that why you like it here?"

"It's the start. But there's a lot more."

"Lead the way, son."

We enter the doors of the bookstore. The owner, James, a black man in his early 40s who looks like the younger brother of Dr. Webber on 'Grey's Anatomy', smiles as soon as he sees me.

James. "Young Vinnie! Welcome home."

James walks up to shake my hand. We proceed to do the traditional black man greeting, all to the surprise of my father. James looks my father over.

James. "Who's this, Vinnie?"

"My father."

"Nice to meet you, my brotha."

"Thomas. Likewise."

Their exchange lacks the flavor of mine and James'. It is more business-like. More grown. More ego. I didn't even know James had an ego until this moment. But I guess all men, especially black men, possess an ego. It just shows itself at different times for different men. James knows how many tears I have shed over the pages of a book. He is aware of my pain. He does not know where my pain derives from. But in the six years I have been coming into his store, he has only met my mother. So, to see my father with me this time, he sensed something...

Skepticism.

James. "So, how are we doing this, Vinnie?"

"Can you grab a few books for me? For him..."

"I sure can."

I smile. As does James. A book connoisseur's connection.

"Get him Baldwin's 'Fire Next Time', Morrison's 'Sula', Whitehead's 'The Underground Railroad', Butler's 'Kindred', Diaz's 'Drown'... and, Baldwin's 'Another Country' –"

"If that's the case, we should throw him 'Giovanni's Room.'"

"I don't know if he's ready for Giovanni. Another Country is a good gateway to Giovanni, don't you think?"

My father watches this discussion over literature happen with earnest. It is not that my father does not read. He is one of the smartest men I know for a reason. He has risen to the top ranks of his profession for a reason. He is hard-working, brilliant – and totally unaware of why I am the way I am.

My mother is dead...

It was her. And these books. They shaped me. Placed the paintbrush in my hand, indoctrinated me into the world of intellect, articulation and constant intake of information. I crafted the persona that is now me through these actions, through these people, through these words. And now, my father will go on a similar journey. For only in this way, will he ever be able to meet me where I am.

"Hold those until we leave. Those will be the ones he reads next."

James. "Next?"

"That isn't what we will be starting him off with. And this order is for here. He will begin reading here."

"So, what are we getting?"

I turn to my father. His eyes have never left me. His interest one of intense curiosity. I think he admires the control I have over the situation. He has never seen me in my element - not at this level. I am one with the literature. It runs through me, and off the tip of my tongue, in language that sings of the compositions of the writers before me. And I am honored to be their vessel.

"Get him 'The Will To Change: Men, Masculinity and Love'."

bell hooks.

My father does not understand why I chose such a title. I look to James. He reads me. He understands. The simple selection of this book is not simple at all. The complexities of my relationship with my father appear obvious now. hooks' book changed everything for me. I try to read it once a year. I read it for the first time when I was 10 years old. I did not understand it. But I knew there was something there that I was supposed to learn. So, I kept reading it. I kept studying it. Then, as I got older, I began implementing its charges. And with her – and Baldwin – a black woman and a gay black man – I introduced myself to my divine feminine, kissed the hands of Walter, kissed the lips of Jhene, and redefined what it meant to be a boy. A black boy. A free, black boy.

Now, I needed to free my father.

"Interesting title, son."

"It's all in there. It's all there in the title."

"Why that one?"

"Why not? I just need you to trust me."

My father adjusts his shirt. His collar seems to need that in moments when he is uncomfortable. His shirt is perfect when he is perfect. Any imperfection needs adjustment. The bookstore is a perfect imperfection. It can lead you down the wrong road if you treat it poorly. I am delicate with its sensitivities. I mean it no harm. I only want it to provide me with the nourishment that I need. To be my refuge in a time of struggle. I need it to be my muted friend, vocal in its silence, yet revelatory in its execution.

"I trust you."

I must learn to love my father with everything I am...

James returns with a copy of the book. My father takes it from him, spots a love seat in the corner and sits down, cross legged, like his bosses would expect of him.

He looks beautiful...

He opens the pages of his new life, adjusts his shirt and begins. One thing about my father, once he engages in a task, he is fully there. He commits. It would be unbecoming to not. It is why I knew he did not love me. That he did not love me fully. That he does not love me fully. I would have felt that energy at its highest peak. It would have consumed him. It would have consumed me. Like how he is with work…

He took off work today…

He is here. With me. Engaged. Fully. In a piece of me. A part of me. In my essence.

My mother is dead…

But he is here. Alive.

And well.

If only he knew how to paint…

XXXVI

He looks beautiful...
Sleeves rolled up. Shirt unbuttoned twice at the top.
He looks comfortable. I hadn't seen my father like this until
the day I saw my father like this. In that room. Between
those walls. Where death took its cue. And listened.
My mother is dead...
I stand near James. Examine my father from afar,
for now.
His brow furrows on occasion. He changes
positions every few pages. He engages. Disengages.
Reengages. It is fascinating to watch him fight his instincts.
He looks to me for guidance. Makes eye contact with his
tormentor. And I smile. I witness his breakthroughs. I
witness his internal disagreement with what he reads. hooks
wrote her book for men like my father to be uncomfortable.
She wrote it for boys like me to feel comfortable in our
discomfort. She screams within the silence of the pages for
boys to express themselves, to feel, to redefine masculinity
and patriarchal norms, two things my father drowns himself
in every morning before work. Some people call it a
shower.
He took off work today...
"Are you not going to join him?"
"Not yet. He isn't ready for me to join him yet."
"Oh."
"He needs time for the literature to sink in. To
resonate, before engaging with its embodiment in the
flesh."
"Oh."
"You've never heard me like this, huh?
"Not like this, no."
"Welcome."
James looks at me, then to my father.
"Are you comfortable, James?"

"Not in the least."

"It's okay. I wouldn't expect you to be. You're a black man. Your whole life is uncomfortable."

"I can't say I disagree."

James walks back to the counter. It is clear he has had enough of me, for now. I do not judge him. This is a space he is not used to living in. To him, I am a kid, who reads voraciously, loves his mother and speaks with an eloquence that belies his 14 years. But sometimes, within that eloquence, is a level of discomfort that men do not want to see, feel or recognize. It is seen in homophobia across our community. It is seen in unusual intimacy. It is seen, in me.

My father looks up. I catch his eye contact, and within it, I am charged to move. I do not relinquish the contact. But I am moving, towards him, to join him in this journey. There is another seat only a few feet in front of him, at an angle. I choose to sit there. In my hands – Baldwin's 'Giovanni's Room'. My father's ego crushes in midair. His furrowed brow asks me questions. He is concerned about the power structure of this room, of this endeavor. He does not understand its hierarchy. How his son could rule over him in this discussion, this transference of masculine energy. Here, in this space, lives the divine feminine. Through it, masculinity heals. It is here, in this space, my father must heal. Himself. His ego.

I disconnect our eye contact. He does not need me anymore, at least not for a little while. Right now, he needs bell hooks' words. He needs her counsel. He needs her comfort. He needs her rage.

He begins to read again. Finds stability in my being near. I feel connected. I feel him. I feel what he is going through. His journey, sits with me, as I sit here, with Baldwin across my lap. Baldwin is here, with us. He smiles. He chuckles. He recalls when he sat here, himself, gay in theory, gay in action. Black. And gay. And intellectual. And strong. And beautiful. And handsome. And ugly. And queer. And frightening. And. Feminine. And. Masculine. And. Masculine. And. Masculine.

Baldwin was more of a man than many of the men who did not sleep with other men.

My father sits here in that midst. He is in the fire, now. It is full bloom, flame. His toxic masculinity set ablaze for onlookers to watch and see. And I haven't even lit the final match. For my father is still alone, here. He is still tackling all of this on his lonesome. He is fragile, in this, but not quite. There is something missing at his feet. There is something yearning to complete him. There is additional pressure to be placed, to be felt, secured beneath his soles.

What is missing, is me.

I fold the top right corner of the page I am on. I close my book. I leave my seat. I take the few steps it takes to reach my father. I stand over him as he looks up at me. I smile. Then I turn around. And sit down, and, squeeze myself between my father's knees. I am now here, sitting on the floor, in between my father's legs, with my knees close to my chest, at peace.

I can feel his resistance behind me. He does not know what to do with this showing of affection. I can feel his angst. His pride. His ego. But I refuse its strangulation tactics. I will will him to change. I will will him to love. I will. Will him. I will.

I rest my head back, Baldwin still across my lap, open. I close my eyes. I sit in a place of warmth. I sit where madam hooks knows I should. I sit where Thomas Smith claims I shouldn't.

Claimed I shouldn't…

I feel a hand. My left shoulder is no longer alone. It has been graced with the presence of a hand, a strong, sturdy, manly hand. It rests, here, now, and asks for a companion. I take my left hand, place it on top of it. Hold it. Hold this, this stranger of affection. And squeeze. My father's hand is now in mine. Baldwin, open in my right hand. I still read from its pages. hooks, open in his right hand. He still reads from its pages. We are squarely within the divine feminine, now. My father, his son sits between his legs, holds his hand, while reading the words of a black gay man, while he reads the words of a black female feminist who questions everything that defines what he views as his manhood. This is the most uncomfortable place for masculinity to reside. And yet it sits here. And I sit here. Between its legs.

And it is good.

We are one with each other. We are one with the literature. We are masculine energy. We are feminine energy. We are energy.

We are… father and son.

XXXVII

"And this is okay?"

He questions this unknown. The action, one with the literature, but foreign to his instinctual existence, differs from every other emotional forthcoming he has produced in his years. His mother did not need it, so he did not grow up with it. Only my mother could elicit any emotion, and it all revolved around the physical expression of love – at least, that's my educated guess. I had to be created somehow.

My mother is dead...

I still hold his hand in mine. Cover it, more than anything. Squeeze it, again. I do not look up to speak. He only needs to hear my voice, at this time.

"Yes. It is okay. It is welcomed, actually."

Do you not feel that?

"Do you not feel that?"

"I do not know what to feel. I was unaware I was supposed to feel. That I need to feel."

I feel that.

"What is bell hooks telling you?"

"That expressing myself is healthy."

"Is it not?"

"Again, I do not know, Vinnie. This is all foreign to me. I wasn't even like this with your mother... let alone a boy."

A son...

I squeeze his hand, again. Look up at him. Quickly spin around. Put my book down. Take his book from him. Sit Indian style. Hold both of his hands in mine. And look him in his eyes.

"We have to remove romantic love from its pedestal of being the epitome of love."

"What do you know about romantic love?"

"I know that I feel about it as I do about you. As I do about mom. As I do about Walter. Love is love. Love is all encompassing."

"I don't think I understand."

"I don't think you need to. You just need to feel. Everything. It should all come back to how you feel."

My father takes in his surroundings. Partially out of embarrassment, the rest out of curiosity.

"Is that why you brought me here?"

"It's hard to tell my father how to engage in something so far away from his norm. So a book, a book can help say things in ways that I can't. And nobody speaks to this quite like madam hooks."

"My hands are numb."

I let go of his hands. His discomfort buries him in his chair. He wants to be present, but to be present is to be vulnerable, something my father has worked his whole life not to be.

"Do you remember the hospital room?"

"Of course, I remember."

"What did it feel like to you?"

"It felt like my wife died."

"And the tears?"

I am fighting back my own, pulling at him to find consistency within his attempt at deflating his ego, subduing his toxicity.

"The tears… It was the first time I had cried since boyhood."

"And what about the other night? When you cried in my arms?"

We are dancing within the gaps of our respective generations. I am asking of him questions that he should be asking of me. I am becoming the man our ancestors feared, while engaged with a man our ancestors are proud they raised.

"It upset me. I do not know you–"

"–But you at least know now that you should try…"

"How are you doing this?"

Raised voice.

"How am I doing what?"

Joint volume.

"How are you... like this? How are you emotional? Nothing about me is emotional. Nothing about life is this damn emotional. You stand up. You fight. You figure it out!"

"But your equation is dangerous! Don't you get it? You spent decades with tears built up inside you and you think that's okay. There is nothing okay about that. That is detrimental in every possible way. Do you know how good I feel after I cry? Do you know how powerful I feel after I cry? Men who don't cry start wars. Kill. Abuse. Such violence can be alleviated with a simple cry. With a simple touch. With just... feeling. Something. Anything. Other than a need for power."

My father is flustered but engaged. Expressive, within a cloud of stubbornness. My father operates solely through his ego. It is getting through that, that need to immediately push back.

"You bring me here. Give me a book to read that questions everything – everything my manhood is made up of. Through the lens of woman, at that. I feel scolded. I feel incorrect–"

"–But you're feeling. And that's all that matters. You're allowed to express those feelings, good or bad. That's all hooks is getting at."

"I don't want to. I don't want this. I don't... I don't... not from you. Or her."

My mother is dead...

We sit in hushed silence. My father speaks in internal violence. He is at war, right in front of me. Scared. Fighting a war is at its most difficult when both sides have recruited you. Both sides provide benefits. Their pitches are simple – stay in this space of toxic comfort, where you do not question anything that leaves your lips, or, remove yourself from that place, into a realm of discomfort where your son lies, waiting, for you to love, touch and feel in ways you never have before...

"I love you, father."

"I love you, too, son."

"I love you, father."

"I – love you too, son."

"I love you, father."

"I love – you, too – son."

"I love you, father..."

He cries. Tears win the race down his face. It is an ugly cry. That uncontrollable kind. The one you hide from those who only know your mask. I hold my father's mask in the palm of my hand. And my ownership of this metaphor complicates his reality. Its cracks and crevices speak a language I know too well. I fear I understand his fears. That the one language he never wanted to share with another, converse with another, is now available to him, in the flesh. A flesh that is half of him, and his only living reflection.

My mother fed his patriarchal norms, as an active attraction to his intellectual Neanderthal. She did not know better. But she was able to sift between our differing masculine energies with the grace of ancestral goddesses of the earth and sun.

My mother is dead...

And all that remains is her widowed husband's cracked and distraught ego in the palm of the hand of his antithesis.

The ego is a lie...

And as my father's lies within my grasp, I could crush it, leave it for dead, never to be resurrected again. Easter would never be the same. But three days may be all I need.

His embarrassment has subsided. This public place saw my father's face at its most vulnerable, its most uncomfortable. It is one thing to cry within the walls of your home. But it is another to break down in front of strangers with judgmental eyes. He handles it, morphs his ego into a contraption conducive to hosting such a thing. My father has to be great at whatever he does, so watching him figure out how to be great within his own vulnerability is a true test of his Capricorn.

He passes. Maybe not with flying colors, but he passes. And in this moment, that is all that matters. I watch him, wipe tears from his face, while lacking the urgency of his – seldom – but past cries. My father wiped tears like an arsonist struggling to light a match. His tears, signs of disrespect to all he built himself to be. But at this time, he allows the stains. He allows the residue to shout its reasoning for being there. He does not hide the cry. He sits with it, lets it manifest its destiny.

There is an explosiveness to it all. An explanation as to why men crying makes others cry. It seems so unnatural, so wrong, so inadequate. Our programming is so ingrained, that watching a man cry makes you cry but rarely out of empathy, almost always out of sympathy. We await our sorry. A man's emotions should come with an apology.

So, they say.

He should not express himself.

So, they say.

We should not express ourselves.

So, they say.

Emotions thrown back in our faces by those who ask for the emotions in the first place.

Hell hath no fury like a man with stunted tear ducts...

My father is a stunt man no more. His tears enlightened by the freedom of strangers. He smiles through the pain. He smirks through the pain. He chuckles through the pain. There is a sense of disbelief within the pain. He does not know how he got here. And yet, he is here nevertheless, present to an unknown filled with touching parts of himself that he was unaware he possessed. The parts of him that my mother would never touch for she was too busy loving me to put forth the effort needed to change him. Changing him requires time, and I am young, and timeless, a vessel of wind and Baldwin and hooks, molded into the perfect specimen for such an assignment. My father reached this moment under my guise and I am proud of this. The irony in that he is learning more from me than I have from him is not lost on me. I will not relinquish this power.

I will relinquish this power...

It does seem wrong in a sense. I have to break him down in order for him to bring me up. I cannot become the man I want to be without him, but I will not become a carbon copy of the man he is right now.

Or, better yet, the man he was yesterday.

Or, better yet, the man he was when...

My mother is dead...

When she died, a piece of my father died with her. He does not yet know what piece that is, but it is being filled by elements of life my father has kept at arm's reach for decades. His mother was not one to coddle, hug, hold, kiss, caress, touch... love. She softened in her later years – days – like the last week. She now rests in our guest room, as she sifts through her past, while uncertain of how long she will be part of the present, if she indeed has a future, in the mold of this changed woman who finally recognizes the damage befallen her son and her ex-husband due to her feminine display of toxic masculinity and patriarchy.

The greatest weapons of a patriarchal society are women who scream its praises from the mountaintops. Who make sure the sissies are destroyed before they make their first decision. A society attracted to the Neanderthal in all of us. How erect our genitalia determining our plight.

187

Yes, that last sentence was my own. I am well-aware of my personal ego strokes as our countless strokes are all we are judged upon. Whether inside or outside of a woman, it is in this space that our level of manhood is determined. Our male peers can discuss us all they want, but it is under the judgmental eye of women that our true masculinity is determined.

And it is in this space, that I die.

My father was all man to my mother, his mother, both fans of his, if in different ways. His mother, constant in her relentless pursuit of his self-esteem, proud in the fact that he never wavered, stood tall and allowed his balls to drop. She was pleased with this turn of events as her ex-husband fled in the wake of her Capricorn. My mother, comforted by never wanting for anything material, she was willing to sacrifice her emotional needs for his sense of security. My mother wanted a home, a son, and to be able to work when she wanted, on what she wanted. My father was the perfect man for such a role. He was as perfect for that role as he was imperfect for the role of father.

Yes, I can love my mother more than anything to grace this earth, heavens and the wind while recognizing who is truly at fault for my plight – her selection of my father to be my father.

I can't talk, though. My grandma, my father and my mother were just the beginning of what became my own litany of flaws. I cannot blame them for their humanity. I can only blame myself for the perverted way in which I exude their inadequacies while defaming them for the very things that swim through my blood, and crawl from my throat to be spit upon the masses.

I understand the level of my ugly.

Where did this blood come from?

I sit here. At home. In my room. Wrists sticky. Wrists bloody. I have not cleaned myself off yet. I let the blood attempt to stain my skin. Like my father and his tears, it is a fight I have yet to determine if I want to win or not.

It is late. It is dark. I see no point in letting light into this room. Not now. For my activity is one of darkness. It is one of misunderstanding. It is one of loneliness. It is something for me. For Walter. For Jhene. The only people who understand my why. Understand the purpose of my continual pain seeking, all the while engaging in a growing love for my father. It is incremental. It is patience in flesh. It is dire straits personified.

This must happen...

I still do not trust it. I do not trust him. This journey, to reach a point of reconciliation, is an arduous one. It cannot be dealt with a delicate touch. It must be raw, elbow grease. I will sleep well tonight knowing he cried today. In a public place, my father – the Capricorn – went to blows with his ego and came out victorious. Bruised, beaten, yet, unafraid. He found a new conversation to have with himself. One centered around the possibility of vulnerability. An existence his bone structure denounces, the strength in his jawline crushes, his teeth chatter to the beat of a thousand mistakes, all with the sole task of reminding him that he must fight any and all things that go against his internal status quo. An explanation used in his scarring of my psyche, for his anger towards me despite my youth, despite my son status, despite my love for the love of his supposed life, was always centered around how much he could not understand me. And what is not understood, must be destroyed.

It is time to rest, for tomorrow continues the death and rebirth of a relationship given up on long ago. And only through the wind and a visit from a repentant grandmother, did it ever stand a chance.

Oh.

And me.

Me, too.

I might have something to do with it.

XXXVIII

A breakfast, of sorts. I sip on the oxygen. Breathe in, breathe out. I awaken to the melody of my own heart palpitations. The rhythm, melancholy, yet, consistent. Thorough in its dedication to completion, it will not let me die here. Not here. Not yet.

Wearing long sleeve shirts is wearing on me. The constant need to protect myself from the judgment of others, sometimes, I just want to scream all of my secrets at the top of my lungs and swallow their expectations whole. I want to give my father direct insight into the levels to which my pain goes. Run his fingers along the intricate design of my scars, all calculated marks painted by insecurities, longing, dissatisfaction, and – a box cutter. I want him to feel my elevated skin, the diversity in which I choose where it is I want to cut.

I want him to wonder. I want the depth of his imperfect methods of raising his son to spark a fuse in his soul that forces him to do better.

I want him to do what he did yesterday.

I relished in the unknown my father found himself in. He touched me. He held my hand. He placed his ego in my grasp, and left it there, for me to do with as I pleased. And I was pleased. We all must be broken down before we are rebuilt, and my father's foundation is among the sturdiest of them all. To break him down will take time, patience, effort and guile.

I just have to make sure I am not broken down with him.

As I leave my room to give this day its opportunity to prove something to me, to prove to me that it is worthy of living, I ponder whether or not my father's slumber has sent him back in time, back to a place I do not fit in. Or did it further solidify the harsh realities and truth that were bestowed upon him in that quaint bookstore. I will learn the answer to these questions as soon as I look in his eyes. His eyes will tell his story. His eyes will tell the truth. His eyes will determine if this is a day worth living to its fullest.

I close my bedroom door to see my father and his mother, in the same places I found them yesterday, when my father offered to spend his day with me, his son, for once. I walk towards them. My father looks at me.

And I am loved.

He does not need to say anything. 'Good morning' would not be good enough to replace the simple eye contact I just received.

Oh my.

He just smiled at me. My father is a handsome man. He is even more handsome when love is in his heart. It shines through his exterior, his humanity glistens, radiates, blooms. I am taken aback by the power of this man. And, he still, has not said a word.

Grandma. "Good morning, Vinnie."

"Good morning, Grandma Smith."

Father. "Good morning, son."

"Good morning, father."

"Breakfast looks the same as yesterday."

"I think it did its job yesterday so I thought we'd try it again."

"It indeed did its job."

"Indeed."

I am smitten by this man. This man that stands before me. This man who is set to embrace his fatherhood. This man who is set to embrace – me.

But who am I to speak for him? This is all conjecture, all fodder, all dreams and magic. I am incapable of truly knowing what is on this man's mind unless he tells me. I do feel like I know him fairly well based on the information he has provided to me. But those deeply ingrained mechanisms that determine whether he speaks or stays silent, honors or betrays, loves or hates, are not available to me. It is slightly frustrating that he can keep so much from me. But it does not mean I will not try. Maybe, one day, we will share heart palpitations in a way that my mother and I once shared. Maybe we can be one, like I am with the wind.

Maybe.

Maybe…

"What do you do outside?"

In left field is where you would find this question because that is from whence it came.

"Just, hangout. With Walter. Few of the boys on the street. A couple girls on occasion."

"But what do you do?"

"Boy stuff, I guess. Ride bikes. Play football. Race."

"Race?"

"Yeah."

"So… do you win?"

"What's my last name?"

Grandma Smith. "That's my grandson."

"So, you do win?"

"No other way to participate. If I'm not winning, I'm not racing."

"So, you wouldn't race me then, huh? Because that would mean you'd be losing, and you only race if you're going to win."

"Come again?"

"Who do you think gave you that last name?"

"I don't want to embarrass you, Pops."

I've always wanted to call him that…

"All it takes is an official challenge and we can settle this right now. In front of your grandmother."

I look to Grandma Smith. She looks more engaged than we are. No wonder so much competitiveness seeps through the pores of my father and drips from the blood of both of us.

"I will beat you in a race."

"You're going to regret doing such a thing, son."

He smiles. I swoon.

Grandma Smith. "This is the moment we have all been waiting for..."

...What?...

I look at my father. At Grandma Smith.

My father looks at me. At Grandma Smith.

Grandma Smith looks at my father. Looks at me.

My father. Grandma Smith. Me. All eye contact.

Are we laughing?

Yes, yes we are. Hysterically.

Family...

"That was a good one, Grandma."

Grandma Smith smiles. I took the Smith off the end. She wants that. I gave it to her. Seemed fitting. I do not remember her ever making me laugh before.

My father. "I'm going to change into some more comfortable clothes."

"Comfortable clothes aren't going to save you."

"They're just easier to jump up and down in celebration. Don't want to rip a hole in any of my slacks for –" *Altogether now...* "–That would be unbecoming."

I smile. He smiles. She chuckles. He leaves to change his clothes.

"I guess I should do the same then."

Grandma Smith. "Oh, I thought you young boys could just get up and go?"

"I prefer to prepare prior to embarrassing folks. And this will be the ultimate version of that."

"I see. Well, don't let me stop you."

I walk to my room, confidence through the roof. My father would not dare step to me on an athletic plane. Intellectually? Absolutely. I give the man his due when it comes to the brilliance of his mind on an intellectual level. But athletically? Yeah, he lifts weights on a regular basis but sprinting from one speed bump to the next, like me and the boys on the street do, is not something he seems too adept at succeeding in. Hopefully, this is just a ploy to hangout some more, and he is just speaking to my competitiveness to get me all riled up. I do not fault him for such things. I would operate in the same light.

I throw on some sweats and a long sleeve T-shirt. My entire wardrobe is skilled in protecting secrets. I have trained it well.

I leave my room to find my father in Nike basketball shorts, Nike mid-socks, some brand new Nike running shoes, a tank top that has 'Columbia' across the chest and a big ol' cocky smile.

"You ready, son?"

Naw.

"That I am."

"Then let's go. Mom?"

Grandma Smith. "Yes?"

"Time me."

Grandma Smith smiles and I am starting to feel like I have been set up for the okie doke. This is a full-blown set up. But my pride, instilled in me by the very man who stands before me, will not allow me to back out now. I will beat him. I just need to figure out how.

I might need the wind for this…

XXXIX

I stand at our makeshift starting line, my father next to me, bouncing up and down like a thoroughbred in heat. He is really taking this seriously. His reasoning, I do not know. But nevertheless, this activity is about to go down and it is about to go down now.

"On your mark…"

Grandma Smith is nearby, stopwatch in hand, as she prepares to time her son's race for the first time since the 1990s. That's a guess, but I think it is a pretty educated one due to all the hoopla behind this race of ours.

"Get set…"

My father legit gets into the starting blocks like he is ready for the World Championships. This is not a game, ladies and gentlemen. This is not a game.

"Go!"

My father takes off. But so do I. We are neck in neck, stride for stride. I pick up a little speed, create a bit of separation from my father. A little more. A little more.

A little more…

My father is 50 meters away from taking an L to his son. An L he cannot afford to take.

"Ahhhh!"

I turn to see my father pull up lame. He clutches his left hamstring, relegates his stride moot, his ego buries itself in the ground with each limp.

I stop running. Jog back to him. And just as I am leaning down to check to see if he is alright, this man takes off running. Seriously.

"Hey!"

But it is too late. My father has all the lead he needs to render himself victorious. As this cocky bastard back pedals to the finish line, sly smirk across his face like he has just pulled off the greatest coo of all-time, I do not know what to do with my reaction. I watch him, as he breathes heavily, clearly exhausted from this activity, but the victory provides him with enough energy to still strut like the prehistoric peacock he truly is.

I walk up to him, cautious, unaware of what exactly is his reasoning for such blatant cheating. He smiles, places his hands on my shoulders, weighs me down with his tired upper body, and prepares to speak, words I hope will do something to give me a better sense of what this moment means.

"Like Malcolm X said: 'By any means necessary.'"

He smiles, that handsome smile he saves for those rare moments where love is in the air. He is love, right now. And I feel it, his love.

And we both laugh. Oh, do we laugh!

"I really thought you were hurt!"

"I really thought you wouldn't think that. Go for the win first, then worry about the opposition's fate."

"But you're my father!"

"Yes, so I felt like if you would Malcolm X me, you would Malcolm X anybody… I clearly Malcolm X'd you."

Sounds like something I would say.

"Well… you're right about that."

He puts his arm around me as we head back towards Grandma Smith.

"I wasn't that fast when I was younger. I stole this Columbia shirt from my roommate in college and these sneakers are for comfort and comfort only."

He laughs this all-knowing laugh. We stop walking.

"Always look for an advantage. Always. Whether it is psychological or physical."

Or emotional…

I just like that he is telling me these things as if I don't know them already. But then again, at least he is telling me these things. My earthly father has resembled James Baldwin more than this man ever did. I am glad he seems to have decided to reclaim his place.

"Was this all a ploy from the beginning?"

"Only if you proved to be faster than me, which you clearly were about to."

He pauses for a second before he continues, contemplates his word choice.

"You're better than me at a lot of things, Vinnie. Just wish you could see what I do well."

Hmmm...

"I know you're smart and you provide for your family."

"Is that not enough?"

"Do you do anything more?"

"I come home every day to you. I came home every day to your mother. My coming home every night is how I say – said – 'I love you'. I don't understand why that can't be enough."

His 'I love you' does not look like mine.

But does that make it any less loving?

"As men, we love in different ways, if love is the term we must use. I am trying to learn your way. But my instinct is just to provide. My father – your grandfather – tried to provide, and it was never enough for your grandmother. I promised myself to provide at a level where it could not be questioned. That I was indeed there."

So much more than that is necessary but I feel a strong desire to let him have this, to let him have this moment. His explanation is understandable – albeit still not enough – but this is his belief. This definition of 'there' is interesting at best, baffling at worst. His physical form is here. I always know where my father is.

He never betrays me in terms of location. He is either at work, the gym or home. Nothing differentiates too much. His consistency is both his strength and his weakness. I look to diversify his being. Add some versatility and nuance to his existence. He seems to be taking some of this in, showing me a playful side he did not show before. A playful side still contained within the confines of his reflexive tone. He is still him, with additional flexibility. When dealing with the complication that is I, flexibility is a necessary skill. My father is showcasing that he has said skill. This is good information to know.

"I never felt you loved me."

I just said it. I had to. I had to let him know. I had to give him a glimpse into my level of disappointment in his version of love.

"Never loved you? How could you think I didn't love you? I was here."

"Physically, yes. But emotionally is where I reside."

This conversation is over, now. But it is continuing, still. We may not be using words any longer but I know my father is replaying in his mind all of the various moments where he belittled me, took me for granted, spoke with condescension, blatantly insulted me, all in the name of tough love and discipline.

We return to our walk to my grandmother. After a few steps, he wraps his arm around my shoulder and pulls me close. I laugh a little.

"Is this what you want? Huh? Do you need more of this?"

I can feel his smile.

"It's a start."

"Out here wanting hugs. My mama didn't hug. So, I don't hug."

"Your mother was wrong."

"bell hooks tell you that?"

"Among others."

A slight pause. A pregnant pause. Nine months. Water broken.

"Why the long sleeve shirt?"

He noticed...

"It's chilly outside."

"No, it's not."

"Then it's chilly inside."

"It isn't chilly in there, either."

"Then it's chilly *inside.*"

I point to my chest, it encapsulates my heart. This is where it tends to get frigid. This is from where I receive my directives to cut... and cut... and cut.

I'm starting to know where the blood comes from...

XL

Two hours since…

Would you like to go to a baseball game with me?

Emotions run through me. So unexpected. So left field. I am going to see a left field. And a right field. And a center field. Bats. Balls. Gloves.

Would you like to go to a baseball game with me?

We raced. We laughed. We talked. We talked some more. He asked. I answered. He showered. I showered. We got dressed. We left. Grandma sleeps…

I sit here. In the passenger's seat. Look out the window. Breathe fresh air. From the cracked window. Above my head. Seamless.

Would you like to go to a baseball game with me?

Oxygen flows through my nostrils, and back out again as carbon dioxide, continuing one of the many bodily miracles that prove that I am, at least somewhat, alive.

Would you like to go to a baseball game with me?

My father, I am just now meeting. A man of many faces. A man full of surprises. A man who listens to his mother. A man with a new mother. A man with a smile. A man who smiles.

A man who loves.

Would you like to go to a baseball game with me?

He chats about the game. He wants to watch the game. I do not care about the game. I want to watch him.

Watch him be beautiful. Watch him be engaged. Watch him be the best him – at least, I hope so.

Would you like to go to a baseball game with me?

We park. We get out. We get in line. He is excited – about the game. I am excited – about this man. This myth. This legend. This love. This father. My father.

Would you like to go to a baseball game with me?

We grab food. Him – a hot dog, Cracker Jacks and a large Coke. Me – nachos, a frozen lemonade and cotton candy.

We take our seats. He gets comfortable. Smiles. I get comfortable. Smile. This is us.

Would you like to go to a baseball game with me?

Game starts. At least, I think so. Cheers. Jeers. Claps. Boos. Cracks. Bats. Catch.

At least, I think so.

I pay it no mind. I just watch him. His facial symmetry is perfection. He is truly a beautiful man. Strong. Handsome. Debonair. My father.

Would you like to go to a baseball game with me?

We have great seats. At least, I assume these are. He wants to be close to the field. I just want to be close to him. We have found ourselves in this vicinity before. But never emotionally. Could I actually be getting an emotional father? Is he positioning himself with the wind?

Oh my, I hope so.

Would you like to go to a baseball game with me?

"Are you enjoying yourself, Vinnie?"

Yes, yes I am, father.

"This is fun. Thank you for bringing me."

"Thank you for wanting to come. We should have done this a long time ago."

"I agree. Something about being outside…"

"Yeah… You like your snacks?"

"All gone."

He laughs. He is beautiful.

"I'll take that as a yes."

It is a yes.

Would you like to go to a baseball game with me?

Yes, yes I would. And I did. And it is wonderful.

My mother is dead…

Oh. I have not forgotten. I have only reallocated where my love is and for how long.

I feel the wind blow.

"You feel that?"

"Feel what?"

"That."

"What?"

"The wind."

"Oh."

"The wind... that is mother. She says 'hello, my dear'."

My father closes his eyes. He breathes deeply. His face clenches. His face, rigid. He takes in the wind.

"I talk to her often. Mostly apologies, really. Just wish I had known. Wish I had been there."

"But you said you're always there?"

My father opens his eyes. Stares at me. I ponder the relevance of my question, but still await an answer.

"I guess I really wasn't, huh? Not like I am at work. I am work. But I need to be a husband first. A father... first."

"I don't think it was malicious. Not anymore."

My father wraps his arm around me.

"I appreciate that, son."

My mother knows more than anyone how much I need this. Even I did not recognize how starved I was to feel my father's warmth, to create my father's warmth, to reignite my father's warmth. He is reborn, as a father, as a man. His mother, tied his emotions together in a secure knot, handed it to me, and – alongside his ego in my other hand – we are crafting a man we can all be proud of, without looking at his pay stub.

The game ends at some point. By the number of people getting up and leaving, I suppose it is over. My father applauds his team. I do not know which team it is. I do not know which teams are playing. I do know that I am here with him, and I am loving being in this space, in this energy. Filled with love, wind and reciprocation.

"I love you, father."

"I love you too, son."

"Grandma is probably sleep, huh?"

"A lot of years of life, a lot of reasons to rest."

I feel that...

We get to the car and I find myself attempting to look out a window that only provides me with darkness. It attempts to steal my joy, but I won't let it. I return its glare with my rays of sunshine. A son's shine. I feel like the son of a father.

God the Father, God the Son and God the Holy Spirit...

My father, his son and the wind...

This is reaching spiritual levels. I wonder what the rhythm of his heart palpitations feel like. I wonder if his heart beats to a reggae beat or is it more neo soul like...

My mother is dead...

The wind bangs against our car door, asks to enter, to make its presence known. I lower the window ever so slightly, only to hear the wind howl into our vehicle with the vocal chords of a soprano banshee. It feels chilly, with a calming element to it. The hairs stick up on my arms as my body temperature shifts. It is cold in here now, but for all the right reasons.

"You feel that?"

My father takes a deep breath. Oxygen. Carbon dioxide.

"Hello, my love..."

He believes...

My father senses the moment. He knows my mother is here with us right now, as a family. A family that loves as much as it provides. Or, at least, acknowledges that love is just as important. My mother knew that. My father is learning that. I was born like that, and Baldwin and hooks nourished me over time.

And my paintbrush...

I still wish he knew how to paint. He will never know what it feels like to be one with the canvas, one with

204

the brush, one with me. It is the part of our relationship that can never be. And this fact gives our relationship a ceiling, something neither one of us can afford to live under.

But we will find our own paintbrush, our own palpitation, our own rhythm, within this newly cemented father-son dance we have begun.

We pull into the driveway at the house. I am sure I do not want this night to end. My soul is too joyous, my sensitivity heightened, in the best of ways. I feel everything, right now. I am being, right now. I am one with everything.

I... almost love my father with everything I am...
We walk inside. I smile. He smiles. I swoon.
"Want to watch some TV?"
"Um, sure."

My father looks at me. I look back at him. Our eyes have a separate conversation. I have never spoken to my father in silence before. This is something my mother and I perfected. It was an artform in our hands. This is the first moment in a long journey to reach that point. But this feels different. I feel my father reading me. I feel my father feeling me. He is understanding my wants, my needs. But the question is: Will he fulfill them?

"Maybe not TV. Grab a couple of books."
Are we about to read?
"You still reading 'The Will To Change'?"
"Yeah. It's a lot to work with. But I'm getting through it."
"Proud of you."
"Proud of me, huh?"
"Yeah..."
"Go get the books. I need to sit on that couch."

I happily grab his book out of his room, then grab Baldwin's 'Giovanni's Room' for me. I hand him his book as we make our way to the couch. I stare at the pointless TV in front of us.

I won…

He sits on one end of the couch. I sent on the other. He cracks open his book. I crack open mine. We both find ourselves in the depths of our respective pages. Page 72 for him, page 36 for me. Pages turn at similar paces. With every few pages, I look up to find him smiling, either at the book or at me. It is the bookstore, with more intimacy. We are home now. We are in our comfort zone. Together. As father and son.

I scoot over. Rest my head on his shoulder. He looks down at me, smiles, runs his hand across the top of my head. He still reads. I still read. But I am his son. And I will be close to him, whether he wants me to be or not.

He wants me to be…

I close my book on page 53. His, already closed on page 88. A successful trip down literary lane. I have never been this close to him, in so many ways, with so much context. It's a surreal feeling knowing that this is possible as long as we put forth some work, some effort, some understanding, in each other. It is us, and it is beautiful.

And now, we must rest. He has begun his journey already. I consider joining him. I could use some sleep. And I would love to rest upon his shoulder forever. I rise up and down with each of his breaths, my eyes still open, staring at the pointless TV in front of us. I contemplate my next move. Sleep…

Or…

I forgot about something.

Or…

But I don't need it anymore.

Or…

Yes, I do.

Or…

No, I don't.

Or…

But…

I'm starting to know where the blood comes from...
...
...

...
But he loves me...
Where did this blood come from?

XLI

I awaken from a slumber reminiscent of eternal graves and resurrections. My father, resurrected within a parental framework we can both fit in. He was a father to me yesterday, and last night, and embarking on this day after, the possibility of returning to that space of love and reciprocation is all the reason to live this life today.

My glee runneth over!

He took me to a baseball game...

He let me in, to a locale I am so unfamiliar with, yet, I know as a place I need to be. I am proud of myself for never giving up the fight for him, even when I added to his reasons for his emotional absence, where we have arrived was always the end game. He was always my end game.

I need to converse with my father. I run into the living room, only to find my grandmother sitting there, drinking coffee. She smiles in my direction, and suddenly, I am reminded of the separation from my father – and how much his job plays a part in it. He is there now, unable to see me off to school because when they call, he must answer. He did not know I would call him myself this morning for the morning after is not something he is used to yet. He does not know how to act the night after love is in the air. He prefers to exit in the dead of morning, never to speak to the one in which he spent his evening. I am an emotional whore in this sense. Used, heartbroken – and longing for the next time he calls for me.

"He wants to be here, Vinnie."

As if she knew exactly what I was thinking.

"I know. But, providing…"

"I attacked, berated and chastised your grandfather for the very thing we must praise your father for now. He tries, in his own way. It is how he loves. By making sure that his family is taken care of."

"I am learning to be okay with that, Grandma. But

just as he is adjusting to how I love and need to be loved, I am doing the same in accepting how he views it, too."

"I know you are, Vinnie. I know. And I am glad I am here to witness you both blossom. I almost feel like I may have had a hand in it."

Her laugh, reminiscent of joyous gravel. Unmistakable in both its pain and electricity. I both want it to never end and want her to hush, all at once.

"You did, Grandma. You definitely did."

She smiles, holds back her gravel joy, and leaves us in a silence befitting such a relationship as ours. So much unspoken, yet, our energies understand one another, if nothing else does.

"You ready to go back to school?"

"Not exactly."

"Just don't get into anymore fights."

"I will do my best."

"But if you do…"

"…Make sure I win."

"That's my grandson."

Grandma Smith hands me a brown bag full of lunch. I am somewhat surprised at this gesture as she does not seem like a woman adept at putting together such a motherly endeavor – and she is about three years behind the acceptable age of a paper bag lunch – but she is forgiven. Her heart is in the right place. And I will need to eat at some point. So, all is well.

I kiss Grandma Smith on the cheek and exit out the front door. I look left to Walter's house, pause, take a deep breath in and – the wind speaks. I must go now, for this is a walk that must be done alone. Companionship is not necessary for the silence I must endure as I journey to a place of learning – and people. Lots of people, with their judgmental eyes. But I will give them the benefit of the doubt on this date.

I am a stranger in a lot of ways now. My mother dies. I am suspended. My presence at school is a monster with no regard for time. I am someone you somewhat need to prepare yourself to see. My teachers need to know that they will have me to deal with for the 57 minutes I am in their class, otherwise, my sudden presence, or lack thereof, can stymie, stifle and crucify even the most veteran of teachers. I took pride in that once. It is not one of my more relished accomplishments any longer.

The wind tussles with an intruder. Breezes by me with a negative twinge I am unaccustomed to. A feeling of past joy – current pain – envelops me, swallows my energy and regurgitates its inconclusiveness. There is confusion in the air, the wind, a foreshadow within the shadows.

And a hand on my shoulder, breathes heavily the very air tussling with its existence.

"Where have you been?"

"Hello, Walter."

"Where have you been?"

"Suspended, just like you. We were suspended together."

"You know what I mean."

"I don't."

"Whatever, man…"

I sense tension…

"Did I do something?"

"No, and that's part of the problem. Where were you? I didn't see you all weekend. I needed to see you all weekend."

"The whole weekend?"

"Well, yeah."

"I spent it with my father, parts with my grandmother, parts with all of us. It was a beautiful time that I would love to tell you about one day."

"I don't want to hear about your heaven when I am still in hell."

"Do tell."

"Naw, I'm good. I would have, but. Naw. Naw, I'm good."

"As you wish."

"Whatever, man…"

"Are you going to be alright?"

"Am I going to be alright? Yeah, whatever, man."

"We can talk about it, if you like."

"I don't."

"Very well."

"You're 14, Vinnie. Remember that."

"I appreciate the reminder, Walter."

"You know what?... whatever, man."

"Fourteen, indeed."

Vestiges of an old married couple. I love him. And I am loving my father. And I am loving my grandmother. And I – think – I am loving Jhene.

It wasn't always like this…

My love is working overdrive. Something, somewhere, must take a break. I have loved Walter the longest. Our love is – presumably – the strongest. It can persevere through a sabbatical better than the others. The others are too fresh. The foundational strength Walter and I possess is that in which the other three will seek to produce as well. But my humanity may not be able to withstand providing such energy to so many entities. Once upon a time, it was only my Walter and…

My mother is dead…

The only entity capable of coming between that love was my paintbrush, where my mother was a participant and Walter is politely indifferent. It caused us no harm. But this, this could be a different animal. A Walter with a sawed off direct line to my heart could be dangerous to all of us.

"My father loves me now, Walter."

"So?"

So?...

Oh... I see...

I don't like this look on him. I don't like this voice out of him.

I didn't know he knew how to hurt me...

I spot Jhene in the distance. Or, as this moment requires, a timely escape. I exit this current conversation with the rugged white boy in a white T and jeans, and walk in the direction of Aaliyah in Avril Lavigne's wardrobe.

I can smell the shock on Walter's breath. How could I ever leave him? The air of betrayal follows me into the outstretched arms of this petite girl whose unwavering love for me continues to astonish.

She wraps me in her black girl magic, pulls me close, closes her eyes and holds on tight. She is in my chest now, the place she should always be. But I do not have time for her to be here, anymore. I hold all requisite space in my heart for the man in my home I call father.

She still manages to nudge her way in anyway. For her love only needs a mustard seed of space. Her love is of the unselfish variety, comes and goes as is necessary. When she arrives, it is as if she has never left.

"I missed you."

"I missed you, too."

"How was your weekend?"

"I spent it with my father."

"Oh, really. And how was that?"

"Love. It was love."

"I love that."

I smile. She smiles. I feel understood, in this moment. She senses how much I needed that, that weekend. There was no...

So?

Only a smile and an understanding between two shared souls, in emotional matrimony. She holds my arm in both of her arms. No need to hold my hand when the gravitational pull that are my wrists are below, or, above, my hands, depending on your viewpoint. I tend to lean towards my wrists being below my hands. The tips of my fingers are a starting point no one dares to start from.

She dares...

I need Walter to dare, with me, for me – again. He dared a lot in our collective past but now he only chooses truth, his truth. He is turning our friendship into a selfish game of take and take. The give is gone.

Aren't I the selfish one?

I don't want to be. Not now. Not ever – again. For before, I was. I admit. I made my pain, mine and Walter's. His true pain is hidden, and when discussed, it is handled flippantly. I purported my dream of killing his father, allowed it to represent my loyalty, when in all actuality it is a placeholder for something of a lesser variety.

It scares me, in this moment, that Walter represents a placeholder for my father, and my father now wants his spot back. He never lost his spot. It was always his. I just never had the gumption to warn Walter of his coming doom. Part of me thought it would never come, that I would never need to relay this information to my best friend. Another part of me knew it was only a matter of time before the world provided my father and I with the steel cage necessary for us to rumble towards reconciliation, and reciprocation. We only needed...

My mother is dead...

Tragic times call for tragic measures...

I take Jhene's hand in mine. We walk to first period. Better yet, we walk to her first period. I will be late to mine. And I do not mind. As long as she is safe and secure, I am thankful.

But I am not here. Not at school. Not really. I am there. At home. With my father, who is not there, either. Yet, he is.

Period 1... Math... Ms. Williams...

When you add Thomas Smith to his son, Vinnie Smith, you get joy. Black boy joy! Oh, boy!

Period 2... English... Ms. Chasity...

I cannot put us into words right now. Beautiful is not enough. Immaculate, might come close. Wondrous. It is Thomas. It is my father. It is Vinnie. It is I. And it. Just. Is.

Period 3... World History... Mrs. Ward...

Buddhist countries speak of peace, love and tranquility. Smith homes speak of confidence, hard work, intellect – and now, love. We, Thomas, and I, are a country in and of ourselves.

Period 4... Art... Ms. Scott...

She missed me. And I missed her. My paintbrush sits idle in my room, in a home I share, with Thomas Smith. A piece of artwork I am still learning to deconstruct. I will paint him one day, in a glorious way. And it will scream of black boy joy. And it will be good.

Period 5... Sign Language... Silence...

I sit next to Jhene. She holds my hand under the table. It is warm, soft, calm. No words necessary. Words are unnecessary in this room, in this language. Like eye contact, and smiles, exchanged between Thomas Smith, and his son, I.

Period 6... Physical Education... Mr. Curtis

I sprint into the arms of my father, Thomas Smith, the man who lives in our home and holds the key to unlocking an emotional bond with physical touch sprinkled onto it. Rest my head on his shoulder, run his hand through my hair, hug me, protect me from all physical harm. Educate me on the ways of being man, without being, man. Toxicity is not the goal, but physical embodiment of the soul is attainable, through this father-son tango.

I am home now...

He is not. Still in the land of milk and money. My hug, my love, will still be here when he arrives. Until then, Grandma Smith can keep me company. Her presence alone saves lives. She saved her own, and brought her saving grace into our home, and saved my father, thus, saving me. And I am eternally grateful for that.

I knock softly on the guest room door. No answer. I squeeze the doorknob ever so slightly. I peek inside to find Grandma Smith sound asleep. I love how if we are not here, she is sleeping.

A lot of years of life, a lot of reasons to rest...

I exit her room and softly close her door. She is at peace. I will return to my own.

Sir Baldwin, how art thou?

To you, sir: Though 'Giovanni's Room' has found its way back into my hands, we have not conversed in some time. I hope you find my development to be of your liking. I am less in my own way, letting the world come to me instead of exploding into it. I know, I know, the cutting is something I must break. But is that you talking or the black community? I know it's not our thing, but we have a lot of things that shouldn't be our thing, so this thing shouldn't be that big of a thing. Don't you think? I suppose. I will give it some consideration, but for now, I pray – though neither of us are truly religious people – that you approve of how my father has come around. I will introduce him to you, to us, in due time, but for now, he is in bell's hands. I have missed you, sir. I am struggling with this expansion of my love. I do not know how to distribute its contents to all who need it without shortchanging one, or two. Love was so seamless when so few needed it. But I cannot complain about what is on my plate when I asked to eat. Fill my plate up with love, let it overflow, and I will figure out how to clean up the excess. Oh, Sir Baldwin, you understand me like no one else can. Thank you so much for your ear...

I do not know how or when I fell asleep.

I do know that the timing of such rest is odd. I do know I am supposed to be awake right now. But let me brush my teeth before interacting with my family.

I walk to the bathroom, take out my toothbrush and toothpaste, brush my teeth. I feel refreshed. Like, the next words out of my mouth will sing of freshness and life.

A faint sound...

My father must be home!

This sound is different...

I move closer to my bedroom door as the sound becomes clearer. I know the sound well. It is the sound of tears of the heartbroken.

I exit my room to find nothing in the living room.

Where is that sound coming from?

I search the house, ears peeled for any sign of where the sound is coming from. And I finally catch it. It is coming from the guest room. I move closer to the guest room door and it is clear now. And it is not Grandma Smith crying.

It is my father...

I open the door to find my father as he lightly cries, rocks Grandma Smith back and forth in his arms. A lifeless Grandma Smith. Grandma Smith is no longer with us.

My grandma is dead...

I rush over. I position myself behind my father. Hold him.

"I am so sorry, father."

He cries harder, balances holding her, and leaning into me for comfort. He does not know which one he needs most. Tears begin to run down my face.

I rock him. He rocks her. My family. Rocked.

Again.

XLII

She did what she came to do.

Grandma Smith apologized to her son. Grandma Smith initiated a reconciliation with her son and her grandson. Grandma Smith left this world in the arms of the one man she truly believed in.

She did what she came to do.

She left knowing that her son is headed down a path of manhood, and fatherhood, that she can be proud of. That the damage she caused to his psyche and ego in his youth, did not destroy him at the levels it did his father. She salvaged her son, and in that, salvaged her own relevance on this earth. She did something good. She rectified her own participation in patriarchy, in toxic masculinity, by placing the antithesis to both in view of her son. She knew I was the only one with the capacity to lead my father down a road he always refused to go. But with her guidance, with her push, with her will, she got him to finally look my way, and now, there is love in this home. Yes, there is death. Yes, there is mourning. But there is love. And that was not always the case.

I walk into the guest room. My father spends a lot of his time here now. Not doing anything, really. Just standing in the space his mother once occupied. I understand his mindset.

My mother is dead...

There is no right way to grieve. We all do it in our own way, at our own pace. My father is a different man now than when my mother died. There isn't just the initial explosion of emotion and then frigid silence after. He feels now. He touches his feelings, and they touch back. He is in tune with his humanity, and for that reason, he mourns differently. He allows himself to be present in his grief. Not to run from it because it is unbecoming, or against his alpha male stature. He is secure in the necessity of emotion when feelings are under attack.

"Father, are you alright?"

He turns his head to acknowledge my entrance into the room but still does not say anything.

Still me. "She was a guest on this earth, and left us while staying in our guest room. There is poetry in that."

I do not know what to say. The silence, deafening. My father, in a reflective, almost meditative state, with a focused intent to cherish each breath taken. That is what breathing is. We are taking our lives back. If we stopped breathing, our lives would end. Each breath is a defiant act, continuing a fight against an inevitable end. We march on with each breath taken. I will continue my march, and I hope my father will continue his, too.

"I am always last to know..."

My father speaks in a tone I do not recognize. My curiosity heightens.

"I am always last to know. The people in my life, the women in my life, do not tell me they need me until it is too late. I do not want to be late anymore. I want to be here. I want to be present..."

He turns to me, looks at me with a deep yearning for acceptance.

"...You're my last hope to get something right, Vinnie."

"How badly do you want it?"

My father wraps me in his arms, rocks me side to side, my face deep in his chest. He holds me. It is significant.

He lets me go. Smiles slightly, and walks back to his room. I stay here, breathe in the past and present. So much life has lived in this house that no longer does. But we have to continue to live the lives that are still here. We cannot die while alive. That would be disrespectful to those who have gone before us.

My own room calls for me. And so does an old friend.

I have not painted in so long...

I sit on my easel. I place my paintbrush in my hand. I am in my happy place. Death surrounds me. Feminine energy lacks in this household. Nevertheless, I am gleeful. My grandmother passed. But her death is a reaffirmation. I have my father's undivided attention. He has nowhere else to hide. He is mine now and I will cherish him for as long as he is on this earth with me.

Happiness splatters onto the no longer blank canvas. There is no purpose here. Only the abstract expression of a young black man, with no earthly mother, no earthly grandmother, but an earthly father, who no longer resembles that of James Baldwin. He is now his own man, his own entity, reclaiming his position in my heart where I have waited for him for years.

My grandmother is dead. But this paintbrush is so beautiful...

Splash!

Oh, how I love to paint! The sporadic expression of all that is me. There are no faces on this canvas. No shapes to discern what it is I am actually looking to create. All that is here is emotion. Or is it emotionless? It all depends on the view. And that is what makes it art! I will tell you what it is and you will not need to understand why I claim it as such. You will only need to know that it is mine to claim, and you have no say in that claim. I am claiming this canvas now, as an expression of glee between myself and Thomas Smith, my father, a man I am now safe to say is my father. One who feels.

She needed her rest after years of living...

And now, living rests in my hands. And living is what I will do.

Oh, what is this? I have run out of red paint. I know I have some here, somewhere. Ah. Here it is.

Oops.

Wait. No, I got it. It is right here. That was a close one. For there is nothing that will usurp my joy in this moment. I am life. I am full. I am clear. I am Vinnie Smith. A black boy, full of joy, with no mother, no grandmother and a newly minted father who was there in the flesh all along. I am loved. I am appreciated. I matter.

But...

...

Where did all this blood come from?

XLIII

We are handling this one differently.

No spectacle. No public reverence. No public outpour. No screams. No violence. Just, silence. Reflection eternal. This death is Grandma Smith's final plea for my father and I to be as one. And we are listening.

School happened a few times. I went. I saw Jhene. I – think – I loved Jhene. I went to class. Teachers let me be. I appreciated that. I left early a couple times. Maybe a few times. Pops needed me. Or, at least, I needed him to need me.

Work happened for him a few times. It usually serves as his safe space, his refuge. But he has struggled to produce. The partners have sent him home. There is an emotionless solitude he has found within himself. It looks familiar.

It looks like me.

We hug when we see each other. Every time. No more relaxed moments. Everything has a purpose. We love on purpose. We care on purpose. We smile on purpose.

We cremated her on purpose.

Again, no funeral. No hoopla. We think she would have wanted it this way. Besides, I am not sure we would have known who to invite. She left where she lived to come visit us and no one called to check on her. When she wasn't sleeping, I do not remember if she ever was on the phone with someone who wasn't my father. She was alone. And at peace. She had final tasks to complete before she left this earthly space and, once those tasks were accomplished, she bid us farewell. We are on our own now.

Our last funeral was enough funeral for us. Going through that again – even if it wouldn't be *that* again – is still something we would rather avoid. Grandma Smith was ours and ours alone. My father's mother, and my grandmother. Thoroughly flawed, just like us.

Today is the day we return Grandma Smith to the wind, to the ocean. She will not stay with us much longer. Her ashes are not ours to keep. She is to be with the earth she left, now.

Just one more piece mother nature would like returned to her.

My father remains in a solemn state. He is starting to feel his loss more. Retroactively mourning my mother, proactively mourning his. His shirts, not as crisp. His slacks lack a crease. I recognize him as him, but he is not him. He is a man who feels, now, and feelings alter our appearance. It makes us diverse in our interactions, fluid in our being. It is what makes girls and women such fascinating specimens of existence. They are constantly in flux, consistently inconsistent, yet, you know exactly what you're going to get. It makes absolutely no sense. And that is what makes them so beautiful. Such magic.

Feminine energy is God's energy...

I watch my father. He preps for our exit. Gathers himself. Lacks the meticulous nature of his life prior to bell hooks. Prior to me. Prior to mourning. Prior to – feeling.

I grab the urn off our kitchen counter that holds the remains of my grandmother. It weighs more than she ever did. Figurative in reality, literal in context.

My father leads me outside. I follow in his shadow, not wanting to crowd his solitude. I am happy to be a follower nowadays, patience turning into an attribute I can actually claim as my own. I know where my father lies his head, I know where he rests his soul, and I know that he feels. I am in no rush any longer. I can be patient. Until he returns to me. Whole.

We get in the car. I rest the urn across my lap. My father stares. Not at me. But at the urn. His eyes say 'goodbye'. He takes a long, meditative blink, then starts the car.

My father, his eyes on the road. Me, my eyes on the

urn. I begin to see my grandmother. Her transformation from difficult to discerning, palpable. It shows it is never too late to do better. Never too late to grow. Never too late to...

...Love my father with everything I am...

Almost there.

Thank you, Grandma Smith. Grandma. For setting the foundation that allowed me to get my father back, to get him at all. My memory doesn't remember a time where he was here, present, with me. He is present, now, and it is because of you. You touched a part of him that dropped him to his knees and reminded him of what matters, reminded him of what he had right in front of his face all this time. You showed him that anyone can reinvigorate their heart, and love.

I do not shed tears over you. It does not feel necessary. You did what you were supposed to do. You did what you came to do. You gave my father his heart back and, in return, he is now able to give his heart to me. I hold it in my hands, as I inch towards simultaneous palpitation.

That day will come...

I am thankful. Not sad. You lived the life you were supposed to live. And despite the damage you may have done along the way, you remained human. And you found a way to say sorry. Not many humans reach that point, or live long enough to realize it is something they need to say.

We arrive at the beach. My father gets out. I get out, urn in hands. We walk the sidewalk until it connects to the beach. The wind blows, speaks in one of the romance languages, fluent, and pure. We both breathe it in, breathe her in. Exhale.

My mother is dead...

And so is my grandma. And we sit in this revelation. Sit in this truth. Two men who only lose our women. Cursed masculinity tortured by the divine feminine, it must be taken from us in order for us to learn from it.

We stand at the edge of the sand. My father looks to me, half smiles. I return the favor. We remove our shoes, hold them in our hands, baring our feet. We take our first steps in unison. It is quiet here. Not much fuss on a weekday morning. Folks got school and jobs. And we are doing ours. As sons, grandsons, and, men. This is our work. It is tireless, and freeing. A recognition of a common sense of manhood, despite different lenses.

Each step is pure. Each step is magical. The sand tickles our toes, its warmth battling our body temperature for supremacy. I find comfort in its depth. Its ability to let me sink, but never let me fall. It is like being raised by a black woman, by the wind, by God.

My mother is dead...

And she is here, with us, to pay her respects for her newest angelical peer. I wonder what form my grandmother has taken in the universe. I know she will show herself to me in due time. I hope she shows herself to my father, her son, before me. I want him to share that connection, then share it with me, like I did, with my mother, the wind.

It is getting muddy, now. The water mixes with the sand to create a new substance altogether. We are closer to the completion of our journey. More water than sand, now. The water, cold, wet, yet, perfect. We are almost three-fourths water. There will always be a connection between us and it. It is family. And this is a reunion. Our ancestors are here. The wind is present. The water is wet. The sand is hot. And I, Vinnie, am with my father, Thomas, and it is good.

I open the lid of the urn with shaky hands. The wind circles us, this family, as only it can. It awaits our delivery. It awaits this final piece of Grandma Smith's earthly journey. The wind will take her where she needs to go, to where she is needed. Ashes to ashes, dust to dust, she is a must. Necessary now, more than she was in the flesh. Her job, almost complete.

My father stares at me, at the urn in my hands. There is patience in his eyes – and a tear. Or two. He is present. He lacks arrogance, in this moment. There is vulnerability in this place. We can feel pain. Together, as father and son.

I start to pour out my grandmother's remains but with each second that passes, with each ash turning to dust, my father's emotions heighten. He starts to shiver, and shake. Borderline convulse.

"Stop! Just stop!"

I stop.

"She is your mother, pops. We will do as you wish."

He breathes heavily. Then, the wind...

My mother is dead...

He calms down. Breathes, again. His chest moves up and down as the oxygen clears his spirit. My mother is feeding him, fueling him, allowing him to find peace in this endeavor. She is loving him, all over again. Providing comfort in a way sacred only to her, to them, to us. My father continues to gather himself. He looks like himself again. His strength has returned. He is Thomas, and he is ready to say goodbye to his mother.

"Let me do it."

I hand my father the urn. He stares at his mother's remains.

Breathe...

He slowly begins pouring it out. A goodbye in spilled remains, caught in the wind. But the wind – its comfort, its guide. My mother and grandmother were not close. But they will be now. For now, they have a common goal. To watch, follow and comfort my father and I, as we live this life without them. A household, devoid of the divine feminine, is a household lacking in essential elements of spiritual survival. But we will find a way to persevere. We don't have a choice.

"You did good, father."

"Just, tired."

"I know... I know."

We walk back to the car, put on our shoes on the way. The sand, still hot beneath our feet, but it is the last piece we leave behind. First, it was the water. Then the mud. And now, the sand. Parts of us forever, shared pieces of this moment. It is just us, now. We have the wind, and whatever spiritual form grandma decides to present herself as in the future. But in the flesh, it is us. It is I, and it is him. Father and son.

I smell death...

A particular scent, one I recognize in times of mourning. I would want my father to have to mourn me. I know children are supposed to bury their parents but, burying my mother was enough for me. I could not go through something similar again. I would want to die explosive. Not by explosives, but, with a story to tell. Dying in my sleep, or a disease taking me away in the middle of the night after months of fighting it does not fit my life's narrative. I want to die with spontaneity. I want to be in the utter midst of living and then, leave. No warning, no signs, just an exit. An exit befitting the life ending. My life is not one to end within the context of the mundane. Oh, no. It will be spectacular. One for the ages, and I want my father to be the one to carry it.

My father, he can die slow. His death takes away all that is him, and makes him watch it from the outside. No more work. No more steel gaze. No more success. No more accomplishing. Just a slow rot. And this is not out of a lack of love. This is for him to slow down, marvel at his death, so he can, in turn, relish what was his life. He must be put on permanent pause, before the inevitable stoppage. He must sit alone, waste away, while he remains at peace with what he has done, and what he has lost. He should die slow. Yeah, slow.

Walter, he should die screaming. Guns a blazing. His white T-shirt, drenched in red, blood-soaked – everything. His death needs to be rock star worthy. A steep fall from grace. A bludgeoning. A stampede. A machine gun. A trench coat. A stereotype. A manic white boy death. A death that gives my ancestors a hearty laugh, a sigh of relief. One less white boy to grow up to be a white man. He should die screaming. Yeah, screaming.

Jhene, she should die smiling. Among flowers and the trees, skipping through the afternoon breeze, only to lie down on her back, look up into the sun, close her eyes, feel the wind, and the wind recognizing her as her extended family, extending her hand, and taking her to where all the other angels are. She belongs with the rest of the angels, flying and free. Free to manipulate the madness into bliss and beauty. She deserves no pain. I just hope Aaliyah welcomes her with open arms. They have a lot to talk about. She should die smiling. Yeah, smiling.

Rick, he should die… at my hands. I want to slit his throat with Walter's very own box cutter. There is nothing else to add.

Except...

Is Walter the one I would kill for now?

Yesterday changes things. Rick's death might be in Walter's hands, now. I don't know if that level of sacrifice is befitting our current relationship. The kind of love once bestowed upon Walter is a love I would have sacrificed it all to protect. But now, I am not just protecting Walter, or the wind. I am protecting my father, and – I think – Jhene. Yeah, Jhene. The dispersal of love is profound in this sense. I love too much, so do I really love at all? How much love can a woodchuck love if a woodchuck could chuck love? I dunno. This is when feeling our feelings feels fruitless. I do not want the responsibility of having to love so much, of having to love so many. No one man should have all that power. No one boy should have all that power. Not I should have all that power. I am against counterproductivity and killing Rick in the name of Walter, when I could question whether or not my one death defying stunt should be used for others – Thomas and Jhene – causes a pause too strong to disobey. It would be counterproductive to assume that Walter receives my one act of true mercy. I could relocate my mercy killing. Someone else might need it later. I have to recalibrate. This decision just became that much harder.

Damn you, Walter…

XLIV

I sit on the curb, outside of my home. I have been here for some time now. I do not know why this was the place I wanted to spend my time after leaving my grandmother to rest in the wind and in the water, and yet, here I am. Something about being able to see every house on this street, with each sharing its own story, its own history, its own peaks and valleys, provides a sense of comfort that I unknowingly need right now.

I hear a door close behind me. I know it is not my home. I turn over my left shoulder to find Rick, in a dingy wife beater, cargo pants and black boots, leaving his home. He hurries to put his things in his truck, but locks eyes with me just as he closes the backdoor. We hold this moment, rehash the last time we saw each other, when Rick ran me out of his home and into my father's arms for the first hug of many since. Rick shows no love in his eyes but I say 'thank you' with mine. Rick's actions literally sent me running into my father's arms, and there was no place I would rather be at that time. My thank you only lasts a few moments, though. I eventually land in the place of disdain where Rick currently resides.

Your death will be swift, sir...

If only he knew of the number of times I have imagined the ending of his life, Walter's escape. My father taking Walter as his own and Walter and I officially becoming brothers. I would share my room with Walter. Share my blades with Walter. Share my love with Walter. We would trade horror stories about our fathers and talk about what it was like to watch Rick suffer at the hands of I, and the hands of us. It would be a splendid occasion, filled with love, justice and peace for all those left to live in a world without Rick. A sloppily put together excuse of a man whose hands have beaten and bruised his son to a point of virtual no return. Walter has only had me to lean on through his strife.

And I don't have room to love him at that level anymore...

Rick smiles, a curse smile full of mistakes and anger. He hops in his truck, backs out of his driveway, shows me his teeth one last time, then pulls away. I am so transfixed on what just transpired, how the devil could attain a driver's license in a country under God and indivisible, that I do not feel the new energy next to me. It smells a lot like a sandlot. Dirt and white boys sandwiched between one black boy pitching a shutout on a mound lifted just above all of them. For I have risen above the other boys that surround me, I deserve this heightened level of responsibility. And I will take on all comers who decide they are ready to hit anything I throw at them. And first up, the originator of all things white in my life...

Walter...

"Sup, stranger."

He sits.

"Oh, hi... Walter."

"What you doin' out here?"

"Just thinking."

He snickers.

"Figures. You're always in your own head."

I sigh.

"Yeah, you could say that."

"My dad is gone." So, matter of fact.

"My father is here." So, matter of fact – that.

"We livin' different lives now."

"I just finally got what I have wanted this whole time."

"And you would get it by – what is it? – any means necessary?"

Such snark.

"Why want something if you aren't going to do everything in your power to get it?"

"True. And I want you. I want you back. By any means necessary."

He stands. I don't.

"You can have me. Just not at the level we once were. I'm stretched too thin, trying to love everyone."

"Everyone? Who else is there?"

He must not have been watching.

"You... My father... My mother... My grandmother... Jhene..."

"Jhene? That weird, skinny chick is in the way of us?!"

She is so much more than that...

"That's your perception. But it's more than that."

"Like what?"

"My father reclaimed his place in my heart. And I needed room for him to fit."

"So I'm the one that gets removed? We're supposed to be family!"

Now, I stand. We're face to face, now.

"You're not blood!"

"What's blood got to do with anything?"

Pain.

"Everything!"

"Man, fuck your father!"

Jealousy.

"Watch your fucking mouth!"

"Fuck him. It's like you've completely forgotten all you went through because of him. You started fucking cutting because of him. And now, you're all googly eyed because he hugged you a couple times, shed some bootleg ass tears and took you to some wack ass baseball game. But I was there for all your gay ass bullshit. That was me! I did that!"

Rage.

I do not know where it came from. I do know where it came from. My right arm raised, my fist clenched, my eyes set on the target. This would mark the first time I punched Walter without any playfulness attached to it. This would mark the first time I hit him with the rage of an only child.

His jaw is mine now. I connect. It sends him into shock. A level of disbelief only found within the walls of his own home.

He raises his right arm. Cocks it back. Straight arms it. Throws a quick punch, full of jealousy and rage. It connects. Simmering pain scatters among my facial structure as it battles the pressure of such force.

I raise my right arm, hand opened wide, in a vice grip, towards Walter's neck. In unison, Walter does the same. My hand reaches his neck at the same time his reaches mine. We both squeeze. Or do we? There is a hesitance in our actions. A fight within the fight, not to fight. I want to hurt him, but not maim him. I want to show him my anger, but not destroy him. And his energy is saying the same.

My hand around his neck holds him up but does not damage him. His hand around mine, turns red not in pressure but in pushing back the possibility of pressure. We are two friends whose love for one another stymies any aggressiveness after that first punch. It is a borderline silent back and forth we engage in, our heavy breathing the soundtrack to a fractured friendship severed by jealousy and fathers.

There is such poetry in this violence…

But even its poetic framing does not erase the fact my best friend and I are at odds, physical odds with each other, and we have never been asked to come back from this. I still sit here, in this violent poetry, yet, I am already crafting the story we will tell of its unraveling. There is something about our caution within this violence that says we will be alright but we have not been speaking the same language lately. Maybe I am speaking the language of my father and I, and I am completely wrong about this quatrain when it is indeed in fact a haiku, a 17-syllable execution at the hands of a literary giant and his pupil, who has crinkled and crumpled the page in which his learning has always taken place in order to exert his freedom at its highest volume.

Scream, Walter, scream!

I have always wanted to write poetry with him. It makes sense for us to find our literary rhythm within the confines of pain, jealousy and rage. It is a language that we both at once speak, a language that proactively surrounds our core selves and initiates our behaviors and responses to surrounding stimuli.

I let go. My arms by my side as he continues to hold my neck in his hand. His anger slowly usurped by frustration and sadness, and the unknown of what his life will be like once he lets go of me. I have found my comfort within his rage, rest my chin between his thumb and pointer finger and await my fate. But nothing about this is fatal. He lets go. I regain my breath at a steady rate almost too fast for comfort. I am back in control now, at least, of my body. But of this friendship, I do not know what it is now, nor what it will be. I just know that now, we have written our first poetry, and it is indeed, a tragedy.

XLV

He walks back inside, takes what is left of our friendship with him. This poetic violence ends sans punctuation. Elliptical, if anything. At least, that is the hope. For a period at the end of this sentence, or worse, an exclamation point, would end it all. It just needs time, we just need time, to acclimate to this new world order. This world where love no longer finds itself in isolation. But it is spread amongst a select few, a deserving few, who love in return the vessel from which the love originated.

I.

No Roman Numeral. Just the simplest recognition of self. My love is the love that my few cannot live without. I accept this responsibility, despite the difficulties it creates within my own emotional expression. I do not want to lose the propensity to love each entity at the fullest capacity, but something has to give. The only one fighting me is Walter. And it is understandable. With the wind no longer in human form, the rest of my love is new love. And that new love must come from somewhere. And that somewhere is Walter, the only remaining member of my original love triangle. I am geometrically opposed to stretching into a pentagon, but it is necessary at this time. I do not want to surrender Walter's side, but it is entirely up to him. I can still love him. I know I can. But if he feels this love is all or nothing, which is how we have always treated it, then I will have to learn to live a life, sans my Walter. And that is not a life I want to live, but it is a life I will learn to live.

I walk back into my home. My movements, that of loss. I suffer. I suffer loss. I live an existence of suffering, and loss. Whenever I gain, I eventually lose. There is no time where my gain usurps my loss. It is either even, or loss is winning. Loss is winning, now.

My mother is dead...

And so is my grandmother. And I am not willing to kill my friendship with Walter just yet. This night, these moments, this poetic violence, needs time to marinate, simmer a bit, find what it is it is going to be. But as of now, it is going to be loss. It is going to be pain. It is going to influence my every day. Because who am I without my Walter? A rock in a hard place, who is having a hard time. I did not stand up for him in the ways he stood up for me. I did not. I was selfish, per usual. It was about me. He was there for me, and I was not there for him, and he sensed it. Cried for it. Screamed for it. Fought for it. And I did not come through. I only scolded, relegated his feelings to secondary status, and floated this idea that he was not the one to hold down my heart in the first place. He was a placeholder. And my father was ready now, to be who it is Walter had been all along. I emotionally cheated on someone. Deciding who I was in a relationship with in the first place is the hard part.

My father sees me, and immediately senses something is wrong. This is a skill he developed recently. In recognizing that I am not the same person throughout the day, that minute by minute can cause seismic shifts in mood and demeanor, he is learning to sense when one of my shifts occur. He knows this one is not normal, not my usual. It is, indeed, seismic.

"Are you ok, son?"

I burst into tears. He wraps me in his arms, pulls me into his chest.

"I had a fight... with Walter. Verbal. Physical. Everything. He's my best friend. I don't know what happened."

"You do know, Vinnie. Just have to admit it to yourself."

I look up at him. He does not know what he has asked me to do.

"You, father, are what happened. You are what

happened."

My father looks down at me.

"How, son?"

"I had always kept a spot for you. Always held a spot for you. I never knew if you'd claim it, or if you even knew it was available. I just knew I had spot for you, if you ever wanted it."

"A spot where?"

"In my heart."

"Oh, son..."

"We love, now. I know you love me. But I didn't always feel that. And, and, Walter was always there for me. Listening to me go on and on about what was missing between you and me. He was there for me when nobody else was. And when mom died... he was who I leaned on the most. But with grandma coming, and you coming around, Walter isn't as needed as he once was and he is mad about it. And I don't blame him... you said be honest with myself, well, he was honestly a placeholder for you. I was just waiting for you. I was in need of you. And I have you now... don't I?"

"You do. And I'm not going anywhere."

He holds me in his arms some more. I feel safe here. It is not my mother's bosom, but it is close. Love is in this region. It is obvious to me, now. Love, in a shape and form I never recognized before, is here.

My father removes me from his body, an action I refuse to let happen at first. But see, my father is strong.

"I have something I want to show you, Vinnie."

He walks to his room, pep in his step. I am left to sit within my emotion, to wonder what to make of this moment, and whether or not my father has the capability of bringing me out of my doldrums. He has his chance now.

He comes out of his room with a bunch of rolled up pieces of paper, reminiscent of the multitude of rolled up art I have under my bed. He unrolls them one by one, and to my surprise, what lies before me are some of the best pencil sketches I have seen in quite some time. There is an eloquence, an intelligence within the contextual makeup of each piece, a subtlety only a true artist could execute so flawlessly.

I wonder whose work this is...

"Wow. This is a phenomenal collection of work. Where did you purchase these?"

My father smiles. It is a proud smile. One of... wait... is that personal pride? Am I missing something here? I am missing something here...

"These are mine, Vinnie. This is my art."

No, no one so rigid, so calculated, so meticulous, could produce the grace and finesse required to produce the artwork before me. It can't be.

"You're kidding, right?"

"I am not. These are mine. I have some going back 16 years."

"16 years? You were doing these before I was born?"

He chuckles, clearly getting a kick out of my shock.

"That I was. Did your mother ever tell you how me and her met?"

"She didn't."

"We met at a wine and art – something or other. But basically, you could drink while creating something. It was our place. We would frequent it often before you were born, but once you came along, I became more career focused to make sure you and your mother never wanted for anything."

"Wait, so if you're an artist, and always loved art, why were you always so against my own? It was like you despised me for it."

"I was jealous. You live a life, you have a mind, I wish was my own. I always felt the need to be how I am because that's how I put food on the table and clothes on your back. That's how I provided. I had to work and work some more. I could not be an artist and provide for you and your mother. Anything along those lines had to be laid to rest. But you came along and took everything I ever wanted to do as an artist and made it who you are as a person. You bleed this."

If only he knew...

My father takes my hands in his, looks right in my eyes, and utters the most beautiful sentence I have ever heard.

"But I have always wanted to paint."

If black men blushed, I would be blushing right now. My father wants to paint. He wants to be me. He wants to be part of the most sustainable aspect of who I am. My father wants to be... a father.

"Can you teach me?"

Oh my, God!

I am smitten with this man!

He keeps doing and saying things. And I keep listening and swooning. I love him. And I am so thankful that I am allowed to love him, now. He isn't angry at my love. He isn't jealous of my love. He is, now, open to my love. He uses my love as energy, knowing he always has it to come home to.

But I have always wanted to paint...

These words left his mouth so effortlessly, as if it was not a secret that held the weight of a thousand tongues. This was the one thing I thought put a ceiling on us. The one piece to our complicated puzzle that would not allow us to reach the summits my mother and I reached. But it is there no longer. He is an artist, just like his son. He is an intellect, just like his son. He is love, just like his son. And now his son recognizes, just how much, he is like his father. Something I have fought to disprove for the majority of my short life. I did not want him to be seen in me, when he was not – seen. It seemed unfair. As if he did not have to do any work in order for me to be his clone, his return, his better.

But now...

We walk into my room and I take out both chairs to sit in front of the easel. I motion for my father to sit down on one of them. He obliges. I take out one paintbrush. Then, on second thought, I take out a second – just in case.

I take out various cups of paint. Place them on the easel. Bright colors necessary, dreary shades secondary. I grab a cup of water from the row of water cups I keep on my dresser. They come in handy for a plethora of things, like cleaning paintbrushes and...

Where did this blood come from?

I live a life of diametrically opposed thoughts, feelings, concerns – people. My cups of water serve in the same capacity, a cleansing locale for something so beautiful, and something so disturbing. But both are, something.

"One more thing..."

I grab rolled up pieces of paper from under my bed, all parts of my father-son collection.

"These are some of the pieces you missed seeing at school that night you couldn't come."

As my father rolls open the pieces of paper, he starts to cry.

"They... they're beautiful, son. Absolutely stunning. You have such an amazing talent, and I am so sorry I never told you just how much I admire your pursuit and growth within it."

Now, I'm crying, too.

"Thank you, father. That's all I have ever wanted from you. To be seen, heard, understood, appreciated, and, uplifted. I just want you to be proud that I'm your son. All the weirdness, all the quirks, all the different. All of it. Just love me and show me off for all the world to see."

"I will do better, son."

"I know you will. I know. I believe that."

"So… can you teach me?"

I can teach you…

I sit down next to my father. I grab a paintbrush – one.

"Son, aren't you left-handed?"

"That I am."

My father gets up, motions for me to switch seats with him. My left hand is now on his right side. The magic is awaiting us.

I dip my paintbrush in red paint. Fitting, for such an occasion. I hand the paintbrush to my father. I take his hand in mine, just like my mother would.

My mother is dead…

"Like this, this is how mom would do it…"

I paint with my father. Make mistakes with my father. Laugh with my father. We are at times regal, other times sloppy. Our rhythm moves back and forth from comfort, to chaos. It feels like those early days with my mother, when she battled my impatience with a patience all her own, waiting as my innate talent rose to the surface and I began to see what it is that I have here. And here, now, is a father, with a paintbrush in his hand, and his hand in my hand, and we are one. And it is beautiful.

My father. "This is so different than pencil sketches."

"In what way?"

"This feels more… free. Would I be wrong in that thinking?"

"Not at all, Pops. Not at all."

We continue our dance, develop a rhythm reminiscent of Motown vinyl records. Make music on a canvas meant for exploration, I want to explore us. I want to manipulate manhood, blind the status quo, resurrect Baldwin and kiss male caricatures with smirked lips. I want to confuse tradition, lynch logic, hang hyperbole, intertwine intimacy, validate sanctioned vanguards. I want to say hello to men, smile, and they smile back, all the while secure in every bit of masculinity we can wrap our rugged, soft, scarred, delicate hands around. I want to hold my father's hand, and he not recoil in disgust because I am his son, and he is my father, and we are allowed to feel. I want to be. Be free to engage in complex forms of intimate interaction with formidable foes forever forgotten for fervent follies frequently frolic freely. I am every bit as inadequate as Guggenheim Fellows are failures. I repeat, I want to be to inadequacy what Guggenheim Fellows are to failure. A marriage born out of sheer disdain for the mundane, I will renegotiate masculinity's deal with societal norms and determine new terms for the remainder of the contract. The current terms are insufficient. Boys like me, men like my father, must gather as one and hug and kiss and cry and feel and not be ashamed, not be tortured souls with colossal concoctions of emotions caving in our collective chests.

Breathe...

Him. "I hope we can continue to interact like this in the future..."

We will...

"...I'd really like that. But your father needs rest."

Sleep, father...

He gives me a long hug. Rocks me side to side, breathes me in, fully in tune with his ability to feel.

He lets me go, smiles, leaves my room, and shuts the door behind him. I listen for him, until I cannot anymore. He is gone in flesh, still here in spirit.

Breathe... Baldwin...

Hello, sir...

Where...

No?...

Where did...

Not anymore?

Where did all...

Is it time?
Where did all this...
It can't be...
Where did all this blood...
The time is now...
Where did all this blood come...
I finally have the strength...
Where did all this blood come from?
It came... It came from... It came from nowhere...
No more box cutter. No more blood. No more pain.
No more.

I have learned to love my father with everything I
am...

XLVI

Today, my father returns to work and I return to school – supposedly. When I woke up this morning, and saw that my father indeed left for work, I felt compelled to stay home.

I am not in the frame of mind where school is possible. I am too far gone from the realism that is school buildings, school teachers and schoolchildren. I would only hinder the collective progress of my peers and their overseers by drifting into a dreamlike state where my father and I skip through meadows, read Baldwin, meditate, and fight toxically masculine crime with spears and nunchucks.

I would say we used box cutters as the sharp object in our weaponry, but I threw all of mine away. As of late last night, I no longer own box cutters. I no longer own my cutting. It is without a home. It is without me. And it is better this way.

For I love my father with everything I am...

We painted together. An activity I thought was lost to the wind. I was under the belief that painting would be a solo endeavor for the rest of my days but here he was, this entire time, yearning for the opportunity to put paint to canvas, for me to hold his hand in mine, to attempt to produce a type of art he had always wanted to accomplish, but never pursued.

I didn't let him know that I pencil sketch, too. I want him to have that. It is only right that he assumes responsibility for that art, for that craft, without the knowledge that I am also adept at such things. The ego must be stroked, if ever so slightly, and I do not want to completely murder my father's confidence by diminishing every advantage he perceivably has over me. I must leave him with something, something to carry. Least I can do is give him this.

I want to give him this...

In my hand, I hold the completed painting we started last night. My father did not seem to think it would amount to anything special, but I went to work, turned our collaborative effort into an abstract image depicting what it means to be blood relatives – hence the red. I painted in the language my mother and I once spoke in silence. A language we both learned over time, and if my father and I are to reach similar plateaus, he must see what is possible when spirits are aligned, blessings abound and paintbrushes listen to the commands of those that control them.

I am giddy. I am life. I am love. And I am itching to show this abstract art, this concrete love, to my father. So, I am going to surprise him, at his job, with this painting. I have never walked the presumably hallowed halls of my father's place of work. I am unaware of the surroundings they place him in, the amount of light that enters his office, nor the number of suits, ties and pantsuits that frequent its hallways. That life is separate. All I am prevue to is the income that follows my father, that feeds me, clothes me, and puts this glorious roof over my head. His job provides at the most surface of levels, but it also gives my father his sense of purpose. It is who he is, and I must learn to respect that at a higher level. If he is willing to meet me where I am in regards to my painting, it is only right that I recognize the singular importance of the work that makes him whole.

For I love my father with everything I am…

And I must get this painting to him. It is all I want right now, all I need. It is a must. So, I must, utilize the latest wad of bills left on my dresser. Just a few bills, travel money minimum, travel and some food maximum.

The dream, though, is to ride the bus to my father's job only for him to take me to lunch, then find somewhere for me to relax, read some Baldwin, eat snacks and wait for him to leave. I want all of his co-workers to gawk at how much more handsome I am in person than in all the pictures my father has in his office. I want to be inundated with questions about whether or not my father is the same at home as he is at work. He is, or, at least, he used to be. He is much more loving when he comes home now. Do you all feel his love here? No? That's unfortunate because that's all I feel, all the time. Yeah, that's what I would say. That's what I would want. That would be the dream. I want them to feel jealous of my being able to get all of my father while they are left with the steel-faced gaze he has finally removed from inside the walls of our home.

For I love my father with everything I am…

And within this context, this concept, of love, I must be open and honest about my truths, my past and my consistently dangerous behavior. I must be upfront about the devastating artwork that befalls my skin. I have to tell my father the who, the what, the when, the where and the how something so passionate, something so intimate, something so wrong, could be happening in his home without his knowledge, against the skin he is partially responsible for scarring.

His name is written in these scars. Hieroglyphics. Historical adages. Lyricism. Cuts canoodle with moonlight, glisten under the heat of the sun. The universe knew what I was doing. My mother learned upon transitioning to the wind. I am sure she has informed my grandmother of the same. Walter found me in bathroom stalls, provided me with my weaponry. Jhene kissed my insecurities, loved my inadequacies, and joined me in the inaction of my pain. The only one inside my love's pentagon with no knowledge of my truth, of my longing, of my loathing, of my mistakes, of my pain, is my father.

And that ends today.

I will deliver our painting, eat food he has purchased and deliver the news, without hesitance or fear. For I believe in this version of my father. I believe he is ready, worthy and willing to receive me in my entirety.

XLVII

This bus smells like an anxiety cocktail. Dead-in jobs, eviction notices, six years at community college, two-week alcohol binges, spread out like manifested disease.

And I am its humble host.

I love the anxiousness of the bus. I love the urgency. I love the desire to exit quickly. I love the dogged elegance of someone who can wake up, go to work, make someone else some money, then go home and feed their families. It doesn't matter that they are unhappy. It doesn't matter that there is no upward mobility. All that matters is that they have fed their families.

I love the nomadic spirit of the bus. The craftiness a mother of two develops when she is on her third eviction notice and must seek out housing for her and her two young sons. She figures out a way. An eviction notice is just another chance to do better, for God to prove Her worth. Ain't nothin'.

I love the elongated patience of the bus. The ability to stay taking courses at a college, four years beyond the time you told your family and friends at your high school graduation you would be transferring. But the way life is set up, community college is a safe haven for those working multiple jobs. It is academic patience in its totality. It is education at its own pace. It isn't forced. It is understood, and it doesn't matter when you get it, as long as you get it. Six years be damned.

I love the explosiveness of the bus. Screw a job. Screw school. Let's just down this alcohol without a care in the world for two weeks. Not answering to no one. Not answering to nobody. I just want to drown. I want to make Kendrick Lamar write a remix to it. I want Junot Diaz to write a sequel to it. I just don't think right now is the right time to care about right now. Just give me 14 days, and I'll be better for it. Let me be worse, so I can be better. Let me see what worse looks like, so I can prefer better. It's just a drink. Be merry.

This is my stop.

I hop off the bus. I now stand in the midst of where dreams are made of. We, my father and I, made our dream last night. Or, at least, we started it. But I finished it, though. And I have it rolled up, placed between my arm and my torso. And it is magical. A canvas with a little black boy joy sprinkled on it.

I walk up to the building door. I push it open. There is someone at the front desk. She is a woman. I will speak to her, now. But first, she will speak to me.

"Yes, how may I help you, young man?"

"Do you know where I can find Thomas Smith?"

"Give me one second."

I am his son.

"Ah, yes, he is on the third floor. The office of Tyler, Price & Murth."

"Thank you."

"No problem, young man."

I am his son.

I take the elevator to the third floor. Taking the stairs on this day just seems counterproductive. I want to be taken care of today. I don't want to have to do anything but be a black teenage boy who loves his father and wants to surprise him with a gift they created together. Then be treated like a prince for being so talented and thoughtful and all those nice things people say to people they love and appreciate. That's what I am here to do and I am going to do it.

I reach the third floor. The elevator door opens and I am immediately at the desk of another woman, but she is the receptionist for the office in which my father works, Tyler, Price & Murth. The party should begin here. Here goes the celebration of me. Right here. This is where we are. This is where it will be. We will celebrate here. This is it. Right here. This is the place.

"Hi."

I am his son.

"Yes, may I help you?"

I am his son.

"Do you not recognize me?

I am his son.

"Am I supposed to, young man?"

I am his son.

"How long have you worked here?"

I am his son.

"Long enough to know I do not have to answer that question. Unless there is someone you would like to see, I am going to have to ask you to leave."

I am his son.

"So, you really don't know who I am?"

I am his son.

"Yes."

I am his son.

"I don't look familiar?"

I am his son.

"I'm calling security."

I am his son.

"I am Thomas Smith's son, Vinnie."

I am his son.

"Son? Thomas has a son?... I've worked here eight years and never knew that. Hmmph. You think you know somebody…"

I am his son!

"You didn't know… you didn't know he had a son?"

I am his son!

"I may not have noticed–"

I am his son!

"–Where is his office?!"

I am his son!

I am his son. An eight-year receptionist does not recognize me. Does not see me. Does not know I exist. How can that be? How is that even possible?

I walk away from her. His office is my destination. Names on doors. White names. And esquires. Money everywhere. Degrees everywhere. Musty education. A lot of knowledge. A lot of knowing.

But you didn't know he had a son...

I hear her footsteps behind me. She is shouting. Enters my ears. Translates into gibberish. I assume she wants me to stop. I will not. I must see this office. This place of closed off inaccuracies. This place of lies. This place of absence. This place of ghosts. This place of utter bullshit.

Found it.

I open its doors. My father is not here. Great. He doesn't need to be. I look around. I see his bachelor's degree. I see his law degree. I see photos of him with incorrectly important people. I see photos of him with black folks. I see photos of him with white folks. Look, there are even Mexicans and Asians represented.

And on his desk, photos of my mother, Annette. So sweet, so beautiful, so much like the wind.

Where am I?

I do not see me. I do not see me anywhere. There is no sign of me. I am not here. I am not anywhere. He denies me in here. He denies me at work. They do not know I am here. They do not know I am anywhere. How can that be? How is that love? How is that fatherhood?

His shelves, disheveled. His chair, on its back. His desk, flipped over. His papers, scattered. His pictures, broken. His office, tornado. Name the tornado: Vinnie. I am that tornado. And I have hit. And I have hit hard. Destruction is what I do. Destruction is what I must continue to do. I must destroy.

I must destroy these tears. I hate this emotion. I do not want to deliver on this emotion. He does not deserve this emotion. I want to destroy this emotion.

Why must I feel every emotion? I do not want to feel any emotion.

I want to sever all emotion. I want to eviscerate all emotion. I want to slaughter all emotion. I want to annihilate all emotion.

Fuck bell hooks...

I want to hide from all emotion. I want to run from all emotion. I want to cower from all emotion.

I want to cry... I want to scream...

I want to leave... I want to die... Fuck James Baldwin...

But first, I must leave. I do not know how. Security on its way. Receptionist on my tail. I must find a way out. I must leave this place. I must...

Run...

Showcase my abilities. Football has its purpose. Sprint like no other. Gas these enablers. Leave everything. Leave it all. Exit. Stage left. Please. Exit. So necessary. By any means.

Run...

Explode through the front door. Bus not needed. Wind at my back. Sprint. Devastation in our wake. They all know me now... I bet they all know me now...

I am his son...

I find myself in a tight, taut jog. No stride wasted. I am a stallion on sidewalk. The Preakness in flesh. I must reconcile this mess. My father failed his test...

I am his son...

But only behind closed doors. The baseball game, a setting where his colleagues would not find him, loving, caring and protecting me. That was the only public sighting of our love. The bookstore – that place is way too quaint, obscure, and random for six-figure incomes and enablers.

The funeral – do they even know my mother is dead? How do you leave me out of that story? It's all so blurry. I need water. I am exhausted. Rage drains.

I have been running for 20 minutes...

I am so sorry, Baldwin... but fuck you...

I have been running for 40 minutes...

I am so sorry, bell... but fuck you...

I have been running for an hour...

I have been running... I have been running... I have been running...

I am home now, standing in the driveway. And I do not know what I am going to do.

Oh.

That.

XLVIII

I stand here. In front of my home. Still.

Walter...

I feel his energy as he stands next to me. He stares, like I stare. He breathes, like I breathe. His pose, adjacent to my own.

Still. Breathing. Pain. Seething.

I look at my oldest friend. My jaw drops. His face, littered in scars, bruises. A black eye adorns his once ruggedly handsome face. Purples and reds wrestle for attention on his white skin, search for notice from someone, anyone.

Walter reaches into his pocket. He pulls out a box cutter. He plays with it a little bit. Lets the sun hit it, do a little dance on its blades. It is a wondrous relationship between the two, the blade and the sun. And I watch this tango for at least a minute, as they frolic among each other between the fingers of this white boy, in his white T, and his blue jeans.

Walter. "I have an extra."

Walter hands me the box cutter without even looking at me. I do not know that I need it. But he knows that I need it. Or maybe I do know that I need it, but I just won't admit it.

Oh.

That.

This gift I now hold in my hands is an apology in our world. Walter always seems to know when I need something, when I want something. I don't stand outside of my home and stare at it in the middle of the day, on a school day, without it having something to do with my father. He knows this. I know this. We know this to be true.

He stayed home, too. His beaten up white skin too much of an announcement of what goes on behind closed doors for him to show his face on a school campus of nosy

252

adults and children, alike. He is not trying to answer the litany of questions. His mother is dead, and his father died a long time ago. What is left over is a zombie in full apocalyptic form. A zombie I am no longer willing to sacrifice my own existence to kill. Walter, my dear friend, you must decide what to do about your zombie, for mine has come back to life, and killing it is now my life's ambition.

Walter walks slowly back to his house. I have not moved from my position in front of my home. I wonder what this place truly means besides representing the locale of my darkest moments, my biggest fears, my most treacherous enemy. Figuring out what it represents is something I need to come to grips with before I take my next step. It is clear to me that it is four walls, that houses all of my things, my mother's things, my father's things, a couch or two, a kitchen, some kitchen appliances, shoes, socks, long sleeve black shirts, black hats, black slacks, pillows, pillow cases, combs, brushes, rubberbands, carpets, rugs, television sets, dressers, mirrors... mirrors... mirrors... mirrors... mirrors...

I can't see...
Something is wrong...
Run...
No, not there...
There...
...
Here...

I am here now. Furniture scattered about. Broken tables. Broken chairs. The couch, moved at least six feet to the left. Silverware misplaced. And broken... mirrors... mirrors... mirrors... mirrors... mirrors...

I can't see...

Anything but, the shards of glass on the floor, and, Walter – bruised, beaten, and bloodied. But his blood-soaked T-shirt is nothing compared to what lies beneath his feet. Cargo pants soak in blood. A wife beater soaks in blood. Both cover the legs, and torso, of a formerly alive, Rick. Rick seems to have two necks now, a slit, perfectly sliced across the middle.

I didn't have to kill him...

Walter sensed my hesitation. He knew he could no longer wait for me to take care of his situation. I was no longer a weapon at his disposal. He had to take his skin into his own hands. Every bruise, every scar, every drop of blood, severed Rick's throat, and put him on a first-class flight to hell. The earth and its inhabitants all breathe a sigh of relief.

Walter has not acknowledged me. He simply sits, looks straight ahead, and breathes an awkward rhythm. His breaths scat a melody reminiscent of jukebox catastrophes during Southern jaunts through costume parties meant to persuade racism to take a day off. More succinctly, his breathing scares me. It isn't human. It is inhumane. Cluttered oxygen. A natural born killer's carbon dioxide. I am standing in the room of a murderer, breathing in the air of a murder, and all I want to do is give the perpetrator a hug and tell him it is going to be alright. That this is the type of blood that should be shed. Rick's blood did not deserve to flow through his body anymore. It needed to be coughed up, strangled, flooded down his chest until it stained his last moments with remnants of a war within himself he could never win.

I bring myself to join him. I grab him up under his arms and drag him from under the weight of his victim. Walter, legs numb, cannot move his lower body on his own. The bloodstains, and inability to move, shows how long ago this went down, how long ago it was that I was standing outside waiting on my own father to return. I wasn't waiting for my father to return. That is a man I have not met yet. Or I keep meeting. I do not know which one to believe anymore.

I hold Walter now. It is uncomfortable. It is unbecoming. But we are becoming. We are becoming human. This death, this constant death that surrounds us, it is not unlike the death so many have endured. This inaccurate assumption that death comes in respect to time and space is something we humans have convinced ourselves to be true, when indeed death hits hard, hits fast, and hits, often.

The best way to get over loss is to lose something else…

And here we sit. A black boy and a white boy, best friends. And the ugly is gone, now. Aesthetically displeasing, yes, but there is beauty in freeing yourself. Walter is free, now. Free to enter the judicial system. Free to enter the foster care system. Free to be whomever it is he is meant to be. Utilize his white privilege and shed some tortured white boy tears, shed some years off his sentence, be slapped on his white wrist for doing some white boy shit. It was only a matter of time before his inner white boy exploded with the rage of closed bedroom doors, cursed out mothers, stolen from fathers, rock n roll posters, Marilyn Manson lyrics, and – the history of American whiteness.

I start to smile. It is not something I want to do. It is not something I planned to do. It just happens. I smile. Boy, do I smile. The irony of violence is that violence is often used to eradicate it. It is both victor and victim. Cause and effect. Yin and yang.

Father and son…

I sit here, my best friend weighs heavy in my arms. It smells. Death conducts nostril destruction at an octave few parties can reach. Death guzzles down all senses until you are forced to only smell. It attacks the very existence of breathing for it is not a fan of such an activity. Breathing breeds life and death is an opponent looking for an edge. So, it gathers an aroma befitting that of decay and fecal matter. I cannot stand for this much longer. But I have been here for much longer, than I had hoped. I think Walter has this, now. I think the numbness has subsided. Mine, not his. I can only pray for his. Pray for him. But, my prayer is also for me.

Don't forget...
Oh.
That.

XLIX

My bedroom, such a beautiful place. I love it. It is all mine. And it has four walls. I love four walls. I love when walls come in fours. It is my fave. Yep... yep... yep. My absolute fave. Four walls. This is how I want to live.

I litter. Throw garbage outside of the car window. Leave trash on the ground. Kick trash cans over. Rebel. And now, my bed litters. Or, gets littered – on. Whichever works for you. Now – littered with a small collection of art I may or may not have been saving up to deliver to my father as a humongous gift, show of gratitude, or something or other. One of those frivolous things kids who love their parents do, or kids who are loved by their parents would do. Whichever one suffices in order for us to continue.

All this art, all these stories, all in one place. Every painting, its own distorted manifestation of beauty. This cockamamie concoction of wasted considerable time. I could have spent this time kissing Jhene's inner thoughts, rescuing Walter from himself, or, or, anything, else, other than depicting a failed relationship I could not let go of, over and over again. He continued to fail me. He will always fail me. He will never be what I want him to be, and he does not deserve my paintbrush!

My mother is dead...

Oh, I'm sorry, do I mention her too much? I just, she serves as my only reason to live. She is dead. She will be dead. Until I am dead. And she will still be dead. Only we will be dead. Together. Forever. Dead. But I am alive. And will be alive. Until I am not alive. And ready to join her. Among the dead. And the dead, shall set the living free. My father will be free then. Alone, and free.

I should leave him alone...

These paintings contradict – the vibrancy of happiness seen for only moments at a time, in contrast with depression, and loathing, that seeps through its delicate

257

paper construction. They are all of this, and none of this, and want no part in this, detrimental dichotomy.

I pick up a painting, hold it on both ends to let it breathe. I rip it to shreds. Toss it to the floor in colorful, or, black and white, pieces of memorialized garbage. I pick up another. Rip it. Shred it. Dispose of it. Speed up my process through an actualized demonstration of complete and utter rage.

Breathe...

I take in the wreckage. It is some of the best artwork I have ever produced. Abstract, yet, concrete in the execution of its execution.

I grab a paintbrush. And some paint. And I walk out.

I have one more masterpiece left in me...

The door closes behind me. Not my bedroom door, but, my father's. I am here now. In his room. Staring at the biggest, grandest, most awe-inspiring canvas a young painter could ever ask for his paintbrush to grace. Above my father's headboard bares nothing but white. A white wall, with no hanging painting, no artwork, no picture, no ego, no nothing. It is bare. And it is reaching out to me to end its sorrow. It wants me to utilize its space, to mark its skin, with the one piece missing from my repertoire.

I am painting now. I am painting my father's wall. I am disgracing it. And, loving it. All within regal strokes of precision. My face is coming together. His face is coming together. Our faces are coming together. One by one. It is I, and it is him. We are one. We are art. We are, father and son. Immaculate imagery. I am the paint, and the paint is me.

Where is he?

I bet he stayed around a bit longer to clean up the mess of my tornado. Dropped on his office with the fury of emancipated youth in downtrodden communities across this great nation of ours. His stunned silence akin to the second

258

after the realization of death, which is not at all a realization, for to realize something is to be alive to realize it and death ends life which would end realizing a realization for the dead is now incapable of doing a task only designated for the living.

I am alive now!

And I am painting at a level unbefitting my youthful inexperience for I am only 14, just 14, and my mother only taught me everything she knew in the short time she was able to teach me. And I had so much more to learn! She had so much more to give! But...

My mother is dead...

And I am creating art, with or without her, with or without him, it is art that never leaves me, it is art that never dies, it is art that survives, and, this art will survive – this.

I am done, now.

Done painting. Done with art, for art's sake. But, then. There's that.

Oh.

That.

A masterpiece that deserves no introduction. I must cut now.

No, no, I must. I must cut now.

No, no, no, I must. I must cut now.

A complicated reintroduction into seduction. This blade, a mistress of the highest order. Keeps quiet, knows its role and is there at a moment's notice.

Notice, this moment...

Come back to me...

For each solitary drop of blood, is for the wind, is for my mother, is for my grandmother, is for Jhene, is for Walter, is for my father, and, is for me, for me... for me... for me...

I must be selfish with my skin, now. Stay here. Sit here. For he could not introduce me to the piece of him that

259

matters most to him, that mattered more than I did. He could not. So, I cannot. Not do this.

No, no, no, I must.

I am sorry… to no one.

I am so sorry, father… but fuck you…

Drip… drip… drip…

Ecstasy…

The here and now…

Elapsed time…

Unconsciousness, or… subconsciousness…

Outside of this room, I hear a voice. A beautiful, beautiful voice.

Father…

"Vinnie?! Vinnie, are you here?! I have something for you, son!"

He checks multiple doors. Presumably mine. Presumably the bathroom. Presumably the guest room. Presumably…

I sit here. Below this painting. Wrists dangling at my sides. Neck held up like an infant – not at all. I am dangling. I am not whole. I am blood. I am art. I am son. He is father. And I…

…sit under this masterpiece and I wonder: Is there a place in heaven for a male? For a black male? For a black male cutter?

I am one of a kind, so they will tell you. But I am one of many. Silenced by the hierarchy of masculinity and our minimum involvement in its creation, initiation and subjugation. I am a fatality of toxicity. I am one with the wind. I am kin to the fallen.

My father drops the gifts, the money, the paintbrushes, the paint, the bags of items to be used to recalibrate our love and leaves them on the floor, as he rushes to my side. Crying. Wailing. Sobbing.

Like a girl.

It is unbecoming. As he looks to wake me from my

unconsciousness. I refuse to wake up from my unconsciousness. He needs to feel my unconsciousness. The pain of my unconsciousness. He needs to love me back to life...

He picks me up in his arms. Takes me outside. I slip in and out. Out now. Oh, in again. Oh, out now. Oh, in again... still in... still in...

Say something...

In his arms, I say the words I know are true...

"I knew you'd come..."

He bursts into tears. As...

... Walter is walked out of his home. In handcuffs. Blood-soaked white T-shirt and blue jeans. He looks beautiful.

They put him in the backseat of the police car, just as they notice that I am unconscious in the arms of my father – Thomas Smith – with my wrists enveloped in blood, and caution signs. An ambulance, already here for Walter, rushes to me. Looks to help me. Such ironic juxtaposition. White boy arrested. Black boy saved. White man killed. Black man saves.

Stereotypes be damned. It is a new world order.

And you will feel it.

Won't you?

ACKNOWLEDGEMENTS

To the people who had a special impact on the completion of my first novel, 'Vinnie: a love letter'.

To Tiara: You truly showed out. You were with me from beginning to end. I do not have this book without you. You read every word I wrote. You were my lead beta reader and my proofreader. But more than anything, you were my rock. When I reached that moment when I felt like I was talking about Vinnie too much and you said, "No, no, no. This is a HUGE milestone in your life! It's worth talking about!" That meant the world to me. It showed me that I truly had the support system I needed to get this book done. I love you.

To Michele: Impressing you was a big deal for me. You are one of the most brilliant people I know and for you to fall in love with this story, read it all the time – even when you didn't have the time – really meant a lot. You stood by me and pushed me to make this story the best it could be. I relied on your truth. I knew you'd tell me if something was awry. Thank you for being my friend, my lil sis and the voracious reader you are. I could not have done this without you. I love you.

To Mike: You already know, bro. You're my best friend. You let me stay in your home for those magical four days when I was able to finally just sit down and write. You and your family made my sprint to the finish line possible. You have always supported me, no matter what it is that I am doing, and for that I am truly thankful. You are my brother for life and I love you. Now, I can actually watch you read this thing…

To Ian: My cuzzo. Blood couldn't make us any tighter. From childhood, to my days hosting Lyrical Exchange, till now, you have stood by my side. No one supports me on a day-to-day basis, in person, like you do. If it's important to me, it's important to you and I never take that for granted. You are my family and I am grateful every day to have you in my life. I love you.

To Christina: It's hard to express how much you mean to me. You are one of my biggest supporters, cheerleaders and one of my very best friends. You constantly want to know what's going on with me, and when it was all about Vinnie, you listened and encouraged my journey from beginning to end. I love you with all my heart and my appreciation for the depth of our friendship grows daily. Just knowing that you're proud of me is all I need. I love you.

To Ra: My brother from another. Ever since your arrival to San Diego coincided with my own return, we have been inseparable. From starting Lyrical Exchange to me passing on the hosting reins to you to us both having touched Final Stage at the National Poetry Slam for our poetry slam teams, we have built an unshakeable bond. You are one of only a few people who actually call to check up on me. No text. Almost always a call. Your spirit is one that I hope my future son has one day. We're brothers forever. Let's continue this journey together. I love you.

To Jay: Big bro. You practically came out of nowhere. But I am blessed and thankful for the bond and brotherhood we have developed in a short time. You are always available for sage advice and were my only male beta reader. You put your money where your mouth is in your support of me and I will be forever grateful. You've proven to be a true friend. I love you.

To Dominique: The OG best friend. Since 10th grade, you have supported me and been there for me in every possible way. We don't even talk every day, but I know I can come to you with any and everything and you will show up and show out. You love my projects almost as much as I do, even designing the cover art for the Kindle version of this book. You mean more to me than you could ever know. You've watched me grow, make mistakes and continue to fight for what I want. No one, outside of my family, loves me as unconditionally as you do. You are what friendship is all about. I love you.

To Kristyl: You know I love your life. We have one of the more hilarious friendship stories and I wouldn't change it for the world. I love listening to your stories and I appreciate your ear when I have to tell you one of mine. Your consistency is a trait I truly admire in you and you being borderline overprotective of me is awesome. You always have my back no matter what and keep it real with me always. I love you.

To Courtney: We talk once every six months and it is always three hours long. It's like we are right back in college, laughing and enjoying each other's company. Your brilliance is what made me hit you up to be my content editor and you did it without hesitation. You were an integral part of the final stages of getting this book to the level it is now and I thank you for that. Your excitement and support of 'Vinnie' is everything. I love you.

To Iman: My creative soulmate. To think we are still friends after meeting over a decade ago due to a mutual friend on Twitter. Your spirit, drive and tenacity in pursuit of your creative dreams keeps me going. We are both Virgos, innate perfectionists and both need a support system around us who will be there no matter what. You have been that for me, and I hope I have been that for you as well. You are one of the most talented people I know and I am thankful for our friendship every day. Our art will touch lives and I can't wait to share the stage with you one day to tell the world, 'We made it.' I love you.

To CJ: My dear friend. I am so glad we are back to being every day, all the time, friends again. You are everything I want my nieces to aspire to be. Your independence, your drive, your ambition, your heart and your support are such admirable traits. You stay on me and push me because you believe in me and what I am capable of – even when I don't believe it myself. You humble me, then hug me, and that is usually all I need. Thank you for being there for me for over 20 years. I love you.

To Anjanette: Sis, your energy and support is second to none. Thank you for always believing in me, letting me vent to you when I'm going through my emotional ups and downs and proving that friendships can come directly from the work we do. You are amazing. I love you.

To Keyauna: You have been clutch. Thank you so much for being my second pair of eyes for the book release party planning and just being a presence when I needed one. You talked me through so many scenarios with the release of this book and were down for me and this project. I appreciate you and our friendship. I love you.

To The Black Caucus: Carroll, Carr, Brown, Prater and Wilson. I'm putting your last names because that's just how we do. Y'all are more than colleagues. Y'all are my friends, my family. Our bond is forever. Thank you for always letting me be me. I am your crazy little brother. And I am here to stay. I love you.

To Riv: Who knew that you turning down my first idea for your website would turn into this? You were the first to believe in Vinnie and your website provided the first platform for these characters to prosper, and I thank you for that. I always tell people: You do everything I do, only better. I will chase your talent forever. And if I ever get close, I know I will have made it. I love you.

To EB: We made magic happen on a regular basis and you were just as excited about this project as I was. Your vision for the promotional videos and teasers truly made this project come to life. You gave Vinnie the visual component it lacked. We produce dope s**t. And I am forever grateful. I love you.

To Azadeh: My RISE coach. I wrote this book simply because I needed to. But you were the one to make me see it differently. You made me recognize it as a source of change, conversation and love. You made me see this project as something worthy of more than I was originally willing to make it and I will be forever grateful to you for your guidance. I love you.

To Gina: Almost at the last minute, you became the final piece to the puzzle. You were one of my biggest cheerleaders and helped plan some major moments during the weeks leading up to the release. We have been friends since I was in 10th grade and our friendship ages like a fine wine. Thank you for always being genuine and supportive. I love you.

To Jzov: You were a calming force when I was going through a lot and you didn't even try. You were just you and it was appreciated. You even gifted me a rough draft of this book's back cover. I am forever a fan of yours and I am grateful for our friendship. I hope it continues to grow over time. Thank you for not letting me fall apart.

To Davell: We figured it out, bro. I called you that morning in June because I knew you could help me market and promote both myself and this book and you've done much more than that. You helped keep me focused on the things I am not good at. I can do the writing stuff all day but putting myself out there in the right ways is always a struggle. You provided that expertise, that balance and I thank you for that. I love you.

To Aubrey & Kris (Wit A K): I was in dire need of your expertise, talent and skill and you both came through for me in the best of ways. I thank you for that and I love you both.

To Kizzie: Iron sharpens iron, bro. Thank you for always showing me what it means to be a successful, proud and consistent black man. Your support and legal advice are always welcomed and appreciated. Thanks for being you. I love you.

To Joe Mac: Thanks for showing me the ropes of this independent author gig. It is much appreciated. Your honesty is always refreshing. Keep scribin', fam! I love you.

To Chante: You were one of the first people to truly dive into this work. For that, I am forever grateful. Your genuine reaction to this piece gave me a sense of what to expect from readers. You are appreciated. I love you.

To Khea: Your exit from my sphere was the emotional jolt of energy I needed to finish this project. In the oddest way, the pain of losing you is the only reason this book was completed. It was the most painful trade. I still shed tears over it. I often wonder if I would make that trade over again. It once was 'no', but time has taught me otherwise. I needed to be released from the hold you had on my self-worth and self-esteem. I found a support system that wasn't conditional. You left me for good and every tear that has followed has strengthened my resolve. You were my best friend, my first love, and that will be treasured always. I made a host of mistakes and I am sorry you were the one that I had to make them with. I am a better man because of you. I know what I deserve, I know my flaws and I know what I bring to the table. Our pain will forever be found here, in this space, in the words of 'Vinnie'. You are the spirit of this literature. I could not elicit emotions from my readers if I didn't know what they felt like myself. The anger, the love, the pain, the joy, the reflection, the longing, you provided all of that. So, for that, I thank you. And, despite everything... I will always love you.

I just want to say thank you to the various factions who support me, through and through, no matter what I do – even when it's wrong.

Thank You To: The Banks family, Clark family, Cummings family, 104B, RISE San Diego Familia, We Will Rise, Get Lit Coalition, Young Brother Book Club, Hampton University, Morse High School, Lyrical Exchange, Black Expression, San Diego Poetry Slam, Elevated!, Glassless Minds, Diamond Leadership Initiative, Gompers Preparatory Academy and San Diego Urban League Young Professionals.

We did it, y'all! I hope you all enjoy the book and continue to promote literacy to our youth. Literacy saves lives. Education saves lives. I know it saved me. And now, I have something to add to the literary sphere that cannot be taken away. And it feels, oh, so good…

Love,

Ronald Preston Clark